A MOTHER'S ANGUISH

The letter had come in the morning's mail, a common white drugstore variety envelope with a single sheet of lined tablet paper. The contents of it was no more than a roughly scratched out message. But it was a nightmare from which Susan couldn't awaken. *Your kid's alive. Do nothing till I tell you. If you go to the cops, I'll know and I'll send you back her eyes.*

Susan put the letter down, the touch of the paper burning like fire against her skin. A maniac had written this. A maniac who held her child . . .

Susan sat in the silence of her baby's room, the light of late afternoon fading into evening dark. She moved to the slow rhythm of the white rocker against the wooden floor. *Rock-rock. Rock-rock.* Like the sound of a heartbeat. Like the sound of a baby's heartbeat.

And Susan wondered: *Is my baby still alive?*

CRADLE
OF FEAR

MEG GRIFFIN

ZEBRA BOOKS
KENSINGTON PUBLISHING CORP.

DEDICATION

To all the children of my family day care, especially Noelle, Paige, Emily, Sydney, and Stefanie.

ZEBRA BOOKS are published by Meg Griffin

Kensington Publishing Corp.
475 Park Avenue South
New York, NY 10016

First Printing: March, 1994
Printed in the United States of America

Chapter One

The slab-sided blue van slowed and parked across the street, its black-tinted driver's window rolled up tight. No one got out. The man inside was patient. He knew the schedule. He'd been watching the house for days. Never in the van. This morning was the first time he'd used it. This afternoon would be the last. He waited, his dark eyes peering into the outside mirror.

7:45 A.M. Diane Kendall's steel gray Volvo wagon pulled into the Campbell driveway. Two blond little girls, ages four and three, climbed out of the car, ran to the house, and opened the door. Diane Kendall followed, carrying one-year-old Paige in her arms. A few minutes later, the mother and the two older children got back in the car and drove away.

One.

8:12. Alix Cole's white Cressida blocked the driveway entrance. Carrying six-month-old Chelsea to the front door, Alix knocked once, then turned the knob and let herself in. Three minutes later, she left.

Two.

8:45. Zack Sayers and Susan Richards arrived

within minutes of one another. Fourteen-month-old Jennifer Richards walked to the door of the day care by herself. Her mother followed, carrying the child's pink diaper bag and yellow lunch box.

Zack Sayers was only steps behind the Richards woman, five-month-old Sydney in one arm, her car seat in the other. Sayers remained less than a minute. He sprinted to his blue Honda Accord and drove away.

Three.

9:05. Susan Richards opened the door. Bye-bye, she waved. Bye-bye. She had the usual trouble starting the old red Mustang—cold carburetor. On the fourth try, the engine caught. She gunned it, and sped off.

Four.

The street was quiet. The man waited until he was certain no other cars were on the road. No neighbor watering his roses. No one walking his dog. He started the engine, backed up, and pulled the van into the Campbell driveway.

He was wearing a tan London Fog jacket, pockets big enough to hide the gun. He heard the children as he moved up the walk. One of the babies was crying.

The doorknob turned easily in his hand, as he had known it would. It was always unlocked at this time of the morning when parents dropped their children off at the Campbell day care. He pushed it open, stepped inside and closed the door behind him, his hand slipping into his pocket against the gun.

Chelsea and Paige looked up from the toys when he entered the living room. They stared at him, Fisher-Price people fisted in their tight little hands. Chelsea sat in her walker, chewing on the head of a rubber giraffe. He smiled at her and moved to the kitchen. The gun was now in his hand.

Christine Campbell hadn't heard the door; he could see that. Sydney was crying. Holding the baby in one arm, she took the bottle out of the microwave and started to shake it over the sink. A stream of white formula squirted across the windowpane.

"Damn!" she said, setting the bottle down and tearing a sheet of paper towel to wipe the glass. Sydney screamed louder. "Okay, okay." Christine snatched the bottle off the sink and turned around.

The look on her face was a question she didn't have time to ask. He fired. One bullet to the head and she dropped. Her body crumpled to her knees, then slipped dead-weight to the floor. Sydney rolled from Christine Campbell's slack arm, down her hip and onto the kitchen tiles, unharmed.

Unscrewing the silencer from the nose of the Browning 9mm, he slipped it and the automatic back into the deep pocket of his jacket. The baby was still screaming. He picked Sydney up. Standing directly over the body of Christine Campbell, he fed the baby a little of the formula in the bottle, enough to keep her quiet. There was no hurry. The dead woman's eyes stared up at him.

Turning around, he saw both Paige and Jennifer standing just inside the kitchen doorway, watching. He smiled at them and asked, "Want to go bye-bye?"

Four car seats were belted to the upholstered chairs of the van. He took the babies from the house one at a time, making sure the straps were secure, metal belt clips fastened.

Closing the van door, he went back into the house and collected the four diaper bags, bottles, and lunch boxes from the refrigerator. He looked around. Nothing out of the ordinary. Nothing disturbed. Walking out the door, he spotted Chelsea's pacifier dropped onto the tray of the walker. He scooped it up, slipped it into his jacket pocket, alongside the silencer and the 9mm, and walked out.

9:20. The blue van backed out of the Campbells' driveway, eased onto the quiet neighborhood street, and drove away.

At 5:15 that afternoon, Diane Kendall's Volvo wagon bumped over the corner of Christine Campbell's ice plant flower bed and coasted into the vacant driveway. Three doors opened as the two children and Diane each exited the car.

"Wait for Mama," she called to them, as the girls ran ahead.

Four-year-old Emily Kendall opened the still-unlocked front door and ran inside the Campbell house. Her sister Noelle followed. Diane sat in the car writing the check for the week's day care fee. Christine always liked her check on Monday, a week in advance. She was filling in the amount when Emily came back to the car.

"Don't bother Mama now, Em. I have to finish this. Go see Christine, I'll be right there."

"Mama," Emily said, her face drawn into a solemn little mask, "I can't find her. I can't find Paigie, too."

Diane stopped writing the check. She got out of the car, took Emily's hand, and walked up to the Campbells' open front door. Noelle stood at the coffee table playing with the toys. Everything else was

8

silent. A finger of fear pressed ever so slightly on Diane Kendall's heart.

"Christine?" she called. Where was everyone? Where was Paige? "Chris?" she called louder, moving from the living room to the kitchen. Maybe she'd taken them outside to—

The body stopped her. The hole in Christine Campbell's forehead stared up at her like a third eye, dull and unseeing.

"Oh my . . . oh my God." Diane's hand flew to her mouth, stopping the words, stopping the thought. Her heart skittered as she turned and ran from the kitchen, racing from room to room screaming, "Paige! Paige!"

But the baby wasn't there.

His name was Daniel. From Foothill Boulevard in La Cañada, he took a right onto the Angeles Crest Highway, following the single lane winding highway into the San Gabriel mountains and the alpine community of Wrightwood Village.

The sheer-drop road slowly gave way to a wide expanse of pine and California live oak. Only an hour and a half from La Cañada, the air was cooler in the mountains by ten degrees.

The babies were crying; they had been for a while. It was loud in the closed van, but Daniel doubted if anyone else could hear them. He turned onto Park Avenue, the main thoroughfare of town, passing Holiday Foods Market, Kato's Kitchen, Wietz's Country Store, a bar called Yodeler's, and an Arco Mini-Mart.

Continuing to the east end of the village, the street curved into Lone Pine Canyon Road. The houses in this area were generously spaced and isolated, well over two hundred feet apart. It was an affluent neighborhood with BMWs, Mercedes, and Porsches sprinkled like expensive seedlings on the loose-gravel driveways. Each property was separated by a stand of trees for privacy. Behind these walls of trees, visibility to the next-door houses was blocked. With this buffer the sound of voices wouldn't carry, not even a baby's crying.

Daniel pulled into the driveway before the two-story redwood cabin. A wide attached garage sided the house. He drove the van into the space, got out quickly and lowered the garage door. It was dark in the closed garage but he knew his way around. His fingers traced the splintery wall behind him, finding the light switch and snapping it on. The rough-planked room came into view—paint cans, shovels, spiders, and all.

The babies were still crying. He heard, but ignored them a little longer. The door connecting the garage to the house was unlocked. Its knob turned easily in his hand as he entered. The hall was dark and windowless. Waiting until his eyes adjusted, he let it remain dark and went on. Through each room of the house. Through the upstairs bedrooms. Standing absolutely still at the top of the house, he waited, listening for any noise of a pressure on the stair, or a floorboard's creak.

Satisfied that he was alone, he turned on the lights and worked his way back down to the garage. The babies were red-faced and howling. He released one car seat harness and picked up the smallest child first. Her skin was damp and clammy, hair plastered to her head with sweat from prolonged crying.

10

"Come on, Sydney." He tucked her under his arm like a football and carried the infant toward the house. "You can be first."

Chapter Two

By the time Jack and Lydia arrived, the babies were silent. The beat-up Dodge Colt swerved into the driveway, its engine missing so loudly, Daniel could hear the report of it from inside the house.

He watched from the upstairs window: Jack, tall and rail-thin, his oily blond hair falling across such deep-set blue eyes they reminded Daniel of sunken tubs. Lydia's close-cropped dark hair reminded Daniel of the gleaming head of a panther, and just as dangerous. He studied them from behind the curtained window, watching how they reacted to each other. He had personally selected these two. For his purposes, he needed to know them better than they knew themselves.

Jack's voice carried up the staircase to the second-story bedroom as he entered the house. "Logan? You here? Hey, Logan!"

That was the name Daniel had given them. No need for them to know who he was. Logan would do. It kept things clean, strictly for the money. That's what these two wanted, why they'd agreed to this, and why he'd chosen them, for their greed.

Daniel pulled the pistol from under his belt, released the safety and slipped it back in place beneath his shirt. These two were question marks. They had no souls. As far as he was concerned, every minute he was with them meant watching his back.

"Jack." He walked down the stairs and into their view. "You'll wake the children. I wouldn't like that."

"Where are the babies?" asked Lydia. "Did it go all right? Any problems?" Her eyes were steady brown tracks moving out of her. Nothing moved the other direction on those tracks, only staring out, watching.

"No problems." It was all he told her.

Jack hadn't spoken again. He was the weasel. Bony, jutting face—something about Jack reminded Daniel of a creature that ought to be living in a hole. He was gamy. Daniel could smell him across the room. Sweat stains darkened the underarms of his blue nonbrand-name Izod rip-off, and across his belly was a yellow blotch that looked like a dribble of day-old mustard.

Of the two, Jack was the leader.

"You should have been here two hours ago." Daniel ignored the rest of Lydia's question, never taking his eyes off Jack. "What happened?" Daniel's eyes held Jack tighter than a worm to its skin, but he kept track of Lydia, too. If either of them moved, he would have snaked back his arm and pulled the pistol from his belt.

"Jack had to have a drink." Lydia said it, the words straight out and accusatory.

Jack stared at him, his gully-wallow eyes empty-looking and creepy, like two doors left open after everybody's gone home.

"Said he'd gut somebody if he didn't get one before we came here. He's okay now. We can handle it."

Jack's dead blue sink holes dared Daniel to step inside, to crash past the ice walls to the nest of vipers beyond.

"If you don't, I will," Daniel said quietly, stomping through the ice-wall eyes and into the nest, rattlers' tails shaking all around him. "You're responsible for the children, the two of you," he nodded in Lydia's line of vision, never acknowledging the woman with a direct glance. "If anything goes wrong— anything—I'll gut you both myself."

Anger danced in Jack's pupils, orbed points of it, swerving and swaying little cobra heads. He wasn't leader of this twosome because he was the smartest. Lydia was scared of him. Of the two, Jack was the most sadistic.

Daniel picked up his coat and started for the door.

"Logan!" Jack called. "Where do you think you're going?"

The words were a momentary relief. They meant Daniel wouldn't get a knife in the back. "Ditching the van. By now, police in three states will be looking for it." He turned back to face them, holding the doorknob in his hand. "I've got some other business to finish. I'll be gone two or three days."

"Two or three days!" complained Lydia. "And what do we do with these brats while you're gone?"

Quietly, with a menace that was understated, Daniel turned a cold glance on her. "Let me explain something to you, Lydia. These brats are your ticket

14

out of here. Without them, you both may as well pour that whiskey over your heads and light yourselves on fire. I'm paying the two of you to do one thing, take care of the babies while I'm away. Good care. Anything less, will make me unhappy. I wouldn't advise that."

"Jesus Christ!"

Daniel walked out, the sound of Lydia's epithet buzzing in his ears.

Daniel waited in the plum-and-ocher reception room. It was after the office's closing hour of six o'clock on Mondays, but well before the eight o'clock cleaning crew arrived for the night. This was California summer. It wouldn't be dark until 8:30. Enough daylight filtered through the slits in the vertical Levolor blinds for him to see without the need for switching on the light. Light might draw attention. He didn't need that. Daniel moved unhurriedly from the waiting room to the doctor's private office.

The dramatic raised-foil wallpaper drew his attention, swirl upon swirl of muted colors blending into rivers of soft mauve and shimmering gold, capturing his fixed gaze in this distinctly unofficelike setting. It was a gallery, a place for Dr. Walker Reinhard to display his success. And he was successful. The room broadcast that fact from its deeply cushioned sofas and designer original chairs, to the expensive oil paintings on the walls. Every objet d'art on table, wall, or floor said prosperity, prestige, and importance.

The room wasn't anything like the doctors' offices Daniel had ever known: cubbyhole-sized examining rooms smelling of rubbing alcohol, or the fifteen-bed ward where his mother had lingered for three months before she died. It had smelled of other things: sickness, poverty, pain, and death. This room held a vase of roses, fresh-cut flowers that willed a softness to the backdrop, a gentleness blocking all fear of needles, nastiness, and knives. It was a rich man's office, and the money showed.

In Reinhard's private office, Daniel collected the files he'd known would be kept within the locked desk drawer. Men like Walker Reinhard never imagined they would be robbed. The files he wanted were in a bulky records' folder, documents with names, addresses, and phone numbers of infertile couples in Dr. Reinhard's practice. He slipped the folder between his shirt and zippered jacket and locked the drawer. This was one theft Dr. Reinhard would not report.

Locking the doors to the private office and the outer reception room, Daniel left the building as unobserved as he had entered it. His car waited two blocks away. He went to it now and drove to Dr. Reinhard's home.

The house on Sunset Plaza Drive was along a blind curve of the narrow road leading up the hill of this exclusive Bel Air neighborhood. The merely wealthy didn't live here; this was the homeground of the very rich. On these curved driveways were parked automobiles of movie moguls, drug czars, a few well-placed actors and rock stars, and a scattering of international businessmen with vague corporate titles. These were the neighbors of Dr. Walker Reinhard.

Daniel waited in the dark. Monday night. He knew that on Monday nights Reinhard always played poker with five other men at the house of a Middle-Eastern businessman. The game never broke up before midnight. And on Monday nights the doctor never brought home any of the young men who often visited here. On any other evening of the week Daniel couldn't have been certain of such privacy— Reinhard liked his boys—but Mondays were absolute; they were reserved for the Middle-Eastern partners, and for poker.

The headlights of Reinhard's Jaguar sliced twin blades of light through the window and onto the living room wall. Daniel sat on the opposite side of the room where the shadows never lifted. He waited, listening as Reinhard parked the Jag and tripped over a raised flagstone of the walkway leading to the house. He heard Reinhard's soft curse, and the utterance, "Where the hell's the lights?"

There would be no lights; Daniel had seen to that. It was a simple matter of switching off the fuse box. He'd seen to the alarm system, too. That had been more complicated, but he was sure there would be no silent alarm going to any police station, not until a skilled technician came and reprogrammed the tangle he'd made of the home protection system.

Reinhard unlocked the front door and stepped into the dark room, hesitating in the open doorway when the entry light failed to work, paralyzed as a deer exposed in the track of a pickup's headlights.

"Come inside, Dr. Reinhard, and close the door." Daniel never moved from his place in the solid dark.

"Who's there?" The fear in Reinhard's voice was unmistakable.

"Gage." It was the name he had given the doctor when they'd made their initial arrangements on the phone. Until tonight, they'd never met in person.

"Gage? How the hell did you—"

"Move out of the doorway, Doctor. Walk to the sofa and sit down."

The sound of fingers fumbling at the switch carried in the dark. "Why don't the lights work? I can't see where I'm going."

"I decided that it might be better if you didn't see me, healthier for you. Now, come inside and close the door. Of course, if you'd rather see me . . ." He let a hardness come into his voice.

The door shut with a bang, and the room plunged back into dark. Daniel's eyes had adjusted to the blackness. He watched Reinhard stumble to the sofa.

"You were told never to come here."

"I make my own rules."

"I don't pay you to make such decisions. You've put both of us in jeopardy. My neighbors might have seen you."

"No one has seen me. Not even you."

"What is it you want? If you've come here to bargain for more money—"

"I have the children."

Reinhard's breath sucked in. Daniel could hear it, and after, the slow sigh of its release. "So quickly? I imagined it would be some time before . . ."

"You haven't been watching the news. We were the lead story at noon and again at four."

"I haven't watched any television in days. I've been busy at the hospital."

"Too bad. It was good theater: the mothers' anguished pleading, the fathers' angry faces, their eyes stern and unforgiving."

"I'm not prepared to accept—"

"There's no need for you to take them now. We'll care for them until everything is ready."

"We?"

"It wasn't feasible to do this alone."

"You said nothing about bringing in anyone else!" The timbre of Reinhard's voice pitched higher with each word.

"The others won't be a problem."

"I don't want to hear any more." Reinhard was moving, his hand reaching for the lamp switch on the table. The dry click punctuated the stillness of the room.

"No, I suppose you don't." Daniel pulled out the set of Polaroids he had taken of the babies and laid them on a table. Reinhard could look at them later. Then, meticulously, he went over the detailed information sheet he had drawn up on each child, everything from age, weight and blood type, to coloring and skin texture. All of which would be important to Reinhard. He didn't need a light to read it. He knew the information on the sheets. When he had finished, he waited for the doctor to speak.

"From what you tell me, they seem perfect. I'll want to check them personally, of course, but they appear to be—"

"Exactly what you asked for," finished Daniel.

"Yes."

"When I'm ready, I'll call you at your office. If you're not in, I'll leave a message."

"Good God, no! Are you insane? No answering

19

machine. I want nothing to trace me to this business, afterward."

Daniel smiled at Reinhard's caution. The doctor was a man who had managed his own affairs successfully up until now. This wouldn't be the first set of children he had handled, but it was the first he had arranged through someone else. His uneasiness with the situation could be detected by every inflection of his voice, in each word he spoke.

"If you're uncomfortable with the idea of me leaving a message, then I'll just keep calling. Of course, if you'd rather . . . I could come back."

"Absolutely not!"

"No, I didn't think you'd want that. Well then, we'll do it my way. Right?"

"Yes, all right."

He had asserted control of the situation, and they both knew it. Walker Reinhard might be paying for the job, but he wasn't taking the risks. Kidnapping was a capital offense, multiplied by four.

"Time I was going." Daniel moved past Reinhard to the back door. "Some things need my attention. You do your part of this; I'll do mine."

"Wait a minute! We have to decide what happens next."

Daniel shook his head. "No. That's your side of this game. My job is getting you the players."

He started out of the room, but Reinhard called after him. "I don't want to ever see you here again, Gage. Understand that? If you come around again—"

Daniel turned back, the hard flat of his voice challenging Reinhard's own. "I think we understand each other well enough. No need for threats. If I bungle things, you won't pay me. If you bungle things, I'll kill you. Simple."

He moved to the door without another word of protest from the doctor. "You'll be waiting for my call."

Before Reinhard could respond, Daniel was gone.

Chapter Three

"Shut that kid up!" Jack had finished the bottle of bourbon last night, and this morning he was suffering from a head as tight and swollen as a helium balloon. Worse, there was nothing else to drink in the whole house, with the exception of baby formula and milk.

Lydia stood at the second floor landing, tightly holding the squalling Sayers baby in her arms. "Stop it!" she shouted to the child, which made the baby cry even louder. Lydia's attention then turned to Jack. "What do you think I'm doing, trying to make the kid cry? Quit complaining. Come up here and help me."

Jack walked in bearing two armloads of groceries, kicking the door shut behind him. He didn't look happy. "I could hear them crying all the way from the street. If I could hear them, other people could, too."

The noise from upstairs was awful. All four of the brats were crying, making him want to plug his ears, but he couldn't do that. He never knew who might be sneaking up behind him. Especially now. Logan was a cool-eyed sonofabitch. He'd have to listen close for him. The man might need killing.

The babies cried loud and hard, especially the oldest two, Jennifer and Paige, each one setting the other off like slow fuses on a line of fire. He didn't know how Lydia could stand to be near them. She was making a mess of it, anyway.

He glanced up and saw the walking kid, Jennifer Richards, tottering toward the head of the staircase. Little noisemaker was about to fall right down the steps. Maybe they'd have some quiet for a while. He stood observing this small act, making no comment or move to stop it, until Lydia came racing out of the bedroom—a squirming Paige fixed to her hip by the viselike grip of one arm—and scooped up Jennifer just as the toddler's foot started unsteadily down the jagged drop of stairs.

"What's the matter with you!" Lydia screamed at him. "You want the kid to break her neck?"

He considered that.

Lydia had never looked so frazzled. "Try to remember what Logan told us, Jack. He wants these babies in good condition when he comes back. He's not a man to make angry. If this one had broken her neck, he'd have killed you. He'd have killed both of us."

How any baby ever survived its infancy amazed Jack. Slobbering, red-faced little demons. Why all parents didn't smother the screeching things after the first few nights . . .

The din in this house made him mean.

Logan had been gone three weeks. They'd had no word from him in all that time. Jack began to wonder if Logan was ever coming back, or if he'd given up on this as a bad idea, especially with all the TV hype.

The missing babies were a big item locally. He

wondered if it had made any of the out-of-state papers. Jack liked being a part of it, watching the anxious faces of the mothers and matching them with the kids upstairs.

He'd watched them on the late night news and thought about what it would be like to be with each of the women. "I've got your baby," he'd whispered to the TV screen, to the worried eyes, the pulled-down mouths. "What would you do to get her back?"

The thought came to him of calling the women and asking that question. He wanted to feel the terror in their voices wash over him, wanted to hear them beg. The fantasy was exciting. Sex was nothing more than a quick release, but if there was fear . . .

Logan had said to do nothing while he was gone. But Logan wasn't here. He might never come back. It seemed stupid to wait much longer. There was money to be made from those little screamers upstairs, lots of money.

And more, there was that other teasing thought of seeing where this fantasy might lead. What would the mothers offer? He could hear their voices. *Anything, I'll give you anything.* Maybe they would.

Jack sat down, pulled the tablet and box of envelopes from the grocery bag, and began writing the first letter.

"It's been three weeks and the sheriff's investigation hasn't accomplished anything," said Alix Cole. "What about the FBI? This is a kidnapping. Four kidnappings! That's a federal crime, isn't it? Isn't it?" She looked to the other three sets of parents for confirmation. As the only single parent of the group, she sat alone and uncomforted by any but her own hard will. "Like the Lindberg baby? I thought the FBI always took over in the case of a kidnapping."

"Wait, Alix," Diane Kendall interrupted. "I know you're scared—we all are—but please sit down. Let Detective Walsh tell us what she's found out so far."

The parents of the four kidnapped children were gathered at the Kendall home, a sprawling California estate in the prestigious hillside neighborhood of La Cañada. The outside patio where the parents had gathered overlooked the Arroyo Seco canyon, the Rose Bowl, and the extended city of Pasadena.

"Thank you," said Detective Second, Jessa Walsh, grateful for Mrs. Kendall's interference. Diane Kendall was a calming influence on all of them. The mothers and fathers of the four missing children were strung out, teetering on tightropes over a bottomless drop. Walsh was there to lead them through it, across to the other side, where if they was lucky, their kids and sanity waited.

"We've taken a statement from each of you privately, and I want you to know that the department has given priority-level attention to this case, actually cases. Each kidnapping is being handled independently of the others, and separate from the murder of Christine Campbell." Detective Walsh tried to focus on the friendliest among the circle of faces. That was difficult; they were all frowning.

Jessa Walsh felt their torment like a second skin smothering her own. It wrapped around her, clogging her pores with the viscous swell of fear covering them all. And feeling it, she couldn't do her job. She had to pull back, distance herself from their agony, and guard against letting down that shield. It was the only way she could help them, if anyone could.

"Will the FBI look for our babies?" asked a whisper-quiet Susan Richards. She was nervously fingering the buttons of her brown cardigan, pulling the sweater folds together, then letting them drop. Her hands were small and white as an old woman's. Blue veins branched beneath the skin, muted watercolor lines on a pallid canvas.

"Mike," Susan turned to her husband and asked loudly enough for them all to hear, "will they help us?"

He didn't speak, but looked to Detective Walsh for the answer.

"They may, and they may not," Walsh started, feeling on shaky ground with this version of a half-truth. "It's just . . . well, there are so many missing children these days. The FBI are brought in only when a case seems to warrant that kind of high exposure or political pressure. At this point, we don't have a solid lead to explain why your children were taken. My guess is that the FBI may wait to see if there's a ransom note."

"If it's ransom," said Susan, "why hasn't anyone contacted us?"

Walsh could see that the Richards woman was barely holding it together. She was someone on the verge of cracking.

"I don't know the answer to that," Walsh admitted.

"Then what *is* being done to find them?" demanded Alix Cole.

"We've had very little to go on. Right now, we're checking all known sex offenders in the area."

"Oh God," groaned Zack Sayers, burying his face in his hands.

"At this point," admitted Detective Walsh, "it's up to the kidnapper to make the next move. We're expecting that any day now. Any day," she repeated for the parents' benefit, then stared past their worried faces to the calming view of Devil's Gate golf course in the distance, and the curved wall of the Rose Bowl beyond that.

Walsh kept her other thoughts from the parents. It had been three weeks without a single contact from the kidnapper, or clue to the babies' whereabouts. Whoever had taken these children and killed Christine Campbell knew how to disappear without leaving a trace. The fact that the kidnapper hadn't demanded any ransom money was a bad sign. It meant either the children were dead, or the kidnapper had other plans for them.

The thought of those *other* plans didn't sit easily on this clear blue California day. It was the kind of worry that could send a parent right over the edge and into a fear straight from hell.

"I say we take this case into our own hands and hire a private investigator," suggested Alix Cole after Detective Walsh had left them. The group of parents had moved into Diane Kendall's living room when the day turned to evening. "The Sheriff's Department is stalled, waiting to be contacted by the kidnapper. They're *waiting.*" She threw the word out to the rest of them like an insult. "We have to do something if we want to see our children again. We have to hire somebody to help us."

Alix Cole was a striking woman, five-eight, with a model's body, posture, and face. Her shoulder-length hair pulled back from her face lent dark drama to her tan complexion and wary brown eyes. She was a study in sophistication, style, and beauty, and a woman whose entire being was quickened with anger. It was a combination too compelling to allow indifference from anyone who saw her.

"I don't know," said Charles Kendall, Diane's husband. "If we get involved, we might interfere with work the investigators are doing, undermine their efforts."

"Efforts! What efforts?" Alix couldn't contain her fury. "I'll tell you what they're waiting for. They're waiting to find our babies dead. That's how they're planning to close this case."

The trigger of that thought squeezed and fired through the fears of each parent in the room. It was a bombshell, shattering their resistance.

"Do you know someone?" asked Zack Sayers.

She nodded. "If everyone's with me, I'll arrange it," said Alix, glancing in turn at each of them. Their faces told her what she wanted to know. "I have a phone number. I'll make the call tonight."

It was after ten when Jessa Walsh stepped into her wide stall shower. Her naked feet touched the cool of the sea green tiles, a damp chill rising from her legs, to back, to arms, easing its way upward into a soft shudder that coursed through her, escaping as a small sigh. The warm spray hit, soothing the ache of knotted muscles along her neck and shoulders.

She was cold, always icy after working on a case

that scared her. This one did. Turning, she let the full force of the water run across the swell of each breast, pulling the heat from the water into her like a lungful of air. Warming.

Slowly she soaped her body with her bare hands, luxuriating in this sense of touch. Firm flesh beneath her palms, smooth and supple. Alive. She reminded herself of that, sliding fingers along each muscle. Left calf, alive. Thigh, alive. Left breast, alive—

The shower door opened.

He touched her. His arm snaked around from behind, pulling her tight against him. She felt the texture of rough cloth against her skin, his pants and shirt, and the bite of a belt buckle jabbing into her back.

Instinctively, she slammed her heel against his shinbone, as they'd drilled into her at the academy.

"Christ," he said, his fingers twisting in the wet strands of her hair, "you kick like a mule."

The fight left her. She let herself slump against him.

"My God, Dillon," she said, turning in his arms, "couldn't you have undressed first?"

The water sheeted the soap from her, trails of milky white cascading down the drain, her skin glistening pearls of water droplets. His breath was hot against her ear, his open lips tasting her, moving down the wetness of her throat.

She rose to his kiss, her hand moving below his belt. Her fingers worked loose the single button of his pants, found the zipper's tab and tugged . . . all the way down.

* * *

Later, they talked about the case. They lay angled corner to corner across the bed, all covers thrown to the floor. Her head rested where his lap would have been, had he been sitting up. His arm lay slack across her shoulder, his fingers idly cupping one breast.

"God, you're beautiful," Dillon told her, sounding like a kid with a high school crush, instead of a street-smart cop. "You're all shades of cream, pink and yellow, with your hair spread out like that over my thighs." He stroked her skin.

She snuggled closer and kissed him where it counted.

She tried to hold on to the moment, block out everything else, but the case intruded. It started chipping away, fragmenting her concentration. Dillon Rhys still held her physically, but her mind was working on a dead woman.

Who murdered Christine Campbell? And why?

Like an instant replay in her head, Jessa saw the victim again in that first clear image: the woman lying sideways, head neatly centered in a pool of brown blood, knees buckled under her as if she'd suddenly dropped. One bullet entry in her forehead. Whoever had pulled the trigger had been a damn good shot. The single entry wound was proof of that.

In this memory of the crime scene, Jessa saw everything again. Saw herself bending down, leaning in close, trying to get a feeling for what had happened. Make the dead woman talk. The corpse's eyes had been wide open, staring. At whom? Had she known her murderer? Could Christine Campbell tell her the name?

"Dillon?" She nudged him and said it again. "Dill?" She stared at him.

"Hmm?"

"Maybe you should go home. I've got some things I need to do."

"What is this? Am I getting the bum's rush out of here? Don't be so subtle, Jess. Just say so if you want me to leave."

"Go home."

"Right." He slid his legs off the side of the bed and stood up.

"Dillon"—she laid a cool hand on his back—"thanks for getting me through the night."

He smiled, and she knew he wanted to stay. That wouldn't work. She had her own demons to battle. In her case, they were kids, babies, for God's sake.

Her workday had just begun.

Chapter Four

"Touch that bowl, Cat, and you're history." The fat orange-and-white Persian's tail flipped nastily back and forth, lashing the floor, waiting in its killer stance.

The feline, a tom of indiscriminate tastes and referred to as simply Cat, lived with John Tripp in a large old Pasadena plank-sided house. It was a two-story wood-frame matron, past her prime but dignified by hip and valley roof lines and a gracious front porch borrowed from an earlier age when people sat outside in the evenings and spoke to their passing neighbors.

The house was a luxury, too big for a man living with only a cat, but Tripp enjoyed the spaciousness and freedom he felt here. It gave him room to stretch out and pile boxes of files in the extra bedrooms. It was his home. The stamp of his taste was all about the place: in floor-to-ceiling bookcases, in a kitchen that contained a restaurant-style range and grill, in a forest-green-and-pale-gray breakfast room, and in a cool, dark wine room behind the door where a washer and dryer used to be. It was his place, the way he wanted it. That was something an apartment had never been.

Tripp had just stretched his long legs comfortably across the coffee table and settled down to his favorite evening snack of Fritos and bean dip when he got the call. It was his night off, Wednesday, and he knew better than to answer the phone. Five years of working for Pasadena Investigative Consultants had taught him that rule. Pick up a call on your night off and they had you. He ignored the noise and crunched another chip.

The answering machine clicked in after five rings. Much as Tripp would have liked to have been totally unavailable to work, his boss took a dim view of investigators who disappeared so successfully they couldn't be reached.

"Tripp," the baton-hard voice of Maxwell P. Grodin sounded over the receiver like the *thwack* of a leather sap, "I know you're hiding in there, Tripper. Goddamn answering machines. You listening? We got something here. I'm reaching out for you. If you're standing there grinning, watching the tape spin around on that goddamn sonofabitch—" The beep of the thirty-second message timer cut off the rest of Grodin's tender sentiments.

It wasn't hard to rate the level of intensity. Grodin was always guts over gravel—a style left over from his days with L.A.P.D.—but he seldom swore. Tripp rewound the tape and played the message again. Two "goddamns" and a "sonofabitch" meant it was something heavy that couldn't be avoided. Scooping a last bite of bean dip from the bowl, Tripp worried his comfortable old dogs back into his shoes and hurried from the house.

At the closing thud of the door, Cat soft-pawed his way to the table and hunkered down, pink tongue furiously lapping warm bean dip from the bowl. A loud contented purr rolled up from him, like the boil of thunder on the Serengeti.

At 8:00 A.M. the next day, John Tripp parked his red Mazda RX-7 against the split-rail fence at the front of Christine Campbell's La Cañada home.

The neighborhood was quiet, a rustic community of tree-lined streets without the intrusive concrete track of sidewalks, moderate wealth, and country club beauty. Home of NASA's Jet Propulsion Laboratory, La Cañada was snuggled against the foothills of the San Gabriel mountains, at the base of the Angeles National Forest.

Yellow crime scene tape denied access to the area, but Tripp was licensed to trespass. A personal call from Maxwell P. Grodin to the watch commander allowed this escorted look-see. It was a professional curtesy the Pasadena firm would have to pay back at some unspecified future time, in information.

A watchdog cop named Nilles waited to show Tripp around, moving step-for-step with him through the crime area. Nothing could be touched, disturbed, or removed. Nilles was a slightly younger version of Grodin, surly and sour. The sour part was breathing down Tripp's neck, keeping pace with him as he moved through the yard and into the Campbells' house. Tripp tried to mentally dismiss the man and focus his attention on the evidence he was seeing.

The place wasn't what he'd expected. It was a toyland: blue elephant slide behind the sofa, Wonder horse against the wall, Christine Campbell's heavy maple rocker beside a miniature child-size version, yellow mesh playpen, infant swing, gray urethane walker, and baskets of toys and cardboard picture books scattered on tables, couch cushions, and floor. That was just the living room.

And in the kitchen, the chalk outline of a corpse sprawled across the terra-cotta tiles.

A halo of dried brown blood surrounded the place where Christine Campbell's head had lain. Branches of her blood, sappers sprouting from the root, now channeled into dry fingers along the once-white floor grouting. He stared at this corona, noting the location, noticing the homicide team's marks on the floor and wall, and the bloodstains.

He tried to imagine the Campbell woman: brown hair curled and neatly combed, pink T-shirt, white polyester pants and tennis shoes. No jewelry. Visualizing the scene this way, it was possible to believe she wasn't really dead, that he was caught in the moment of that action.

Tripp's eyes pulsed with this quake of false life, and he allowed himself to go with the thought that he was standing in her blood. He listened for it to speak to him. To feel something of what she had felt at the last, to pull him into that instant of death.

He stood in the silence of this place until he was again sure she was dead. A body doesn't live with the back half of its head blown off. Convinced, he pulled the Kodak out of his pocket and loaded a fresh roll of film.

The pictures he snapped were for his own use. The crime scene unit would have taken the official photographs, but their pictures wouldn't be the way Tripp saw the scene now. Their images would be slightly altered, the angles different. He kept snapping the shutter lens, letting the camera become his eyes, exposing the entire roll. Ghostly images. Blinking clear of the illusion, he focused on the brown-spattered window, tile counter, and wall. The bits of brain matter, bone, and blood were real; they didn't pretend anything.

An experienced PI, he knew that the most important time in the investigation of a murder was the twenty-four hours preceding the death, and the twenty-four hours after. Too much before that, and the evidence was insubstantial; too much after and the witnesses forgot what they might have seen, or decided against talking.

Tripp was coming into a case that was three weeks cold, which meant his chances of solving it were somewhere between nil and never. Challenging odds. He liked a challenge.

He looked around for about an hour, then with the uniform in close proximity, Tripp followed his own steps back out of the house and across the front yard. The grass was dry and brown. It looked as if it hadn't been watered since the day of the kidnapping and was quickly returning to what all Southern California was without benefit of piped-in water, a barren desert.

At 10:15 that afternoon, Tripp pulled into the driveway of the Glendale house of Alix Cole. He had specifically asked to interview this first of the four sets of parents at her home, in the hopes of triggering some unexpected clue which neither of them realized existed. It had been Alix Cole who had made contact with Grodin at the office. A friend of hers had recommended John Tripp specifically, hence the late night call.

It was an impressive home, a two-story Mediterranean, embellished with wrought-iron terraces along the French windows forming the upper balcony, and a wide sloping lawn which led to an imposing set of entrance steps. Alix Cole lived in the prestigious northeast section of the city, a place where few people knew the names of the neighbors on either side of their property, and fewer still cared to know them. Glendale was a next-door city to La Cañada, where Alix Cole's daughter Chelsea had attended the Campbell day care.

John Tripp mounted the colorfully patterned tile steps, walked up four flagstone landings to the massive double doors, and rang the bell. He wondered that a single mother could own such a house. It told him something about the woman.

When she opened the door, Alix Cole's face said more. Standing in the open doorway was a strikingly beautiful woman. She was framed by the backdrop of a deep Spanish style foyer and before the intricate design of a twisted wrought-iron railing and carved-tile staircase.

Her eyes and hair were a rich black-coffee brown, shoulder-length loose curls pulled back and held on one side by a wide tortoiseshell clip. She was tall, slim, and wearing a simple white cotton dress, her own deep tan accented by the neutral color. Her makeup, highlighting already dramatic features, was sophisticated and minimal: a medium shade of red lipstick, no visible eye shadow, and a touch of mascara. Without any makeup, she would have been beautiful; with even this small amount, she was stunning.

That she appeared beautiful at all, under these stressful circumstances, was surprising. It meant something. Tripp lodged the fact somewhere at the back of his brain, where all such thoughts lingered until he sorted through them. He had a mental filing system for such instinctive reactions. They were coded under the red letter heading: remember this.

She spoke before letting him introduce himself. "You're John Tripp?"

He nodded a hello. "Thank you for agreeing to see me this morning, Miss Cole."

"Alix. I stopped being seventeen and Miss Anything a long time ago. Come in."

Tripp stepped across the threshold into the wide entry hall and looked around. The hall led away from the front door and past the stairway toward the back of the house, where it crossed and connected with a second hallway. This front hallway was open on two sides by Moorish arches leading to what appeared to be a formal dining room on one end, and a sunken living room on the other.

Beyond the dining room with its wrought-iron chandelier, heavy mahogany buffet, formal table and chairs, was a curved alcove sunny with casement windows and light reflecting off the glass of built-in china cabinets. Few houses in Southern California had both a dining room and a separate breakfast room. This house was a place where a lot of money had been spent, and it showed.

"You have a handsome home." That was what it seemed to him, handsome. Not elegant, or beautiful, but handsome in a very masculine style—nothing like the woman before him.

Alix didn't seem pleased by his remark. She looked around at the thick white walls, the curved arches, and the graceful staircase, no love in the glance she gave them. "This is my father's house. He's dead"—Tripp noticed she hadn't said *"he passed away"* or any other euphemism for death— "but the house still doesn't feel like mine. I've never liked this place, never been happy in it."

He reacted to the remark as if he'd witnessed a child being beaten. Her words had that impact on him: the pain of deep, permanent scarring.

He followed Alix Cole down the three steps to the sunken living room, where they settled on the twin sofas of a vivid red-and-gold sectional. A similar color scheme had been picked up in the occasional chairs, drapery swags, and hearth carpet. The generously proportioned room was large enough to carry the colors. White walls gave no quarrel. Tripp's eyes were sharp for such details as interior design, somewhat unusual in a man; it was one of the traits which made him a good PI. He noticed everything.

"There's something I'm curious about," he said. "Who directed you to me?" Grodin had told him that Alix Cole had asked for him specifically.

"A good friend of mine gave me your name over two years ago. I've carried the phone number around with me all this time, only I never thought I'd need to use it."

He let his glance linger. It was a thing he always insisted on, knowing how people found him. Connections were important to Tripp and often were the source of a lead in a case. "And the friend was . . . ?"

"Laura Martinelli."

The name caused a swell of memories to come flooding back to him. Laura sitting across the table from him on the terrace of the Laguna Hotel, wind blowing her brown hair, and the Pacific Ocean at her back. Laura in slim black heels, brown straight skirt, and white blouse, outshining the works of art at the Huntington Museum. And the final image, Laura clothed only in a cream-colored sheet, after they'd made love.

"We worked together for a few years," said Alix, "before I moved to Arizona. She told me about you. When I married, Laura gave me your number. She never trusted Rick."

It had been a long time since Tripp had thought of her, but if Laura had given his name to Alix Cole as early as two years ago, she must have suspected there might be trouble in Alix's future. But not child trouble; Chelsea hadn't been born yet.

Alix didn't wait any longer to ask the question Tripp had been anticipating. "What have you found out about my daughter? Tell me everything. I have to know."

That was normal, a question any worried parent would ask, given the circumstances. Tripp was relieved that Alix asked it. For now, he wanted to assume all four sets of parents were innocent of criminal involvement in this case. Wanted to, but kept a reserve in his thinking, allowing for the possibility that one of them might have plotted to set up the kidnapping, or kill his or her own child and try to cover the act by this complicated ruse. Worse things had been done to children by their own parents. He knew. He'd seen some of them.

"I'm meeting the other parents for the first time today," he told her. "I've gone over what I was allowed to see of the police records, and I've seen the house. I'll be interviewing some of the neighbors. Right now, I—"

"Do you think my daughter's dead?" It was a hard question, posed without any outward show of emotion and coming without warning.

Tripp was still trying to figure Alix out. She put on a tough front, but he instinctively felt that she was terrified inside. "I don't think we ought to assume anything yet."

"I keep thinking about her, about Chelsea," Alix went on as if he hadn't responded, "wondering if she's alive. If I'm absolutely quiet, it seems as if she's still here, maybe sleeping, and then ..." She visibly pulled back from the vulnerability of the thought. "Why would anyone take four babies?" She hadn't broken yet, or given up. Her eyes were fire bright.

"One obvious conclusion would be for black market adoption, couples willing to pay any price for a child, including breaking the law. If that's happened, we can believe that your daughter and the other three babies will be well treated by their captors."

Alix didn't interrupt; the expression on her face told him she knew there was more, and she was waiting for him to say it.

"Or, there have been cases of young children taken for exploitation. That's possible."

She flinched at that, and he was sorry he'd had to suggest it, but unless she was a very good actress—and he didn't discount that as conceivable—her blanched-faced reaction led him to believe she wasn't the one responsible for her daughter's disappearance. At least, that was his gut instinct, and he went with it for the moment.

"I want Chelsea back."

He had no answer for such a statement. Tripp stood up, feeling the suffering in this house beginning to smother him. He said as gently as he could, "I'd like to see Chelsea's room now. Could you take me there?"

The baby's room was upstairs. It was a dream nursery, complete with fairy-tale motifs on the walls, white eyelet curtains at the windows, and a round carpet woven with images of Beatrix Potter characters covering the hardwood floor. It was a happy room, sunny and littered with bright-colored toys on shelves, and stuffed animals beneath the matching eyelet canopy of the antique brass and porcelain crib.

"I spend most of the day in here. I try to stay away, but it pulls at me. I keep thinking . . . will she ever come back?"

Tripp watched Alix hug her arms tightly to her chest, and the feeling of suffocation in his lungs worsened. This room was the one place in this very formal house where he felt any sense of real love. It made all his questions too hard to ask. He didn't want to cause this woman any more hurt. But he did ask. He had to.

"Tell me about Chelsea's father."

Alix's fingers hooked into the soft weave of a crib blanket, smoothing it against her cheek. "Rick was into drugs."

"Selling, or using?"

"Selling. He made a lot of money in narcotics. I

guess you knew that." They shared a confirming glance.

"Did he operate around here?"

"No, Arizona. I came here after we split up. I was afraid of him by then. Afraid of what he'd become."

Tripp knew he was opening a long-closed vault. He didn't force the door, but pushed his way in carefully. "Tell me anything that you think might be helpful."

"If I tell you and Rick finds out," Alix Cole told him without hesitation, "he'll kill me. You should know that."

It didn't seem to Tripp that she was saying this as a threat. In fact, she didn't look as if she cared at this moment whether she lived or died. She was simply telling him. He waited. No urging of his would pry open these secrets. Only the love of a mother for her child. For the baby who belonged in this room.

"Rick lives in Tucson," Alix began, "at least, he did when I left. I don't know where you'd find him now."

Tripp didn't interrupt with questions. He listened while Alix told him facts he couldn't have bought from the highest paid informant. He would turn the information into specific notes later, when he was alone. For now, he was like the baby's crib.

Empty of all thought, and silent.

Chapter Five

Meeting with the three other sets of parents took up the rest of Tripp's day. Each was a pull of emotion, and after speaking with them, he felt drained.

Diane and Charles Kendall had fixed looks of fear on their faces when they opened the door. Charles Kendall invited him into their home with the words, "You're our final hope, Mr. Tripp. Please, come in. We need you to help us find our daughter."

The house was as much unlike Alix Cole's heavy mausoleum mansion as coq au vin was from Kentucky Fried Chicken. The rooms were large and airy, with picture windows overlooking the green valley below. From the spacious living room, he could see a wooden swing set in the yard. Four-year-old Emily and three-year-old Noelle Kendall were playing on the swings. Each little girl was blond and pert. He could hear their laughter. This wasn't an unhappy home.

He gave the Kendalls a little background on what he'd done on the case so far. It wasn't a lot, and he quickly got to the questions he wanted to ask. "Why do you think your daughter was taken?"

"That's easy," said Diane Kendall. "Money."

Tripp waited to see what else would come of the question. He gave it time. There were things stirring in this room, things he didn't know about. He wouldn't jump in too soon. Let it cook a little. Let the answers froth and bubble to the surface.

Diane Kendall sat up straighter in her chair. She stared at Tripp, eyes calm, looking as if she'd come to a decision. "My husband and I aren't wealthy," she told him, "but my father is, extremely, and well known."

Her husband put a restraining hand on her arm. "Diane. My God, do you think you should—"

"This is exactly the kind of information I need, Mr. Kendall," Tripp homed in, right on target, "things you know of that I don't—yet. I will find out, but it'll save us all a lot of time if we could get things into the open right now. Time might make a difference in your daughter's life." He pushed in his sword and let them bleed a while, and think over what they had to say.

A minute passed. Two.

"I don't care." Diane Kendall jerked free of her husband's hand, stilling him in the muzzled silence of her look. "I have to think of Paige. Nothing else matters." She turned away from the visible warning in her husband's eyes. Tripp noticed this exchange and filed away the message. They were hiding something.

"My father, Harper Pierce, is the president of a multinational banking conglomerate," she began. "If our child was taken for ransom, I think it was because of him."

A story unfolded of a wealthy, powerful man who had climbed to the top of an echelon of international bankers. In that climb, he had sacrificed friends, family, and coworkers. Without question, there were enough people who wanted revenge on Pierce to have kidnapped the Kendall child a hundred times over.

"It's something very few people know about," she confided. "I've kept my father's business a secret from most of my friends and all of my business associates. We thought it might be dangerous for us. You never know what people might do to get back at a powerful man. Who they might hurt."

Ideas were moving around like crabs walking in Tripp's head. If Paige's mother was right, and he believed she might be, it could be the reason the Kendall baby was taken. Why all the children were taken. Money was a powerful motive.

But if money was the reason, why not just the one child? And where were the ransom notes? Since the day the children were taken, there had been no contact with the kidnapper. No demand for money. Nothing.

"If it comes to it, if that's the reason Paige was taken," said Mrs. Kendall, "I'll find a way to force my father to pay the ransom. If I have to hold a gun to his head, I'll get the money."

Diane Kendall was an attractive forty-year-old woman, with elegant looks which spoke of well-bred beauty, a cosmopolitan cultural heritage, and a polished, sophisticated femininity. But the hard set of her eyes as she stared at Tripp in this raw vision of truth, was that of a mother tiger protecting her young.

Whatever else he'd heard this day might be speculation, but of this one fact, he was positive. If it came to it, Diane Kendall would willingly murder her own father to save her child's life.

Tripp's gaze shifted to the two blond little girls playing on the swings outside. *What happens to the innocence of childhood?* He watched them a moment longer before he turned away to leave.

"I'm going to do everything in my power to find your daughter," he promised the worried parents.

Charles Kendall stuck out his hand and Tripp shook it, but it was Diane's eyes which touched him with a greater force. Her eyes were those of someone who had been lost and forgotten for a long time. Tripp knew the only way he'd ever forget those eyes would be if he brought her daughter home.

He left the beautiful house overlooking the green Arroyo Seco canyon, the sound of happy children ringing in his ears.

Zack and Carin Sayers lived in a rented two-bedroom house in La Cañada. There was no other side of the tracks in this prosperous city, but there was the dividing line of Foothill Boulevard, the main street of town where markets, restaurants, and small businesses flourished, and where the hillside estates were separated from homes in the flatlands. Addresses above Foothill Boulevard were considered the more prestigious neighborhoods, on the Flintridge side. Residents added the name to their address and claimed to live in La Cañada-Flintridge. It lent a certain snob appeal. The wealthy lived there. Residences below the boulevard were by and large the attractive and comfortable homes of ordinary folk—teachers, nurses, employees of NASA's Jet Propulsion Laboratory, and couples like Zack and Carin Sayers.

It was nearly four in the afternoon when Tripp

knocked on the door of the Sayers' stucco and rock-faced California bungalow. A dog barked from somewhere inside, and Tripp heard a man's voice call, "Just a minute," and then, "Carin, he's here. Put Rocko in the backyard."

A moment later the door swung open, and a muscular, dark-haired man in his early thirties stood in the shadowed entry.

"Mr. Sayers?"

"Yes. You're the private detective Alix Cole hired?"

Tripp nodded. "I'm with PIC." He handed them his card.

"Pasadena Investigative Consultants," Zack Sayers read the card aloud, then turned it over to the woman who joined him at the door. "This is my wife, Carin." Sayers made an attempt at a formal introductions. "John Tripp."

Carin Sayers, a pale and pretty brunette, had large hazel eyes and softly rounded features. Her hair was caught by a scarf at the nape of her neck, and the gathered hair tucked under neatly into a classic ballerina's chignon. She was attractive in a girl-next-door sort of way. Of the three women Tripp had met since morning, Carin Sayers had the gentlest eyes.

He continued to stand before the open doorway. Neither husband nor wife had invited him in.

"I wonder if we could talk inside?" Tripp suggested at last.

"Oh. Oh, sure. God, I'm sorry." Zack Sayers stepped back and made room for Tripp to come through the doorway. "We're a little"—he seemed to struggle for the right words"–we're shaken up over what's happened. Nobody's thinking too clearly right now."

"How long had you been taking your child to the Campbell day care?" It was an easy question, one to get them started. The tougher ones would come later, when he was sure of what he wanted to know from them. Each set of parents had different information to offer, twists and turns in their family backgrounds, a rock quarry of motivations and connections—one of which might lead him to the kidnapper of the missing children.

Carin Sayers answered. "I brought Sydney to the day care when she was six weeks old."

"Six weeks? Is it common for babies to start day care so young?"

Her expression told him this hadn't been her choice. "These days it is. My pregnancy was difficult. I had to stop work two weeks before Sydney was born. That, plus the six weeks of maternity leave after her birth, meant I'd been away from my job for two months. I was afraid to take off more time than that. Legally, I might have forced them into giving me a longer maternity leave, but I worried that whoever came in to replace me might keep my position, and when I came back I'd find myself a file clerk, or something. Plus, with all the hospital bills, we really needed the money."

The Sayers' home was clean but modest. What looked like a second-hand sofa was the central focus of the boxlike living room. Brown tweed-colored carpeting covered the hardwood floor, good for hiding spills and dog hair. There were no books on shelves, no visible signs of hobby, occupation, or casual pastimes. It was utilitarian basic: one sofa, two chairs, a surface-scarred coffee table, and a portable TV on the small chest of drawers in the corner. The TV looked like the size and quality freshmen students took to college. Tripp guessed this had belonged to one of the Sayers' for just that purpose, a holdover from their single days.

What would a kidnapper want from them?

"Did you have any recommendations from any friends or relatives before you took your daughter to this particular day care? What made you choose the place?"

"It was because Christine took babies," said Zack Sayers. "We looked at ten or twelve home situations and a couple of infant care centers before we settled on Christine. Very few day care homes take infants, children under two. Rules for state licensing regulate how many children one provider can care for in a single family home. If they take in infants, the rule is no more than four. If they take older children, they can have up to six. Because of that, most of the family day care providers refused babies under two. They want to watch the maximum number possible."

"We felt we were lucky to find Christine," said Carin. "She liked the little ones best. She was good to them, really loving." Her voice broke, and it seemed as if she closed down, becoming silent beside her husband.

"I'm wondering," said Tripp, "when Christine interviewed you, did she say she preferred to care for infants?"

Zack Sayers hunched closer to the edge of the sofa, as if picking up on Tripp's insinuation. "Yes, she did. She said she had a reputation as one of the few providers who specialized in infants. She loved newborns. Does this mean something? I mean, does this give you a lead?"

"It might," said Tripp. "If the kidnapper knew her specialty and deliberately chose the Campbell day care over one with older children, it might."

Through the late afternoon and into the early hours of night, Tripp questioned the Sayers. To his every question, they had a willing, ready answer. Nothing seemed held back or hidden.

Among the things Tripp learned was that Zack Sayers worked as a computer technician at NASA's Jet Propulsion Laboratory. He had direct access to a huge network of computer terminals around the world and the information they held. Carin Sayers worked as an assistant editor in a movie-based magazine, *Filmline*. Her access was limited to the contacts she made doing celebrity interviews.

When he left the Sayers' house, trails of as yet unasked questions were beginning to twist like writhing snakes in his mind. Had the kidnapper chosen the Campbell day care because of the age of the children? Or, was it for another reason, one which had to do with the kinds of access to information the parents, or grandparents, held?

If that speculation was true, why wasn't there a ransom note? He walked to his car, the barking of a still-confined Rocko sounding in his ears.

Tripp had skipped lunch that afternoon because of the interviews with the parents. He had one more meeting tonight, with Mike and Susan Richards, but decided that he'd postpone it until after dinner. His stomach was loudly complaining with hunger.

He drove to a small steak house called Sparr's on Foothill Boulevard, and ordered a top sirloin, baked potato, and green salad. When the food arrived at his table, he ate like a starving man. It wasn't hunger, really. The feeling was still there after he ate. What he felt was the emptiness picked up from talking to the families of the missing children. What he felt was loss.

It was 9:15 when Tripp parked behind the old red Mustang in the Richards' driveway. An attractive house fronted the La Cañada property, and a long dark driveway led to the much smaller Richards' house in the back. A single bulb beside the door served as a porch light. Tripp carefully crossed the unlit stretch of lawn leading to the house, stumbling over an unmarked sprinkler head.

The glass-fronted door swung open as he was bent over in pain from what felt like a broken toe. He was grateful for the hard-leather brogues he always wore. He had very sensitive feet and needed all the protection he could get.

"Is that you, Mr. Tripp?" A young woman stood on the porch, peering down at him.

"What's left of me."

"Oh, that sprinkler head. I should have warned you. I've barked my toes on it more than once, myself."

Barked my toes was a southern expression. The voice had revealed only the slightest accent, but he recognized the unmistakable idiom. Texas. He had a good ear for regional dialects and jargon.

"Are you okay?" The man who stepped out onto the porch beside her was Californian through and through. If he wasn't a native, he'd been raised here.

It was all there for Tripp, this dialect placement, sure and instant. It was one of the many talents for which PIC paid him his salary.

He stood up and winced only a little as he took the stairs. "I'm fine. It's my fault for getting here so late. It was too dark to see where I was walking. It's been a long day and I stopped for dinner before I came here. If I'd arrived an hour ago, it would have still been light enough to see that . . . obstacle." It was the mildest choice of the words circulating in his head.

"Come on in, Mr. Tripp," said Susan Richards. "We're anxious to talk with you."

She was about twenty, he guessed, and looked like somebody's kid sister, innocent and sweet. He tried not to let the way she looked influence him, but it did. She wasn't much older than a teenager herself, and now her child was missing.

They talked until late in the night. He learned that Mike Richards worked as the day-shift manager of a Lucky supermarket, one of the West Coast's largest chain of food stores. Susan Richards worked as a secretary for the Glendale City offices. Their combined yearly income was less than forty-five thousand.

Tripp's conclusion was simple. If the kidnapper's motive had been money, he'd picked the wrong set of parents in the Richards. Both their cars and home were accurate indicators of their financial status—fresh out of city college and scrambling for that first rickety rung on the ladder of success.

During the night, Susan made three fresh pots of coffee, and the hours passed. Tripp listened to their best guesses of why their daughter, Jennifer, had been taken. "They're all girls," said Susan. "Has anyone thought of that?"

He had.

"Maybe it wasn't for ransom," said Mike Richards, "but to sell them to somebody else. Maybe that's why we haven't heard anything. Some kind of illegal adoption ring."

He'd thought of that, too.

"Jennifer had her first birthday two months ago," said Susan. "She was learning to walk."

"Honey, don't." Richards took his wife's hand. "What's your best guess Mr. Tripp? Can you give us any kind of hope?"

His best guess wasn't something they would want to hear. Four children taken by a kidnapper who hadn't contacted anyone in three weeks wasn't a good sign. He wouldn't lie to them, but he wouldn't crush their hopes without a good reason, either.

"I'll be following up several leads." The positive statement was true. He'd learned enough from his discussion with each of the parents to approach more than one angle.

"Don't let my daughter be forgotten. I know she's alive. I feel it. You keep searching for her. Promise me." It was the last thing Susan Richards said to him.

He was almost moved to tears by the way she'd said this. It had been a long time since he'd cried over a case, even one involving a missing child. Or four. "I'm just getting started, Mrs. Richards. I'm a long way from giving up on her, I can promise you that."

That night, alone in the dark silence of his bedroom, Tripp thought of what Susan had said. "I know she's alive. I feel it."

Could a mother know such a thing? Really know it?

He fell asleep wondering, dreaming of cradles, empty and rocking with the thrumming pulse beat of fear.

Chapter Six

"So let's go over this one more time." Tripp leaned into the question. "What exactly do you mean, you think you saw something?"

Mr. Albert Jacobson seemed in no hurry. He rested his hands over a stomach that looked as if he'd inflated it with a bicycle pump, closed his eyes to concentrate, and said, "I believe maybe I saw the killer."

Tripp sat up so fast, his ankles cracked. They did that if he moved too quickly. Loose joints, his mother always said.

"Tell me what you saw, Mr. Jacobson."

He didn't put any words into the man's mouth. Didn't say—*What did he look like?* If the killer was a man—and Tripp was assuming he was—he wanted Jacobson to say so. The print lifts from the carpet were size twelve, a man's hard-soled loafers. That was the kind of information he'd just as soon keep to himself.

"It was one of them buses . . . no, that's not right. Vans! That's what they call 'em." Mr. Jacobson's face sugared up in delight with finding the word. "A new one," he specified. "It had sliding doors on the sides, like for deliveries."

Maybe he'd been wishing for too much. Tripp eased himself back. This wasn't the lottery. You couldn't expect to go to the Big Spin on the first ticket. He calmed down his buyer's fever, and settled down for a nice "A" ticket ride. Please remain seated until Mr. Lincoln comes to a full and complete stop.

"You saw a van?"

Albert Jacobson nodded. Tripp thought that was all the information he was going to get, but then Mr. Jacobson started up again, his voice hissing like a split tire at the beginning and the end of sentences. Asthma? Emphysema?

"It was blue," Jacobson said. "Dark blue."

Tripp went at this slowly. "You said you saw the killer."

"I didn't say that. No. I said I might have seen him."

"Mr. Jacobson—"

"Now, don't interrupt me. I'll tell you what I know, and then you tell me if I saw something, or I didn't." He said it with a testy little snap to his jaw. "You keep talking, we'll never get nowhere."

Tripp shut his mouth and listened.

"That Monday, I saw a blue van parked outside my house for about an hour. Noticed it because nobody ever parks there, not even me."

Tripp kept his amazement that Jacobson was still driving to himself. "What time was this? Do you recall?"

"Are you going to let me tell this?" the man bristled. "How the hell do I know what time it was? Morning's all I remember. Pretty early. It looked to be hot out, and I was resetting my sprinklers to give the grass an extra day's watering. I don't set my sprinklers to water every single day . . ." He broke stride, taking one long, wheezy breath. "Some folks around here do, but that's a waste, what with the drought and all. Only need to do that in the dog days of summer, and even then, not every single day."

"If you could just tell me what you saw."

It was getting more stifling by the moment in this room. Jacobson must have the heat turned up to ninety. Tripp longed to open a window for a little air. Mr. Jacobson's green eyes were staring at him, that thin-lipped mouth pressed shut. It was going to stay shut, too, unless Tripp said something resembling an apology.

This was the silence of the irritated old. There was no way of waiting it out, Tripp knew from experience. The old had forever.

"Sorry, Mr. Jacobson. I am sorry, really. It's just that I'm sort of in a hurry. You understand. I just need to know what you saw."

"What do you think I'm telling you?"

Tripp nodded, hoping he looked contrite. A bead of sweat dripped off the end of his nose. His shirt was stuck to the wooden chair back, and it seemed his Right Guard had failed.

"Would you mind if we opened the front door, or a window?"

"And let out all the warmth? No-sirree-bobtail. I'm not paying electric bills to buy heat I can keep in the house my ownself. That's just like the young of this country, wasting all the things nature gives us for free."

Desperation inspired brilliance. "Let's go outside."

Tripp ripped his shirt free of the chair and headed for the door. "I would appreciate it very much if you'd show me where the van was parked."

"I can't do that." Jacobson refused to budge. "The neighbors would see me talking to you."

"They've already seen my car in your driveway," he reminded him. "Your neighbors know I'm here. Let's go outside, Mr. Jacobson. Now." He moved to the door and opened it. The fresh air rushed in at him and he sucked it into his lungs in huge, refreshing gasps. Somewhat restored, he walked out onto the spongy dichondra lawn.

Remarkably, Jacobson followed.

"This was where the van was parked?"

Jacobson nodded.

"You say it remained outside your house for about an hour?"

Jacobson nodded.

"And it was blue?"

Jacobson nodded again.

Tripp waited for the man's neuroconnectors to link up, for thinking to jolt in, but nothing happened. Jacobson remained unreflective as a rock.

"Mr. Jacobson," Tripp finally asked, "did you see anyone get out of that van? Anything unusual?"

The man didn't speak. Jacobson, the outdoor mute, stood like a loose-headed statue on the dichondra, white hair swaying side to side. No.

"All right." Tripp gave up. "I think that's enough. Thank you very much for all your help, Mr. Jacobson."

He'd found out zip, but at least this interview was over. He began to think longingly of driving home with all the car windows down, taking a cooling shower, and changing into fresh clothes. His feet were fast-tracking it toward the car when he heard that unmistakable squeaky wheeze. Jacobson was going to speak.

"Hey you, fella! Don't you want to hear about the man I saw going *into* the Campbells' house?"

Tripp pirouetted.

Albert Jacobson drew a long breath, the sound of a balloon slowly letting out air, and whispered, "I can't tell you out here. Too many ears."

Jacobson walked back into the house. The sweatbox. "You coming?" Albert Jacobson called from the porch.

Those green eyes were watching him. Feeling a channel of sweat start to trickle down between his shoulder blades, John Tripp moved like a condemned man, across the dichondra, up the porch steps, and through the door of the oven.

Jacobson quickly shut the door. Didn't want to let out any of the heat.

"Poor baby," Elaine Warner crooned. She handed Tripp a Coors in a tall, cold can. She never did that, waited on him, but tonight she did. She was a woman he had dated a few times, and now was a sometimes sex partner. He didn't love her; she didn't love him. They were together tonight because they liked each other well enough for sex, but that was where their relationship ended.

He was prostrate in a tub of tepid water, a portable fan plugged in on the far wall, blowing a current of cool air across his wet skin. Every so often, he'd dunk his head under and come up spewing steam.

"You shouldn't have an electric fan near that tubful of water. You trying to fry yourself?"

Tripp's eyes did a ceiling roll. "I did that already, earlier today."

She dangled her hand idly in the tub, trickling droplets from her fingers onto his chest.

"If you want to play little fishy," he said, showing signs of life, "I've got a rod you can handle."

She peered into the clear depth. "Do you?"

He grabbed her hand and pulled it down to feel.

"I thought you said you were worn out."

"Never that tired."

"Okay," she agreed, pulling the white cotton T-shirt over her head and sailing it across the room. The bra followed. She had to sit on the edge of the wet tub to unlace her running shoes. His hand copped a feel while she tugged off her socks.

"You're getting me all wet," she said.

"Oh yeah?" He sat up and slipped his other hand around for a doubleheader. "Well, you're getting me all—"

"Never mind." She stopped him, staring down into the water at the standing issue. "I think I see the point."

Her dark blue pants came off, the lace-edged panties, too. She stepped into the tub. He fed his eyes on the curves of her, rising and falling above him. Rising and falling. The water moved with her, pulsing the whole length of his body, like a heartbeat that swallowed him whole.

Her body arched back, and she braced her hands behind her on his legs. He focused on the rounded swell of her breasts as they moved with every catch of her breath. Then none of it was her anymore, just him, feeling ... only feeling. His eyes were fogging and the sound of that pulse roared in his ears, until the heartbeat exploded, shattering the pulse and the fog and the sound.

Tripp, contented and quiet in body and soul, rested. The world was a peaceful, beautiful place. He wanted nothing more than to lie completely still, and drift.

"Let's get out of here. I'm going stir crazy in this place." She poked him with a finger in the center of his chest.

He lifted one eyelid.

"Really," Elaine poked again. "I mean it. I'm hungry."

"You want us to get dressed? To go out to eat? After what we've just ..."

She had the decency to look contrite. "I'm starving."

Sighing, he climbed out of the tub, dripped across the bathroom floor, pulled his old clothes over a still wet body, and headed out the door. To dinner.

It had been that kind of a day.

"As it stands," Tripp reported to Maxwell P. Grodin the next morning at PIC, "we have two possibilities. The Kendall baby has a rich, powerful grandfather. The motive could be ransom."

"And the other?" Grodin's fist was knobbed at his chin, the knuckles working the loose flesh. His face was deeply ruled with lines that over the years had grown into canyons, dark and glowering.

"The Cole baby's parents are separated. According to the mother, the father's capable of anything."

"Of murder?" Grodin specified, reminding him that this case wasn't only a kidnapping.

"Apparently. Alix Cole says he was very heavily into the drug business. The cops have been looking for him, but so far he's snug under a rock."

"What about the other two families? Any leads on them?"

"Nothing much. They seem fairly ordinary."

"Nobody's all that ordinary," Grodin reminded him. "That's one of the things you learn with a few years on Homicide. Trust no one. Everybody has a motive, if you dig deep enough. Each of us is capable of killing. And sometimes it's the person you least suspect who turns out to be the ax-murderer."

"I know, I know." Tripp turned his palms up to signal *enough*. "It's Day One, okay?"

"Wrong." Grodin's fist came down on the desk. "Three weeks ago was Day One. Those kids are out there, if they're still alive. You may be the only chance they've got of getting home."

"Thanks for not putting on the pressure."

Grodin shrugged. "It's the nature of the job." He took some quick notes, then looked up from the yellow legal pad. "I'll get someone to put a few lines out in Tucson for Rick Cole's last known whereabouts. You follow the lead on the Kendall baby's grandfather." Grodin went back to furiously scribbling notes, then glared up at Tripp a minute later.

"You still here?"

"No." Tripp was out the door and halfway down the hallway before he heard Grodin shout, "Somebody get me the phone book for Tucson!"

* * *

The mail carrier dropped the letter into the brass slot of the La Cañada house along with a loose shuffle of five or six bills and advertisement circulars. For hours, it lay undisturbed within the house's inside letter box. Waiting.

Susan Richards was alone. Her husband, Mike, fearful of losing his job at the market, had returned to work after the first two weeks. She'd tried to do the same, to go on as if life could return to normal, but had only been able to start back at the city offices on part-time hours, because she didn't have the strength to be away from the house for longer than that.

She felt she needed to be home in case someone called, in case there was word from whoever had taken her daughter, or someone walked up to the door and brought Jennifer back. But that didn't happen.

She'd cleaned the house, whipping out the demons of her soul with hard labor. It hadn't helped. Nothing had. And now, this.

Susan's hands shook so badly, holding the ink-scrawled sheet of paper, she nearly tore the letter in half trying to open it.

The letter had come in this morning's mail, a common white drugstore variety envelope, with a single sheet of lined tablet paper. The contents of it was no more than a roughly scratched-out message. It was a nightmare from which she couldn't wake.

Your kid's alive. Do nothing till I tell you. If you go to the cops, I'll know and I'll send you back her eyes.

Susan put the letter down, the touch of the paper

burning like fire against her skin. A maniac had written this. A maniac who held her child . . .

"Jenny's alive," she whispered to the bound terror that held her spirit. "Oh God. Oh please, God. Help my baby."

She wouldn't tell the sheriff's team of investigators. She would say nothing about the letter to Detective Jessa Walsh, or to PI John Tripp. She would even hide it from her husband. She was too afraid. All that mattered was that Jenny was alive. Nothing would make her risk the threat to her daughter that the letter promised.

If you go to the cops, I'll know, and I'll send you back her eyes.

Susan sat in the silence of her baby's room, the light of late afternoon fading into evening dark. She moved to the slow rhythm of the white rocker against the wooden floor. Rock-rock. Rock-rock. Like the sound of a heartbeat. Like the sound of a baby's heartbeat.

And wondered: *Is my baby still alive?*

Chapter Seven

Diane Kendall didn't leave her house anymore. The phone might ring. A ransom note could arrive from the kidnapper. Her baby Paige might somehow come home. Each day she checked the crib; it was always empty. Each day she sat for a time in her daughter's room and waited for something to happen. It never did.

Diane had lost all interest in work. Since Paige's kidnapping, she hadn't gone back to her job. The company offered to give her some time and use an office temp in her absence. They wouldn't attempt to fill her position. She told them not to bother. It didn't matter. She knew she'd never be back. Reluctantly, they took her advice and hired someone else.

In the last weeks, she had become obsessive about her other children. Her husband drove the two little girls to school every morning, and picked them up every afternoon. No one else was allowed to drive them. The children couldn't go to their friends' houses to play after school, and their friends didn't want to come to the Kendalls' house. It made the other childrens' parents uncomfortable. After all, something terrible had happened to the Kendalls. Other parents were careful how they said it, but the truth was, they wouldn't let their children come to the Kendall house. It wasn't safe.

While the children were in school, Diane simply waited. She made no effort to do anything. Every movement was a cost of energy, and she felt drained, depleted. She didn't work, cook, clean, read, or care about how she looked. Each day she dressed in whatever blouse, skirt, or pants she could find. It didn't matter if the colors clashed. Who would see her? Nothing mattered anymore.

She found it was nice to hear a voice in the background, something to keep her company. Nothing she had to concentrate on, or listen to very carefully. A steady noise, that was what she wanted. Talk shows were nice. She could sit on the couch and hear the rise and fall of voices, and feel herself distracted by the sound.

Enough to keep from screaming. Enough to keep from thinking about what was happening to Paige. Was she alive? Was she starving? Was she hurt?

Diane felt a familiar panic start to engulf her. In a minute she would stop breathing. In a minute she would faint, and Charles would find her on the floor, again, and there would be more talk of doctors. Her mother had been hinting.

She didn't need doctors; she needed her child.

The talk show host began to introduce her guest. The only word for describing the woman sitting across from the host was soft. She was an image of comforting roundness, from her hair pulled into a spongy-looking bun on the top of her head, to rosy apple-dumpling cheeks, a weighty bosom, and stubby body. She was calm, that was the sense Diane had of her, a calmness that enfolded the woman like a heavy coat. Diana longed for such calmness. She hungered for it.

"My guest today," said Bari Maxwell, the talk show host, "is Rowena Rawlings Crawford, a thirty-four-year-old woman from Millford, West Virginia. Up until five years ago, Rowena lived a peaceful, if somewhat secluded life in the backwoods of Millford."

Diane thought how nice it would be to live in the backwoods of anywhere, how nice not to see anyone. She stared at the woman, feeling again that sense of peace coming over her like a burning light.

"Five years ago, something happened to you, didn't it, Rowena?"

Rowena nodded. A faint smile pulled at the corners of her lips. Like a Buddha, thought Diane, serene, peaceful.

"What happened that day," said Bari, "was an accident that almost took Rowena's life." Bari Maxwell smiled reassuringly at the woman on stage. "It was chilling, the event that changed your life."

Rowena nodded.

Diane was listening, intent on every word, waiting for the guest to speak. She was drawn to the woman, as if there were some connection between them. She felt it. Knew it.

"On that day two years ago," said Bari, "you were walking home from the local market. It was late in the afternoon, beginning to get dark, and you were carrying two heavy bags of groceries. Tell us if you will, Rowena, what happened then?"

The camera brought a close-up on the plain, unremarkable face. Brown eyes stared directly at Diane. Looked at her. "We had no rain on that day, no warning. Nothing to warn a body of what was coming. It was clear sky, sunny. Only thing I recall out of the ordinary was the smell. The air had a burning in it, like a scorched frying pan. Like that," she explained, "only stronger."

Diane knew the smell. It was the way her wok smelled when it was hot, before she put oil into it. She leaned forward, wanting to know what Rowena would tell her. That was how she felt, as if Rowena were speaking directly to her.

"Do you remember what happened along the road?" Bari asked.

"I was hit by lightning. That's what they told me, all them doctors, when I woke up at the hospital. I don't recall anything past that odd scorchy smell. Doctors said a bolt of lightning went right through me, entered the top of my head and went out the sole of my foot."

The audience provided the appropriate muffled gasps. Bari knew how to pump a moment. "The fact is, a lightning strike like the one you have described would kill most people. I think of it"—she paused for emphasis—"a bolt of lightning cutting through your body, head to foot, and I can only imagine the extent of excruciating pain. To have survived that . . ." She let the thought trail off. "You must have been in agony."

The woman shrugged. "That time is gone from my memory, burned out. See this?" she leaned forward. "My hair's white where the lightning cut through my scalp." The camera pulled in close and let the viewers see the wide triangle of pure white hair, startling against the dark mahogany hair of her crown.

Unconsciously, Diane put her hand on that same part of her own scalp. For an instant a shudder traveled through her, from the top of her head straight down. She made a sound when the shock wave hit her, as if she had been electrified. But nothing had changed. She was still on the couch in her living room. She was still watching television. Her breathing and pulse were normal.

But she had changed. Inside, she felt different. Touched by that woman.

Rowena held a small wooden box on her lap. She opened the lid and showed the contents to the camera. "These metal buttons were stitched onto my dress." She dropped the four lumps of metal onto her hand. What lay on her palm bore no resemblance to buttons. "They melted when that bolt struck me. Some of the tins in the grocery sacks I was carrying melted, too. I didn't own none of it, understand what hit me, till I was well again. I saw what them cans looked like, little lumps of metal, and I threw the mess away. I kept the buttons, though, for a remembrance."

"As a result of the lightning strike, you began to notice that something about you had changed," said Bari. "Tell our viewers about how you realized you had become a psychic, that you could see into other people's lives."

The camera did a pan of the audience. For the first time, Diane noticed them. The row of faces were haunted-looking, like hers. Suddenly, she understood. They were there because Rowena was a psychic.

Like Diane, they had missing pieces torn from their lives.

"There were lots of things I just knew, after that," Rowena explained. "I don't try to understand how it works, whether it be a gift from God, or that lightning touched some part of my brain and made it work harder, sharper. Don't know how or why. I only know I see things now, and I never did before."

The story went on, interrupted every few minutes by ill-timed commercials. Rowena told the audience how she had begun working with the parents of missing children in Millford and several surrounding areas. She explained that she was drawn to these families and their pain. As a result of the information given by her visions, the police had located many of the children. Most were found dead.

Three women were selected from the audience. Mothers. Each carried something that had belonged to her missing child: a baby shoe, a teddy bear, a jacket. The women sat on stage, their faces blanched by the strong lights. They told their stories without tears. Diane understood. Tears had been burned out of them. Tears were gone, vanished like their children.

One by one, Rowena touched the objects given to her by the women. She closed her eyes. When she touched the jacket, she gasped. Diane felt the same fear and gasped, too.

"Your boy's asleep," Rowena said gently. "He's at peace. Nothing can harm him anymore." She folded the jacket tenderly and handed it back to the mother. Now, the woman cried. Diane cried, too, tears she hadn't been capable of for so long. She sobbed, sharing the mother's terrible loss.

"We'll take a break," said Bari. A commercial interrupted the tender scene, advertising feminine hygiene products. Diane rushed to the kitchen, grabbed a box of tissues, and made it back in time to see Rowena holding the teddy bear.

Again, Rowena closed her eyes. This time, there was no audible gasp, or any visible sign of disturbed reaction. She held the bear as if it were a child, cradling it in her arms in the same way the mother had. "I'm in a car," she said. Her voice sounded high and strange. "It smells bad. Something over my mouth. Out the window, I can see a house with no roof. There's an old tree by it. The car's taking me to that house. A black dog. I can't breathe . . . I can't breathe." There was a pause, and then, "I can't see anymore."

For a moment, Diane couldn't breathe, either. There was a long silence, and then the second mother asked, "Do you think my daughter is alive?" The mother's eyes were dark, dry wells of pain.

"Her body's out there, buried near that house," said Rowena. "Maybe, in it. She was afraid, your little one. She lived for a while, I think. It's so much better for her now. She's not afraid anymore. The hurt's over. It was a man who took her, someone she knew. He drove a green car, with brown leather seats."

"Oh God," said the woman. "My cousin has a car like that."

Rowena didn't react to this. "She's not real far away from where you live. You drive out to the country. You'll see the house with no roof. That's where you'll find her."

"She's dead?"

Diane wished the mother hadn't asked.

Rowena didn't flinch from the question. "She was so tired. It was too hard to wait. It's all right now. She's sleeping."

The mother's face showed that she had known it, expected it. There were no tears, only the shattered stillness of grief.

Diane wanted to turn away from the program. The pain from those women reached into her. She felt more than she had allowed herself to feel in weeks. Their grief was too close to her own, too hard. Was her baby *asleep?*

She couldn't turn away from it, any more than any of those women on stage could turn away, any more than any of the haunted faces in the audience could turn away. This simple woman, Rowena Rawlings Crawford, could be the only connection to her child, to all their children.

"I want you to look at this last object, a baby's shoe," said Bari, "and tell us what you feel about it, if you can give as any information for our last mother on stage."

Rowena picked up the white satin shoe. It was an infant's size, not as big as the palm of her hand. She closed her fingers around it gently, and shut her eyes. When they opened, a smile was on her face.

"Your boy's alive."

The audience cheered. The mother broke into joyful tears.

"He's with a dark-haired woman. I hear her singing to him," Rowena told her. "She calls him ... Ben, or Brian. She's wearing a white dress, a uniform, like a nurse. He's in a stroller in the park. There's an apartment, a gray stone building, across the street from the park. I see a cab go down the street ... yellow, with markings around the top."

"A checkered cab," Bari Maxwell broke in.

Rowena seemed to ignore the interruption. She was still concentrating on her vision. "He's a happy baby, smiling, looks well cared for. The woman's not the one who took him. Somebody else. A man, I think. Yes. A man whose name ... I can't get it. Starts with an *R*, I'm sure of that.

"I think your baby was given to these people, maybe sold to them in an adoption. He's loved, I see that. You don't need to be scared about him being hurt. They're good to him. He's alive"—Rowena turned to the final mother on stage, touching her hand—"and he wants his mama."

Diane was choking on tears. They were streaming down her cheeks faster than she could wipe them away. She was making noises like some kind of hurt animal. She needed help. She needed help desperately.

The talk show was over. The closing music brought up program credits, accented by the sound of a final applause from the audience. By the time the picture switched to a series of hour-break commercials, Diane was dialing long distance information, asking for the number of the station.

Finally, she was put through to the show's production manager. "Please," she said, her voice unsteady, "I need to speak to Rowena Rawlings Crawford. This is an emergency."

Chapter Eight

Morning was the worst time, thought Lydia, as she spooned another gobbet of lumpy oatmeal into Chelsea Cole's straining mouth. How could kids eat this stuff? It looked like warm wallpaper paste. Probably tasted like it, too.

Jennifer, Paige, and Sydney were all howling for their breakfast. Babies had no patience. She could say "Just a minute" a thousand times, and they'd still be screaming for what they wanted. Babies worked on the principle of: if it's in your hand, you have it; if it's not, you have to yell. It worked pretty damn effectively, too. Drove her nuts, all that crying.

She handed morning bottles of milk to Paige and Chelsea. The noise level changed from loud crying to the sound of snuffled tears and furious sucking. It always amazed Lydia how they could turn off the waterworks like that. Neither of them put out another tear once they got what they wanted. And kids were supposed to be so innocent. Not hardly. They were calculating, manipulating, demanding little egomaniacs.

She had learned something working with these

four. She never wanted to have any babies of her own. Let somebody else feed, diaper, and walk the floor with the little screamers. She'd had enough.

Six-month-old Sydney turned red in the face. She was too young to hold a bottle for herself, and even when Lydia propped it up on a blanket, the kid managed to let it roll away.

"Hang on a minute," Lydia called to the squaller one more time, as if it would make any difference. Nothing was going to shut that kid up until she got what she wanted. Cause and effect. It worked perfectly.

"Dammit!" Jack shouted from the top of the staircase. "You make that one shut up, or I will!"

Jack had been drinking again—God knew where he got it this time—and the likelihood of a killer hangover was better than even money. He had pickled what little was left of his brain. Screaming babies wouldn't help the colossal headache that must be giving him a taste of retribution right about now.

Lydia scooped Sydney onto her lap before Jack could stomp down the stairs and squash her. She wouldn't put it past him. When he was drunk, or getting over a night of drinking, he didn't give a thought to her, Logan, or anybody. He would have stomped the noise out of the kid, and thought better of it later.

It wasn't easy, but she managed to hold the baby propped against her, one hand holding the bottle for Sydney, the other hand-spooning oatmeal into Chelsea's open mouth.

She listened to the sound of shuffling hesitation at the top of the stairs. It would take some effort to move Jack's body down the steps. She didn't think he'd try it, unless something drove him crazy. If that happened, there was no telling what he'd do.

"Jesus, Lydia! Why can't you get off your lazy ass and keep them kids quiet? My head's killing me. Dammit to hell. Put a rag in its mouth, for God's sake."

His feet plodded across the hardwood floor above her. He was going back to his room. He'd fall on the bed, and if they were lucky, he'd sleep most of the day away without giving her too much trouble. If they were lucky. Sometimes, he could be a real pain in the ass. That's when she had to be careful. He was a jerk, but a dangerous one.

Not for the first time since they'd been here, Lydia mulled over the thought that something would have to be done about Jack. Like the screaming babies, he was asking for cause and effect. A little more cause, and she was about to give him the effect he needed. A bullet between the eyes would probably do it.

The oatmeal dribbled out of Chelsea's mouth faster than Lydia could shovel it in. "Had enough, huh?" Lydia tore a paper towel off the roll and swiped at the kid's face, removing the worst of the mess. The baby squirmed and twisted.

"Okay, time for a changing of the guard." Lydia lifted Chelsea out of the high chair, swabbed up the spilled oatmeal from the seat cushion, scooped Paige from the floor, and put her in the much-coveted place of honor, the feeding chair.

Oh God, she thought miserably, *three more to go.*

Chelsea was crawling beneath the kitchen table, going for the plug outlet. Paige was moving fast on new-walking legs toward the forbidden stairs. Jenny, her morning bottle polished off, pulled herself up to stand at Lydia's leg, and reached for Sydney's bottle while picking pieces of Paige's breakfast off the high chair tray.

She'd be glad when Jack was sober again. He hadn't told her what he was up to last night, but she knew it was something Logan would most likely kill him for. Logan *could* kill him for all she cared. Jack never helped her with taking care of the babies. Why Logan had picked him was beyond her. Men could do the stupidest things, picking somebody like Jack to take care of babies. Might as well bury the kids and get it over with. Seems like anyone clever as Logan would have gone for somebody smarter.

He picked me, she reminded herself glumly. Had to give him a little credit.

Money or no money, she wasn't going to stay here much longer. Logan was taking his sweet time making the deal over the babies. Four weeks! How long could it take to ransom the little squallers?

Something wasn't right. Lydia felt it in the core of her bones. If things turned sour, she wasn't going to be the one stuck here holding the kids when the cops pulled up. She'd abandon them and get out of the house before she'd let that happen. The kids didn't mean a thing to her; they were trouble looking for a place to fall.

And while she was thinking about it . . . what the hell was going on with Jack? What about all this running back and forth to town? He was up to no good, that much was sure.

Sydney fell asleep on Lydia's lap. "That's one less bowl of cereal to make this morning," she said to the finally quiet baby. "Wore yourself out with all that crying. I guess you'll do without. That'll teach you."

Lydia carried the sleeping baby upstairs and put her down for a nap in the crib nearest the wall. She tiptoed on her way out, not wanting to wake the sleeper.

It wasn't Sydney she was worried about. Jack was in the room next door.

Jack couldn't resist calling. He'd given the matter a lot of thought, mostly late at night, alone in bed. He wanted to hear the pleading voice of each woman as he bargained with her for her kid's life. He had imagined whole scenarios, mostly ending in plenty of money and sex. Right now, he could use a little of both.

The letter had been fun. It had satisfied a need for a little while. He got a kick thinking about the fear he'd put into that cool-eyed woman. He guessed he'd shook her up good. That had got him off for a while, thinking about it, but the pleasure hadn't lasted. It had been two weeks ago, and it wasn't enough anymore. His needs had been climbing.

He needed to hear their voices.

Jack drove to Palmdale. He thought of Logan as the line connected and he heard the distant ringing. Logan wasn't here now. He didn't have to know everything. Logan didn't have to listen to brats crying and puking all day, either. Second ring.

"Come on, baby, pick it up."

"Hello." The voice was exactly the way he'd imagined it, soft-sounding, young, vulnerable.

"Carin Sayers?" He spoke her name in curt, hard syllables, the way he'd practiced. It was important that he sounded powerful. That's what would work for him, the power.

"Yes, this is Carin." He could hear the slight rise in the tone of her voice. Nervousness? Fear? Excitement? The same feelings were charging through him.

"I have your baby." He said it bluntly. That would be the most effective. Hit them with that, and see how they squirm. He shut up and let her dangle.

"Oh God!" Her voice was way off the tremble scale now. He thought he heard a little whimper. It gave him a rush.

"Where is she? What have you done with her?" She was demanding, as if that would get anywhere with him. Then her voice dropped lower. It was in that pleading tone that he wanted to hear. "Is Sydney alive? Tell me . . . please, tell me."

Now they were getting somewhere.

"I saw you on TV," he said. "You gotta nice shape. Big, pale eyes. I watched you."

She started crying; he could hear it. That was okay. It was getting him excited, pulling all her strings.

"Don't hurt my baby." Her voice sighed and whispered over the line. "What do you want from us? Is it money? Please, give me back my baby."

"Not yet," he said. That was meant to feed her hope, and it worked.

"When can I see her? When will you give her back to me? I'll give you whatever you want . . . only, give me my baby."

Those were the words he'd wanted to hear. *I'll give you whatever you want.* Just like he'd imagined it late at night in his room. It felt the way he'd known it would, a big superblast of a high. Only, he needed more.

"Say you want me." The words were ice cold in his mouth.

"What?"

"Say you want me, or you'll never see your kid again."

There was silence on the line, a terrified white pulse of silence.

"Say it!" he screamed. Goddamn her! Goddamn her! Goddamn her!

"I ... I want you," Carin Sayers cried into the phone. Over and over, until her voice cracked with weeping and choked with the drowning sound of muffled sobs.

Jack heard it all. For a moment, it gave him a measure of peace. Then, without another word, he hung up the phone. He didn't have any more time to waste on this one.

Later, there would be three more mothers to call.

Chapter Nine

Detective Second Jessa Walsh knew that the primary investigation in any juvenile missing person case was the family. Nine times out of ten the perpetrator turned out to be a father without legal custody, an uncle with sexual leanings toward child pornography, or a relative with a history of mental disorders. In most cases, when children were murdered, abused, or stolen, the enactor was someone in the family, someone the child knew. Detective Walsh's first list of suspects, therefore, were the parents of each child kidnapped from the Campbell day care.

Walsh had seen enough of these cases to know. It had been three years since little Amy Peterson's homicide. The circumstances of that case, the clues Jessa had missed, allowed Amy's killer, Amy's father, to accomplish his crime.

Jessa had pulled a six-month leave of absence after that one, reassembling the shattered bits and pieces of her mind into a tougher working order. And she was tougher. She'd learned she couldn't grieve for the whole world, or blame herself for all its misery. Still, at the edges she was too caring. Too fragile.

The problem was she had an unhealthy tendency toward getting personally involved in her work, far deeper than was good for her. She'd been known to quit eating, quit talking, almost quit functioning over a case.

"Ease it back a little, Jessa," she warned herself these days, when she recognized the familiar symptoms. "You're starting to slip into overdrive."

It was damn hard not to care when the victims were kids.

She hadn't suspected Amy Peterson's father, not until far too late. George Peterson had appeared to be a nice man, part of the hardworking middle class, a loving husband, a pillar of the community, until his prints were found on what turned out to be the murder weapon. Those were the prints of a monster, not the man everyone thought they knew.

He hadn't killed his daughter right away. He'd kept her alive for months, torturing her, molesting her, until even a child with as much will to live as Amy, had finally given up. If Jessa had seen through his pretense, if she had doubted his story even a little, Amy might be alive today.

When the nightmares came, the dark-eyed children of her dreams wore Amy Peterson's face. They always would. Guilt lodged in places doctors couldn't find to scrape it clean. Nothing would ever erase Jessa's personal sense of blame in Amy's death. All she could do was try her hardest not to let the same thing happen to another child.

If doubting everyone meant going a little nuts once in a while, then that was a price she was willing to pay. She was sure of one thing; she'd never overlook a relative again.

The relatives in the Campbell day care kidnapping were an interesting bunch. They ranged from Susan Richards, a young woman barely past her teens and looking like somebody's kid sister, to Rick Cole, a South American drug overlord. In between, they ran the full sweep of the spectrum.

It made sense to start with Cole. Go for the obvious. He was the one DEA wanted. The Drug Enforcement Agency could pull some strings in getting the information she needed. They would love to be given a legal reason to bust Cole and haul his ass in on charges that would stick.

From what she'd read in the files so far, Cole had slipped through the fingers of DEA more than once. Even when they'd brought him in, it was hard to make the facts add up to a count that would give him prison time. He had enough money for the best legal minds in the country, and so far, he'd walked.

Jessa didn't give a damn about nailing Cole on drug charges. Her mind-set was single-focused. *Did he take the children?* That's all she wanted to know. The rest of it was somebody else's knot to untangle. All she needed was to find the children, by whatever method that took. She wasn't above doing something illegal to get them back, and she wasn't above shooting somebody to save them.

The most important thing was to find them, and if the babies were still alive, to bring them home.

"Diane Kendall?"

"Yes?" The voice on the other end of the line was unmistakable. Diane knew at once to whom she was speaking, but waited for the woman to tell her.

"This is Rowena Rawlings Crawford. A lady at the TV studio gave me your name and phone number. She said you wanted to talk to me."

"I watched the program," Diane said. "I was staring at the television screen, not really paying attention, and then I saw you." She wanted to tell this woman how the show had made her feel. Except, it wasn't the show. It was Rowena herself who had affected Diana. "When you were talking, it seemed as if—"

"I knew there was someone my words were touching," Rowena said calmly. "All that time I was on stage, I kept knowing somebody was out there, trying to come into my head, trying to reach me. I couldn't tell if it was a man or a woman, just somebody in pain. Now that I hear your voice, I know you're the one. I feel it."

Diane couldn't think what to say. She hadn't expected this.

"I called you because—"

"You called because your baby's missing. A blond-headed little girl. P . . . is it Peggy?"

"Paige."

"Paige," Rowena repeated carefully. "Pretty sound to it, Paige."

The room seemed to be moving in and out of brightness. Diane felt the beat of hard pulse in her ears. "Is she . . .?" Her nerve faltered. "Can you tell me if my baby's alive?"

There was a slight hesitation. "I can't tell you that."

Diane wanted to grab the woman through the phone. "Why not? Those other women, you told them about their children. Please, you don't understand. I can't go on like this. I saw you on that show. It was as if I could feel what you were feeling. I was sure you'd help me. Why won't you tell me about my baby? Why?"

"Didn't say won't. Said can't. Talking to you, touching this phone, all I'm seeing is through your eyes. All I feel is what you know, what you feel. I've got no idea what your child is feeling, not till I touch a thing her little hand's touched, something close to her. You see?"

Diane made a noise that said she did. It was too hard to speak.

"Now, don't take on so hard. I want to help you, Diane. I do. You love your child, and I know you didn't do the least thing to your little girl. I would have felt that right away."

"I can't go on like this. If I don't find her," said Diane, "I think I'll go crazy."

"You push that thought away, honey." Rowena's voice sounded gentle and caring. "I know how bad you're hurting. You send me something of your baby's. Send it right to my house. Got you a pencil? I'm out in the country a ways, but this address will reach me."

Diane grabbed the first thing she could lay her hand on, the family Bible on the bookshelf beside her, and scribbled Rowena's address on the last page.

"You're not carrying this alone anymore, Diane. Hear me? You remember that when times get too hard. I'm here to help you find Paige. Can't promise anything for sure, but I'll do what God gives me to do."

A warmth of love washed over Diane. She felt

Rowena Crawford's kindness like a comforting touch upon her skin. "Thank you. Oh, thank you."

"Hush now, enough of that. You send me something of that baby's. I'll tell you the truth, how I see it. Don't be scared no more. I won't forget you."

After, when the phone was silent and the only sound Diane heard was the thudding of her heart, she stared at Rowena's address written on the Bible's clean, white page.

"Just give me one miracle," she whispered, as if the book could hear her. "Help me find my baby."

That afternoon, she bundled a few of Paige's things into a cardboard carton, a blanket from the empty crib, a small yellow-and-white gingham dress, and a soft toy lamb her daughter never slept without. She almost put a photo of Paige into the box, but at the last minute, she drew it out.

"Please, let this psychic be real," she said to the roomful of threatening silence. "Please, please, let Rowena be real."

With a flame of hope burning in her, Diane drove to the post office and sent the package by Next Day mail.

The Bob's Big Boy restaurant on Lake in Pasadena was a local hangout for them. Dillon Rhys was a fan of the cheeseburgers there. They reminded him of his misspent youth, he claimed, when he used to take his dates to the drive-in version of another Bob's on Colorado in Glendale. Apparently, there was still a throbbing connective link in his brain between the memory of a girl giving him what he most wanted, and the cheeseburgers and malts that had proceeded the act.

Where they ate was no big deal to Jessa. Food was the least important thing on her mind right now.

"That's the sickest thing I've ever heard," said Dillon. He was dipping a long finger of french fry into a side of shrimp sauce, stabbing the air with it while he spoke. "That poor woman. Maybe you should take the phone out, Jess."

"Are you kidding?" she shot back. "I hope to God he calls again."

The call was the first real lead Jessa had been given, if it was a genuine contact from the kidnapper and not a prank caller, some screwball who wanted to get a little attention in this perverse way. She couldn't be sure of anything yet, but it was more than she had yesterday.

The phones belonging to all the parents of the missing children had been tapped since the first day Jessa came onto the case. The tape recorders worked like high tech answering machines, automatically recording any conversation which took place on those phones, and sending the numbers of the callers to a tracing system. The system had given them the caller's location. Up until now, all incoming calls had been nothing out of the ordinary, only talk between concerned friends and family.

This was something else. The problem was, Jessa wasn't sure exactly what it meant.

"If the call was from the actual kidnapper and not a copycat, why didn't he mention a ransom drop?"

"I don't know," said Dillon. He plunged another fry into the ruby-colored sauce.

"Did he contact her to get off on this woman's fear?"

"Don't know." He bit the fry in half, dipped, and bit again.

"He had to realize what a risk he was taking, putting in that call. Anyone with the least knowledge of investigative procedure would have suspected that the phones would be tapped in a kidnap victim's house. Is our killer uncommonly ignorant, or is there another reason he chose to take such a chance?"

"Hey, be grateful that he's screwing up," Dillon told her. "This is the break you've been waiting for."

"I don't like it. The kidnapping was done by someone smart enough not to leave us any clues. The schedule for morning arrivals at the day care had been checked out. Whoever did this knew the routine and walked right into that house. A silencer was used for the homicide. There were no prints left from the shooter. Everything the four babies needed was taken, bottles, diapers, even toys. It was carefully planned. The killer wasn't stupid. This doesn't feel right."

He reached across the table and took her hand. "Look at me, Jess."

She did. She needed something else to see besides the memories of that kitchen with blood on the cupboard doors. Dillon's eyes were blue skies staring at her, drawing her back. He was a good-looking man, dark hair falling in a few boyish strands across his forehead. It always surprised her how much she loved looking at Dillon's face. It was like her own jump back into her teens, staring at him.

"I think you're pushing yourself too hard on this one," he said, his expression completely serious. "Seems as if you want the call to be a false lead, as if you're afraid to admit that something good might be happening. What's scaring you so damn much,

Jessa? Things are going the way you want. Keep telling yourself that."

His advice wouldn't work and she knew it. She was scared.

Maybe it was the way Carin Sayers had reacted when they replayed the tape so Jessa could hear it again. The Sayers woman seemed to be as mild and gentle a person as Jessa had ever met, but she'd started yelling and breaking things when she stood in the room with Jessa, listening to the voice on that cassette.

"It's all right," Jessa had tried to comfort her.

"No . . . no," Carin had yelled. "It's not all right. That monster has my baby. I keep thinking of it, the way he sounds. My God, what terrible things has he done to her?" Carin's eyes were twin nightmares, seeing the images of a fearful dark, and unable to wake up.

Jessa kept worrying the thought until it made her head sore. It didn't seem possible that the kidnapper and the caller could be the same man. She saw one as the organized killer of Christine Campbell; she saw the other as the word Carin had used to describe him, a monster.

There was something in his voice, something that made Jessa more than simply afraid for those missing children. It made her tremble inside. What she had listened to in his voice was pure evil. She recognized it, knew how it sounded, the same feeling she'd had when listening to Amy Peterson's father . . . after he'd told them what he'd done.

If the babies were in the hands of the man who'd called Carin Sayers . . . Jessa hoped they were already dead.

Chapter Ten

"Your baby's alive," said Rowena.

Diane Kendall gripped the phone for support. It was her lifeline, and she held on to it as if she were drowning. This was the only thing Rowena might have said that would have kept Diane alive another week, another day. For a moment, she couldn't speak. Her vocal cords were strangled by the rigid muscles of her neck. A kind of spasm passed through her, and she felt air and voice return.

"Tell me," said Diane. "You saw something?"

"Not like you mean. I see what your baby sees. I think through her mind. She's so little. Don't look at much above a person's knees. Don't know a lot of things she's looking at. Some, I can sense or feel, like if she's scared, or sick. The rest, I have to see through her little eyes."

Diane's hand shook so hard she thought she might drop the phone. "Please . . . there must be something."

"There is. It won't do for you to come apart now. You've got to stay strong for when your little girl comes home. Don't lose sight of that."

"She's coming home?"

"I can't say for sure," Rowena admitted.

Diane hated the woman for torturing her. Probably, this *psychic* was a fraud. How many other desperate mothers' feelings had she played upon? A TV entertainer, that's what she was. It was a sin so terrible, Diane couldn't get her mouth around the words of hate rising in her. She wanted to slam down the phone.

"It's cold in the room. Paige is cold," said Rowena, her voice sounding abruptly frail and distant.

Shivers, violent ones, ran through Diane's body. She knew in that instant, absolutely knew, Rowena was seeing her child. "Where is she? Where's Paige?"

"Crib's sitting on a wood floor. Baby girl's crying, crying. Nobody picks her up. Room's empty, 'cept for that crib."

"Where is she?"

"Don't be talking to me," said Rowena, the words sharp and rushed. "I'll lose her."

Diana swallowed the hard lump of fear. She felt like a game bird trapped in a field of grass, and hunters approaching. They'd be there in an instant, she needed to fly, but couldn't.

"Can't see around the room. Baby's facing down, lying on her stomach in the crib. She's crying so loud. Why won't somebody come?" Silence. "Oh, sweet Lord!" cried Rowena.

"What?" Diane ignored the earlier warning not to speak. "What's happening?"

"Something loud. A door banging open. More light in the room. Somebody's coming."

"Can't you see her? Is she hurt? Who's there? Who's with my baby?"

"The crib's shaking. A man, I think. I can hear him. He's yelling and hitting the bed. Hitting it hard. Been drinking whiskey. I smell it on his breath."

"Where is she?" Diane felt the words burst from her like a cry. And then, in a small and frightened voice, she begged, "Don't let him hurt her. Make him stop. What's he doing? For God's sake, tell me!"

"He's picked her up." It sounded as if Rowena hadn't taken the next breath, her voice flat and monotone. "He's holding her in his hands—not gentle. Poor baby. Oh, poor little baby."

A terrible pressure was building behind Diane's eyes. She felt the pulse of it pounding at her brain, at her sight. The pressure was going to explode. She couldn't speak. Wait one pulse, wait two, wait three pulses. . . .

"She's looking around. I can see the room. It's piney wood, like the floor. Looks like a cabin. Nothing but sky in the window. She's seeing him. I can feel her. She's scared. I see his face. He's thin, pale skin pulled tight over jutting bones, long greasy hair hanging in his eyes. Cold blue eyes. He's looking at her like—"

"Like what?"

"Please no, Lord! Jesus, Jesus! He's putting his hand over her mouth. Can't breathe," cried Rowena, as if the struggle were within her.

Muffled cries followed. *Paige's cries?*

Diane held one hand fisted at her stomach. She bent double, feeling the hard pressure of that hand against tight muscles. She needed pain to ease her of this other suffering.

93

"She wants her mama. Thinking, *Mama*. I can feel the thought coming up from her like heat. Oh, she's dying." Rowena's voice was broken, bleeding with her own tears. "I can feel life going from her ... smothered."

"Stop it," said Diane. The sound barely surfaced. A whisper. "No more. I can't—"

"The light's going. She can't see now. Not struggling. I think she's—"

"Stop it!" Diane screamed. "Don't say any more. Don't tell me." She wanted to throw the phone down and run. To escape. But her baby couldn't escape.

Rowena gasped loudly. It was many seconds before she spoke, but finally she said, "Something happened. I don't know what. I felt her body being sucked back from the dark. She's breathing again. She's alive."

Those were the last words Diane heard. The pounding in her head burst into splintered black. She felt herself slide into the tranquil dark, into blessed unconsciousness, and slump to the floor.

"Quit it, Logan! You're killing him."

Daniel could feel Lydia pulling at his shoulders. She was straddling his back and trying to yank him off Jack. Her fingers were digging into his flesh, but his fist still found its mark on the side of Jack's head.

"He's senseless," she yelled. "He's not feeling it, anyway. You're hurting your hand for nothing."

That thought registered. His hand felt like he'd broken it on Jack's hard jaw. His fist was red and pulpy, but he couldn't tell if it was his blood, or

Jack's. The stupid bastard had been smothering the baby.

Daniel got up and tried to walk away like Lydia was telling him. She was right. Killing Jack would complicate everything. He tried, but his rage at Jack was about more than his trying to kill one of the kids. By this one lamebrained act, Jack could have ruined all of Daniel's plans. He could have destroyed the whole deal. Fury rose up in him again. He stepped between Jack's sprawled legs and kicked him. That wouldn't kill him, but he'd remember it a long while.

"Are you done?" Lydia picked up Paige. The baby was crying in gulps, as if trying to catch her breath.

"Is she all right? Let me see her. Give her to me."

Lydia had to pull Paige away from him. The baby's fingers gripped Lydia's sweater, and Paige screamed when Lydia thrust her roughly toward Daniel.

He took her, but she fought to get away from him. Her body arched backward. "What's the matter with her? Why is she screaming like that?"

"She's scared of you."

"What? Why should she be scared of me? I saved her life."

"Yeah? Well, she just watched you beat the hell out of Jack. Babies work on feelings and instinct. Her instinct tells her you're bad news."

He held Paige at arm's length and checked to see if she was hurt. Her body twisted and struggled to be free. From what he could tell, her neck was fine. It was as red as her face. There were no bruises or marks on her neck. It didn't look as if Jack had tried to strangle her—which was a good thing for Jack and the rest of his anatomy.

95

Daniel noticed Paige's bare legs. "How did she get these bruises on the back of her legs?"

Lydia's whole body seemed to draw up and tighten. "How do I know? Babies fall down all the time."

"Not babies who don't walk." Daniel laid Paige on her stomach in the crib, and removed her diaper. The bruises were visible on the child's backside, five blue marks where a hand had slapped.

Daniel turned around. "Did you do this?"

"No." The pupils of Lydia's eyes were zigzagging around the room. She couldn't stare at him straight on.

He moved closer. "Somebody hit her. Somebody who'd be diapering this child. A hand print wouldn't come through a diaper and clothes like that. It was on bare skin."

"It must have been Jack."

"Jack wouldn't diaper a baby."

"He could have pulled off the diaper," Lydia cried, fear shining in her eyes.

"Why would he?"

"I don't know what he does all the time. He's crazy. Maybe he likes little girls. He could have been trying to—"

Daniel hit her. The back of his hand connected to the side of her face, and she fell back. Blood trickled from one corner of her mouth. Before she could come at him, he hit her again, this time in the stomach.

She crumpled to the floor and sat huddled and gasping for breath. Her long hair hung in her face, and drops of bright blood made a pattern of stains on her white shorts.

"Bastard!" she screamed at him. "I didn't—"

He jerked her off the floor by the twin sides of her open collar. "You hurt this baby again, and I'll kill you."

She swallowed back whatever she had meant to say, and didn't look at him. A woman who'd been hit before; he could see that in her eyes. She'd been beaten, probably all through her childhood, and knew the survival skill of closing down.

He let go of her, and she fell back a couple of steps. "You won't know when I'm coming, and you won't see me," he threatened, "but I'll find you. Understand?"

She nodded dumbly. She didn't lift her head, or look into his eyes.

He started to leave, but turned back at the doorway. "When Jack comes to, if he tries to take out his frustration on this baby, do whatever you have to do to stop him. If he hurts her, I'll hold you both responsible."

She didn't respond, but stood there, staring resolutely at the floor, not challenging him to hit her again.

Would it be enough? he wondered, walking down the stairs. Would his threats keep the baby safe?

There was so much still to do. All he needed was a little more time, then everything would work out exactly as he'd planned. The question was, would the babies live long enough for him to finish the deal?

He'd have to speed things up. Couldn't trust Jack or Lydia. Hurrying might jeopardize his plan, but there wasn't any other choice. It meant he needed to do something to quicken things.

From where Daniel stood on the stairs, he could

see six-month-old Chelsea Cole sitting propped up by blanket and pillow on the living room floor. Her dark brown eyes watched him as he came down the stairs.

Instead of leaving, he walked toward the baby . . . drawing out his knife.

Chapter Eleven

Alix Cole heard the mail truck stop in front of her house. She recognized it because of the distinctive squealing brakes. Usually, the postal carrier delivered mail to the curbside box, unless there was a package that was too bulky to fit.

Alix glanced out the upstairs window in time to see the mail carrier get out of his truck and start up the walk. A minute later, she heard the doorbell. She had been sitting in the large white rocker in Chelsea's room. It disturbed her to have to break the only connection she still had with her child and go downstairs to answer the door.

The stairway was dark. Alix kept the drapes closed all day, all night. Didn't want any prying eyes seeing into her grief. The dark was better. It calmed her when she felt like screaming.

The glaring sunlight was painful when she opened the door. She had to shield her eyes with her hand.

"Package for you," said the carrier. He held a sheaf of mail: a thick bundle of magazines, local newspaper, bills, letters, advertising circulars, and a package, about the size of a shoebox.

"Do I have to sign for it?" She gathered the bundle into her arms.

"No, that's all right. I brought it to your house because all this wouldn't fit in the box. Looks like you got a present." He gave her a cheerful grin.

"Thanks," she said, and shut the door.

She carried the bundle into the living room and set it on the coffee table. The box rested on top, a brown-paper-wrapped package, unadorned by return address.

"What are you?" she asked the box, not wanting to touch it.

She hadn't ordered anything from a catalog, and no one would have sent her a present. She'd lost all relationships long ago. Rick had made sure of that. He hadn't liked anyone else getting too close. Not safe for him.

The box needed opening.

Probably should call the sheriff's team first.

It waited for her to touch it.

Might be from the kidnapper.

She lifted the box. It was so light. Barely weighed anything.

Probably should ask Detective Walsh.

The package tilted in her hands, and she heard something inside slide to the end of the box. It hit with a little weight and a dull sounding thump.

What could it—

And then, Alix was tearing at the brown paper. Her hands shook so badly, she couldn't cut through the twine.

"Come on!" she screamed at it. "Come on, damn you!"

The scissors bit through, the cord snapped open,

and the box lid fell away. A small, shriveled some-thing spilled onto the table.

Alix didn't scream.

She didn't have enough breath.

On the table lay the severed first digit of a baby's finger.

Lydia had to take care of the kid, after what Logan had done. She tore up a couple of sheets and band-aged Chelsea's little hand the best she could. There was no antiseptic in the house to put on the wound, so she poured some of Jack's whiskey over what was left of Chelsea's baby finger, and wrapped the whole hand like a big cloth mitt.

He had cut off the tip of Chelsea's right pinky. Lydia had heard the kid start up, right after Logan went downstairs. She'd almost wet herself at the sound of that scream. A baby, for God's sake. The man was crazy. He'd knocked her around for slap-ping Paige too hard on the butt, but look what he'd done to Chelsea.

She thought about what he'd done to Jack. Logan was capable of killing all of them, and the realization came to her: he probably would, when this was done.

"How the hell did I get involved in this?" she asked herself. "And how am I going to get out of it, alive?"

It didn't make sense. What was it Logan wanted? He had practically beat Jack to death over what had happened to Paige. Lydia didn't think she'd ever seen a man so angry as Logan had looked when he saw Jack holding his hand over that baby's mouth. Logan had come to the house without warning, like he always did, and she and Logan had been talking just inside the doorway, when they'd heard Jack's door crash open, upstairs. It had taken her a minute to realize where Jack was, and what he might be doing. They had run up the stairs together. If she hadn't stopped him, Logan would have killed Jack.

He was so damn protective of these kids, threatening Lydia if she so much as breathed heavy on Paige, and almost killing Jack. And yet . . . Logan had cut off the tip of a finger from a six-month-old baby. She couldn't believe he really cared about any of these kids. He hadn't even bandaged Chelsea's hand.

He wanted the little brats in good condition for when he—

No. Lydia suddenly realized. Logan hadn't even looked at the other three babies, except for what he did to Chelsea. They could have starved to death for all he knew, or cared.

The flash of understanding pulled Lydia up like a rope jerking through her. Logan's plan centered around only one kid, the one Jack almost smothered. No wonder Logan had nearly killed him.

What was it Logan said? Lydia remembered. It was right after he'd backhanded her and punched her in the stomach. *You hurt this baby again, I'll kill you.* Her stomach still hurt from his fist. And later, he'd warned her, *When Jack comes to, if he tries to take out his frustration on this baby, do whatever you have to do to stop him.*

On this baby . . .

In that moment, Lydia began to understand what was happening. The whole thing was all about one child. The kidnapping of all four had been some kind of a smoke screen, a coverup to hide Logan's real motive.

Why was Paige Kendall so important?

Lydia's cash-register heart started pinging. If Logan was willing to put on such an elaborate and complicated show to hide his real purpose, how much must this kid be worth?

One thing was sure, Lydia was going to find out.

Logan hadn't seemed to realize that she knew. That was healthy for her. She had a good idea that if he suspected, he'd reserve the same attention for her that he'd given Christine Campbell—a bullet to the head. A brain shot could stop a whole lot of snooping. Lydia understood the risk. She'd have to be very careful Logan didn't find out.

Being careful wouldn't keep her from looking and listening. She was going to do a lot of checking into things on her own. Learn what was so special about this kid. If the take was big enough, it might be worth killing Logan.

And if she was smart, she could use Jack to do it.

John Tripp needed a vacation. The stress and pressures of his life were squeezing in around him, like being vacuum-sealed. Lately, there had been one too many ugly cases, and not enough sleep. A few days of kicking back was wanted, and no phone calls.

Cat was mountain climbing over the kitchen counters and twin sinks, sniffing from day-old plates, saucepans, and mugs. He had a taste for cold coffee and toast corners, making a leisurely breakfast of them.

"Hey, that'll rot your guts." Tripp poured the remains of the coffee down the drain. "You're a cat, remember? Cats like milk, and tuna, and cans of wet meat by-products."

Cat's tail whipped back and forth, lashing the stack of spoons and saucers.

"Yeah, you're a stalking tiger, but get the hell off my plates." He brushed Cat off the sink with a persuasive push. "I'm not dealing with any hopped up caffeine-headed felines. Find your own drugs. Scratch up a little catnip." He opened the back door and encouraged the overweight tom to wander the yard by tossing him over the threshold.

The phone rang. Tripp let it jingle twice, even though he was standing right next to it, then picked up the receiver. "John Tripp," he answered, in case Grodin was calling. It was midafternoon, and Grodin liked his PI team to sound professional.

"Mr. Tripp," the voice was distressed but feminine. "This is Alix Cole. I need your help."

The name brought a flash of pleasant memory. She was the single mother with dark hair and dark eyes, whose face and body had been the dreams that kept Tripp awake at night, and not about the kidnapping.

"Something's changed?"

"Yes."

"Have you talked to Detective Walsh?"

"No," she said. "I won't be doing that."

He understood. Whatever had happened, and he assumed it was bad, she would be keeping that information from the sheriff's department. It was one of the reasons people hired a PI, to tell him things they wouldn't tell the authorities. Information like this could be an advantage, or a pitfall. He'd seen it go both ways. Sometimes, it was the missing piece that solved the puzzle. Other times, it was the smoking gun, and pointed at him.

"What time would you like to meet?"

"Now." There was a hint of urgency in her voice.

He hesitated for two long breaths. Something about this didn't feel right. She wasn't calling as spokesperson for the group of parents who had hired him. This was private. He recognized the separateness of it. She wanted to see him alone, to tell him something the others didn't know. Something she didn't want them to know.

"I'll be there in fifteen minutes."

The soft click was her only goodbye.

He thought about telling Grodin, and tried to convince himself it wasn't because of Alix Cole's looks that he didn't make that call. He was the PI on the case, not Grodin. The client had a right to her confidentiality, at least until something proved she didn't.

He had business to take care of on the way, and had to stop first in La Cañada. It was nearly sunset when he started up the 2 freeway to Glendale. Traffic was light, and the air clear enough to see a V-shaped wedge of the Los Angeles skyline. From this vantage point, the tall buildings looked like Camelot, or the Emerald City. Something surreal and alluring, from a distance.

Maybe Alix Cole was like that, too. If he let himself get too close, would she still seem so beautiful?

A coyote shot out from the brushy undergrowth along the hillside bordering the freeway, and dashed across the lane in front of Tripp. He avoided it easily enough, and watched in his rearview mirror to see it run safely across the center divider and the three lanes of oncoming traffic.

Coyotes were survivors. They had adapted to people invading their territory of dry hills and countryside. They drank water from swimming pools, ate cat food left outside for pets, or the pets themselves, and used man's roadways to get them where they wanted to go. Some got hit, but enough made it through. There were more coyotes than ever before in Southern California. They were thriving.

Alix had adapted to another kind of life. She was a survivor. But would she make it through?

He drove through the sprinkler green landscapes of north Glendale. The homes in this area ranged from quarter-million to million-dollar estates. This is where the young Alix Diamond had grown up, in this place of wealth and comfort. But she had run away from family and home, with Rick Cole.

Tripp thought about that union. What force had led a young, beautiful woman like Alix into the arms of an underworld drug lord? He remembered the expression on her face when she'd told him, "This is my father's house. I've never liked this place, never been happy in it."

So, why was she here? Was this her refuge from Rick? Or had she come home because her father was dead, unable to torment her anymore, and she could live in his house without fear?

Trouble was a word that seemed to follow Alix Cole. Some people were lightning rods, attracting it. Tripp wondered, did he dare get close?

He parked the RX-7 along the curb and walked up the front steps of the house. Alix opened the door before he had a chance to ring the bell. Her hair showed messy tracks where her fingers had dragged through it. Her eyes looked scared.

"Please," she said, "come inside." When she'd closed the door, she turned to face him. "You've got to help me."

There was something scared and defenseless about Alix that made him want to help her—that little girl who had grown up in this cold house. But there was another side to this woman. She had lived with Rick Cole, and given birth to his child. Tripp decided to move ahead carefully, and watch out for striking snakes.

"What's happened?"

Her eyes told him it was bad. "This came in the mail today." She picked up a small box from the hall table and handed it to him.

He didn't try to guess, but opened the package quickly. "Jesus." He closed the lid and put the box back on the table. He didn't want to touch it. The monster who'd done this thing to an infant had held this box.

"We'll need to have some tests done to verify—"

"It's my daughter's."

"We can't be sure of that."

"I'm sure," she told him. "And there won't be any tests. You and I are the only two people who know about this. I'm not going to notify Detective Walsh."

"This is evidence," Tripp tried to convince her. "There might be something that could be traced back to the kidnapper—the wrapping, the box, anything."

"And I might get more pieces of my daughter in the mail. I won't risk it."

Her words stopped him cold. It was his responsibility to keep the sheriff's investigation informed of any tangible evidence turned up in the case. A PI could get into deep trouble with the law by holding back information. Not that he hadn't done it before, but the circumstances were far different.

He thought about the severed piece of finger in the box, and that room with a white rocker, crib, and baby's toys he had seen upstairs. There was no balance in that scale. It weighed heavily on Alix's side.

"If you're not going to tell Detective Walsh, why tell me?"

"I need your help. Chelsea's running out of time."

All his instincts told him this was true. "Was there a note? Anything you're not telling me?"

"Only that," she said, glancing at the box on the hall table. "What does he want?" she cried. "Why doesn't he tell me?"

"Who?" Tripp felt chills asking her. Had she known the kidnapper's identity all along?

"Rick, of course. It has to be him. No one else would be capable of such . . ." She stared fixedly at the box. And then as he watched, she seemed to cave inward, her body swaying for an instant before she started to fall.

He caught her in his arms, but he was the one who felt weak.

God, he thought, *I'm lost.* Her eyes, full of such torment. And then, she was against him. He pulled her closer. It wasn't quick and frantic, but slow and wary. His lips grazed hers before they kissed, as if testing whether she would allow it. When she moved up to meet his kiss, pressing against his mouth, he knew.

All defenses were down. There was nothing to stop them.

Chapter Twelve

He hadn't planned for this to happen, but there it was. He was with her. She was more to him now than the others in the case, and that would complicate things. He thought about it as he lay in her bed, his hand against her breast.

A disturbing idea came to him. She might have done this deliberately, for just that reason.

"Tell me about Rick."

She sighed and moved his hand away. "What do you want to know?"

"When did you meet him? How long were you together? What makes you think that he—"

"That he did this?" she finished his question. She sat up, running both hands through her hair and bending forehead to knees. The action made her appear vulnerable, worried. "I don't know that he did it," she admitted, "but who else would want to hurt me?"

"I don't know," said Tripp. "Why don't you tell me about him?"

She wrapped the sheet around her, as if aware of her nakedness now. He pulled it over himself, too.

"Rick is the most powerful man I've ever known."

She didn't look at Tripp as she talked. "When I first met him, I was young, and that power was seductive."

"Were you in love with him?"

"In the beginning. For a long time, I guess. He was different then. That was before all the drugs. He changed."

"And was he in love with you?"

"What difference does it make?" Her eyes were angry, defiant.

"It matters." He needed to know how much she had hurt Rick Cole when she left. Enough for him to take this kind of revenge?

She was quiet for a minute, then answered. "He said he loved me."

"Do you believe he did?" He was probing the wound.

"Yes. Are you satisfied? Yes, I know he loved me."

That was interesting. She knew. "And when you left, did he threaten you?"

"No."

It wasn't enough of an answer. She was keeping something back. "He loved you, but he let you walk away?"

"No."

"Then, what?" He was getting angry, too. "What aren't you saying?"

"I didn't tell Rick anything," she said. "I took Chelsea and left."

Tripp let that image linger in his mind. It wasn't hard to imagine an angry South American drug lord, deserted by the woman he still loved, and insane enough to get back at her like this.

"If he loved you, why would he do this?" The questions were hard, but he needed answers.

"I don't know."

"Has he ever killed anyone?"

Her answer came in a voice he could barely hear. "That's why I left."

Tripp was beginning to feel more than a little uncomfortable sitting in this bed. His imagination could fill in the details of armed men in the pay of Rick Cole breaking down the door, and what kind of colorful things they would do to a man caught with the drug lord's wife.

Something nagged at him. He didn't know what it was yet, but the thought jabbed like a thorn when his mind ran across it.

"You know how to reach him." It came to him just like that, quickly and without any doubt. "You do, don't you? Could you get a message to Rick, if necessary?"

She shook her head.

"Are you sure? Maybe someone who works for him? You knew his contacts. There must be a way."

"No. I don't know how to find him. I told you, I ran away. After that, I lost track of him."

She was lying. He was absolutely sure.

"All right." He pulled her back into his arms. "I had to ask."

"Don't you think I'd tell you? Do you think I'd let him do this to Chelsea if I knew how to reach him?"

He held her without questions.

When she was calm, she turned to him again. Her body was soft, silky, and moved over his like warm water. He felt himself rising to her need. But the questions still nagged at him. Was she doing this be-

111

cause she wanted him to help her? How much was Rick Cole a part of this case? What kind of a father would mutilate his own child? . . . if Chelsea was his child?

"Come back to me," Alix said.

He did, and all the questions faded. Everything was the longing he saw in this woman's eyes, and the heat of her body against his. Willingly he let his own fires enter that heat, joining, and be consumed.

It was late evening before Tripp went home. His house stood out among the others for its darkness among the lights on the block. Like an invitation to a burglar, Tripp thought. It was embarrassing. A private investigator was supposed to know better.

He hadn't planned on being out so late. What happened between him and Alix had come as a surprise. He couldn't help wondering if it had come as a surprise for her, too. If she was using him, he didn't want to know it—at least, not tonight.

It had been a long time since he'd felt the way he did with her. Moments like that were rare in a lifetime. If it was going to go sour, he wanted to keep it with him a little longer before the ugliness surfaced. He wanted to remember the way she'd looked today, and to fall asleep tonight imagining her in his arms.

Cat met him at the door.

"You guarding the house? Sorry, old guy, forgot I left you outside."

Meows sounding more like a squawking parrot rose from the tom. He circled Tripp's legs, brushing long orange-and-white hair on the black pants.

Tripp unlocked the door and switched on the front

porch and living room lights. It was like stepping into a picture of abstract art. Nothing was where it should have been. Furniture turned upside down. Lamps thrown on the floor. Wooden chairs with broken backs threatened like jagged teeth.

Tripp said softly, "Hello, Rick."

It was clear to him who was responsible for this. Rick Cole had paid a visit, sometime during the hours Tripp was with Cole's wife. The damage to Tripp's house was Rick's calling card.

He moved through the mess, his anger growing with the evidence of his destroyed possessions. This was his home, and it had been raked over with deliberate violence. The cupboard doors in the kitchen stood open, and the tile floor glittered with shards of broken glassware, china, and the broken necks of wine bottles. Tripp picked up Cat and carried him.

"This is one time I'm glad I left you outside, buddy." He was comforted by the steady purring close to his ear. "I can imagine what they would have done to you."

The phone still worked. He carried with him the phone numbers of everyone involved in this case. Alix Cole's was close to the top of the card. She answered on the second ring.

"Yes?" She didn't say hello like most people, but then, she wasn't like most people.

"Hi," said Tripp. "I don't have to worry about finding Rick. He knows where I am."

"What are you talking about?"

"He's watching you, Alix. He knew about us, today. Do you have a gun in your house?" He thought about her being there alone.

"Yes, I have a gun." Her voice thinned to a breathless sound. "What happened?"

He told her. "I'd say he doesn't want me to see you. He sends impressive messages, your ex."

"I'm sorry. I didn't think he'd still react like that."

Tripp sucked in a deep, slow breath. "You mean, he's done this kind of thing before?"

"Once or twice, a long time ago."

"Jesus, Alix. Thanks for warning me."

"I did warn you!" she cried. "I told you he killed a man, didn't I?"

Tripp wasn't feeling so good. "You mean he . . ."

"He killed the man he thought was my lover."

"Was he?"

She didn't answer.

"Dammit, Alix! Was he?"

"Yes."

He was putting it together. Bits and pieces with jagged sides.

"You saw what he did to Chelsea." She was crying, hard sobs that were painful to hear.

"We don't know who's responsible for that." Tripp couldn't explain why he was arguing the point. Rick did seem like the prime suspect. It was just . . . a man who still cared this much about his wife, wanted her back, knew where she was but didn't force himself on her . . . a man who watched over her the way Rick did . . . would he do such a thing?

"Are you going to report this?" She sounded small and defenseless.

He should. The cops should know exactly what was going on. Grodin would insist. Anything less would be withholding evidence.

"If you tell them, he might kill her."

He tried to think what it would be like, having your child in the hands of a man capable of doing such damage to a house, maybe capable of mutilating his own daughter. If Rick were watching Alix carefully enough to know what had happened today, would he know if Tripp reported the break-in to Walsh, or the police? The answer was obvious.

"I won't report it."

"I'm sorry, I'm sorry," she said over and over. "I should have told you everything."

He couldn't think how to respond. His mind was numb with the shock of finding all his belongings destroyed.

And then, she said the words that chilled him most. "I'd do anything to get my baby back."

It left him feeling exposed, like a bug pulled out from under a rock. What kind of woman was Alix? What did he really know about her? And what the hell did she mean, *anything?*

It was hard to sleep that night. Hard when he realized Rick Cole knew where he lived. Tripp left the mess in the rest of the house, and concentrated his immediate efforts on turning the mattress back on its frame and box springs. By midnight, he could step on the bedroom carpet in his bare feet and not risk being jabbed by a piece of broken glass or splintered wood.

He fell into bed with his clothes on. If the ex-husband paid him another visit in the middle of the night, he didn't want to be undressed when they met. The odds were stacked enough on Rick's side as it was.

He wondered what Rick had done to Alix's lover before he killed him.

Sleep came in fitful dreams. All Tripp could remember was crying children, and a blank-faced man with a knife. He woke a little after three, opened his eyes, stared into the dark, and listened. Had something moved? Was that what woke him?

Lights would make him feel better.

One wasn't enough. Soon, every room in the house was bright. He worked until dawn, cleaning and throwing out the broken pieces of his life. The sofa could be saved, but every dining room chair was shattered. The table had been scored and gouged with the point of a knife. Had the same knife cut off the tip of Chelsea's finger?

When he was finished, the house was little more than walls. He looked around. This was the fury that had burned itself out in the destruction of a home. What would Rick have done to a man?

Tripp thought of the man who'd been Alix's lover. She said her husband had killed him. How? With a knife?

When the sun came up, Tripp turned out the lights, and let the day carry him to a dreamless sleep.

Chapter Thirteen

Jack wasn't up to causing trouble for several days. He wasn't up to much besides holding his head over the toilet, and moaning to an unsympathetic Lydia that he thought his skull was cracked. She left him with a bottle of aspirin, a glass of tepid water, and a cold look.

"I'm surprised you're not dead," she said, as if that were meant to comfort him.

Logan had come close. Every inch of Jack's body hurt. His face was swollen, his nose probably broken, and he had black puffy bruises all over where Logan had kicked him.

The whole thing didn't make Jack happy. He was a sensitive guy. He knew when people were pissed at him. And Logan was righteously pissed. People who got that mad at Jack usually got dead. He couldn't stand the strain of worrying about their bad moods.

Logan was one sorry time bomb. He was going to go off and kill somebody. Jack would just as soon it wasn't him. He was tired of this little game. Four crying babies were enough to drive a man over the edge. Maybe he had pushed it too far the other day;

117

he didn't remember much except the kid wouldn't shut up. He guessed it might not have been too good if he'd killed her. One less profit share. And after he'd put so much work into the little brats.

So, Logan was right about that. But he shouldn't have kicked him like he was a dog. Didn't need to go that far. It made Jack mad to picture himself knocked out and bloody, with Logan entertaining himself kicking holes in Jack's head. Didn't take too much imagining, either. His head was swelled up like a balloon on one side, and kind of caved in on the other.

What the hell was he getting out of this, anyhow? Nobody was making any money. The only fun he'd had this whole time was when he'd called that Sayers woman.

He thought about the call, savoring the memory. Maybe it was time he tried that amusement again. Anything to get his thoughts off this house that smelled of stinking baby diapers. He'd called Carin Sayers last time. What if he called the Kendall woman?

The idea excited him. Even better, it felt like getting back at Logan. He'd call Paige's mother, and tell her what he almost did to her kid. Maybe she'd like to know what Logan had done to Chelsea, too?

The problem was, how was he going to get into town to use the phone? He was in no shape to drive. His eyes were still seeing double. He shouldn't use a phone in Wrightwood, either. Cops could trace the call. He wasn't stupid.

He'd have to wait.

One of the babies was yelling. "Lydia!" he hollered. She didn't answer. "Lydia!" he screamed louder. She still didn't answer. "What the hell?" Grumbling, he struggled his aching body off the bed.

He was all the way downstairs before he realized it.

Lydia was gone.

Lydia drove up the steep hill to the road fronting the Kendall home in La Cañada. She parked along the wide turnaround at the end of the street. Before her was a breathtaking panoramic view of Devil's Gate Golf Course, the Rose Bowl, and the San Gabriel Mountains. From here, the road divided. To Lydia's right, one branch of the Y continued up the hillside to other streets. To her left, was the private road leading to the Kendall home.

It would serve Logan right if she drove up to the front door of the house and knocked. For one wild instant, she could imagine herself doing just that. *Hello, I'm your baby's kidnapper, and I'm here to talk about some serious money.* That would suit her fine. She'd played nanny long enough. Living with four babies, not counting Jack, was driving her up the wall.

It had been risky, leaving the kids alone with Jack, even for a few hours. With luck, they'd all sleep until she got back. Jack had been pretty much out of everything since Logan beat him up. She doubted he'd notice she was gone. That was why she'd taken the chance. She needed to find out about Paige.

Getting out of the car, she stood at the bottom of the private road. From here, she could see the Kendall home. There were no locked gates or guard dogs ... nothing to stop her. If she walked up the road, she might be able to break into the Kendalls' home without anyone seeing her.

It was tempting. This might be her only chance to find out why Paige Kendall was so important to Logan.

Of course, she could get caught.

Lydia was a born risk junkie. That's how she always wound up in so much trouble. One side of her nature was practical and careful, the other side was an adrenaline freak. *Go on*, it urged her, *do it*.

"What the hell," she said, and started up the hill.

The house was practically an aquarium, with wide glass walls facing both the view and the street. The drapes were opened full length, and Lydia could see into the formal dining room and the connecting living room beyond. The floors were polished wood, and the furnishings looked like quality pieces.

Lydia stood for a while, observing. She was hidden from view by a hedge, but could see into the house. This is where Paige's family lived, where Paige had lived with them, before Logan snatched her away. What must it be like to grow up in a place like this? To never know hunger? To live with people who loved you?

Not exactly the way Lydia remembered her childhood. Home was a place her mother brought the men she called boyfriends. There were a lot of men. They provided money for drinks and drugs. Not clothes for her daughter, no new shoes, but the real necessities of her mother's life: a bottle of Stolichnaya, pills to pop, and lines to snort. Whatever drug the street market was selling—she took it all. If her mother had known which of these men was Lydia's father, she'd never pointed him out.

Ten minutes. No one had passed through the visible center of the Kendall house.

"Nobody's home." Lydia felt a rush of excitement as she ran to the back of the property and hunkered down before the kitchen door. In her hand was a narrow metal file, and two lock picks. Lydia had learned in her teens how to enter locked houses. It had helped her survive. In a couple of deft moves, there was the satisfying sound of the bolt clicking back and the handle turning.

She wasn't scared. The sense was a kind of thrill. It was a hell of a lot better than waking up one day broke, old, and alone. One thing was sure: she wasn't going to wind up like her mother.

The door opened easily. She knew about silent alarms but ignored the possibility. Not many people had them. If this house did, well then, her luck was bad. She didn't think about it longer than a couple of seconds. There were other things to consider.

Like, where would she find the answers?

The bedroom seemed likely. Most people kept anything of importance in the bedroom. The reasoning was simple. They wanted these things close to them when they slept, as if by being near, they were guarding them.

Most people were fools. The bedroom was the first place burglars looked. People kept their guns in the bedroom, too.

The house was eerily silent. On a wall of the master bedroom were family photos, pictures of three little girls. In one picture, Paige was held in the arms of an older man. A relative? Her grandfather?

The man looked familiar. Lydia knew she'd seen his picture before and tried to place him. He was dressed casually in the photo, a knit polo shirt and shorts. She imagined the same man in a business suit. Something was there, just beyond the edge of her memory, but she couldn't reach it.

And then, a folded newspaper lying on a bedside table caught her attention. The headline was from the front page of the business section. It was circled in red ink.

CEO Superman. Beneath the headline was the lengthy article: Harper Pierce of Trans-Continental Bank, was honored at a recent gathering of banking's top executives. Pierce—the man who turned Trans-Continental Bank's future around with his tough politics and his cutthroat tactics with competitors—received recognition from his own in a private celebration at the Ritz-Carlton, Huntington.

Lydia opened the folded newspaper, and there before her, on the side that had been lying against the table, was a picture of Trans-Continental Bank's CEO, Harper Pierce . . . the same man as the smiling grandfather in the family photo.

That was the connection. Logan had taken Paige Kendall because she was the granddaughter of Harper Pierce. If Trans-Continental Bank were part of the ransom . . . there was going to be a lot of money.

Lydia took the newspaper with her. She didn't bother to wipe her fingerprints from the door handle, or worry about what she'd touched. The break-in had been clean and simple. Nothing damaged. Nothing stolen, except the newspaper. No one would know she'd been here.

She was walking out of the room when the phone rang. The intrusive jolts of noise startled her. Three rings, then the answering machine clicked twice, and a woman's voice spoke. Paige's mother? She sounded refined, polished, the kind of voice produced in expensive women's colleges.

"You have reached the Kendalls."

"I knew that," said Lydia, mocking the machine and the rich-bitch voice. It aggravated her.

"We are not available to take your call—"

"Not available, huh? Not in the bathroom? Not in the shower?" She was enjoying this.

"—but we would like to speak with you."

"Yeah, I'll bet you would."

"You may leave a message of any length. Please wait until after the beep."

Lydia waited. The machine beeped, but the only message the caller left was the sound of a hang up.

"How rude," said Lydia. She was disappointed.

She glanced at the series of family photos on the bedroom wall before she left. Her resentment of Paige Kendall lessened. "Maybe I wasn't born rich, like you," she said to the picture of the blond little girl, "and maybe I didn't grow up in a house like this one"—she leaned closer to the picture, until her breath was fogging the glass—"but I didn't get kidnapped, either."

Lydia was feeling good when she left. The kitchen door was easy to relock. She'd found what she wanted. Nobody got hurt. She hummed a little tune on the way to her car. Things were starting to look up.

* * *

"Bitch!" shouted Jack. "Goddamn bitch! You take off without even telling me where you're going!" He was standing in the doorway downstairs, babies crawling around his feet.

"Shut up and get out of my way, Jack." Lydia pressed forward and Jack moved aside.

He slammed the door. "Logan would kill you if he knew what you did."

"Logan's not going to know," She picked up Sydney, felt the soggy disposable diaper, pulled the tape tabs, and dropped the diaper to the floor. Only when she had done the same to all four babies did she pick up the wet diapers and throw them away.

"You gonna let them run around like that?" Jack seemed shocked. "This whole house will smell like pee."

"It already does."

"Yeah, well it could smell a whole lot worse."

She gave him a look. "Relax. I'll diaper them in a minute. Let them dry out. They've all got rashes red as welts. You could have changed them."

"Changed them!" Jack's face darkened with anger. "You're lucky I'm still here."

She narrowed her eyes at him. "Where else would you be, Jack?"

"Someplace away from this noise and stink." He looked away from her, as if he were hiding something.

"What are you thinking about?" she asked, stepping closer. "Don't you get us killed by doing something stupid. Hear me?" She made him look at her. "I mean it, Jack. I'd run a knife through your ribs if I thought you were planning something."

Jack's eyes were ugly to see. "You go to sleep in this house, too, Lydia. Don't forget that."

She left him alone then. His words had triggered dark memories of when she was young. The world of night hadn't been safe for young girls, not in a house full of her mother's boyfriends.

She remembered, and her words were as icy as her voice. "Not very strong right now, are you, Jack? Better think about what you're saying to me. Better think. You wouldn't be the first man I've killed in the dark."

He backed down. Eyes first, glancing away, then he stepped back. "You'd better diaper those kids before they mess all over the house."

"I'll do that," she said. "Why don't you go back to bed? Get some sleep."

Jack wanted to kill her. She could see that from his hands; they were balled into fists. That was all right. *Go on wanting it.* Lydia wasn't planning to be around her much longer, anyhow. She was going to figure out what Logan knew, the plan, and then she was going to take it for herself. Before long, Jack, Logan, and the babies were going to be dead—and Lydia would have all the money.

It was enough to make her sing while she diapered the brats, and propped up their bottles on Jack's empties of JD.

Chapter Fourteen

Daniel Cantrell's position at Trans-Continental Bank was as executive assistant to Harper Pierce. He didn't type, make coffee, or answer phones. His importance to Pierce was his connections, and the information those connections could give him. His name wasn't signed on the contracts when the deals closed—he left that to Pierce—but he was the one who made the deals possible. That's what made him worth his salary.

Daniel's office on the twenty-third floor of the Trans-Continental building was set in the center of the Los Angeles downtown skyline. From his office window, he could see the city, and the San Fernando and San Gabriel valleys beyond the L.A. basin. Above the valley, in the San Gabriels, was the mountain community of Wrightwood, where Harper Pierce's granddaughter waited to be ransomed.

It was all coming together. All the players were in place. Daniel's plan would work, if Pierce reacted like a human being instead of a banker. That was the intangible, the pivotal point Daniel couldn't count on.

Did Pierce care enough about the child to illegally transfer TCB's funds? Even if it meant Paige's life?

The interoffice beeper sounded. It was a muted tone, but the noise of it set Daniel's teeth on edge. He loathed Pierce and hated being available to his every call. Soon . . .

"Sir?"

"Daniel, I want your input on something."

"Right there."

By now, Alix Cole must have told the other parents about her baby's severed fingertip. Fear was contagious. The parents ought to be ready to cooperate with anything Daniel suggested. And if things went as he planned, so would Harper Pierce.

Pierce's office was at the end of the hall. His suite faced the sea. On a clear day, Daniel had seen Catalina Island from that window, and sunsets that were spectacular.

The decor was simple, a leather swivel chair behind a modest desk, an upholstered sofa and three accent chairs, and pale green carpet and drapes. The only obvious evidence of wealth in the office were the impressive works of art displayed on two interior walls.

In the four years Daniel had worked as assistant to Harper Pierce, the two men had never developed a friendship. Pierce kept his business and personal lives separate. He didn't buy a gift for Daniel on Christmas, but gave him an impersonal cash bonus. They were business associates, only.

That was why it surprised Daniel when Pierce said to him, "Come in, I need to talk to someone." The man seemed badly shaken.

"Are you all right? Can I get you something? A drink?"

The decision seemed almost too much. "Yes," Pierce answered finally. "Scotch rocks."

Daniel fixed the drink, brought it to him, and stood waiting by Pierce's desk. The old man hadn't asked him to sit, and he never did, unless asked.

"Daniel, you must have heard about my granddaughter's kidnapping." Pierce seemed to notice him. "Oh, sit down. This isn't business, exactly."

Daniel sat.

"I'm sure the gossip has made the rounds." Pierce eyed him, as if for confirmation of this.

Daniel volunteered nothing.

"Doesn't matter," said Pierce. "None of them knows what's really happening. You're not a family man, are you Daniel?"

"No, sir. I'm single."

"Right. Sometimes, I think that's better. Not so much trouble. That's what families are, complications and trouble."

It was a point to offer a comment, but Daniel didn't. Pierce had called him in here for a reason.

"Paige is my daughter's youngest," he said, "a pretty little thing. I've never been much for babies, no patience with them," he admitted, "but with Paige I . . . oh, I don't know. She's such an affectionate child."

Did Pierce know about Chelsea's finger?

"Nothing's happening. We've waited, my daughter and her family. I expected a ransom note by now. At first, I was firmly against paying any ransom, but now . . . why the hell don't they contact us? What is it these people want?"

Daniel leaned in closer. "The police? They must have some leads?"

"If they do, they're damn well keeping it to themselves. My daughter's half crazy with worry. She's hired a psychic. Can you believe that? Some woman she saw on a talk show. Says the woman's telling her things about where Paige is being kept, something about 'piney woods.' "

"When I heard about this turn of events, I tried to put a stop to it, but Diane stood up to me. She's never been strong-willed, always accepted my decisions on matters she didn't understand. But on this, my daughter's got her back up, and she won't drop this phony psychic."

"You're sure the woman's a phony?"

Pierce reacted with his familiar temper. "What's that supposed to mean? They're all frauds, aren't they? Don't tell me you believe in such people?"

"I've never had a reason to deal with one."

"No one with any sense would," said Pierce. "It's got me worried about her—my daughter. I can't reason with her. She's erratic, almost manic sometimes. She's never behaved this way. It's not normal."

"I imagine stress takes its toll," said Daniel.

"Stress? Yes," said Pierce. "It's damn well taking its toll on all of us." He leaned his head into his hands. "My wife acts as if this is my fault. She and Diane have it in their heads that Paige was taken because of my connection to this bank. They don't say it, but I see the blame in their eyes."

"Hasn't there been any contact? Any message from the kidnapper?"

"Nothing," said Pierce. "Diane's going mad with waiting. Her husband doesn't know what to do. I'm her father, understand? There ought to be something I could do. If I knew who was responsible for this, I'd pay to have him killed." Pierce stared pointedly at Daniel. "I know how that must sound, but I don't take it back. I would, after what he's put my family through. I'd do it and never feel a minute of remorse. Damn the bastard!"

"Is there anything I can do?"

"No, of course not. I just needed to blow off steam, talk to someone, you understand? I don't bring this up before my wife or daughter. They're both a little"—he searched for the right word—"fragile with worry. Best not to add to it."

"If there's nothing else?" Daniel rose to leave.

"No, nothing. Thank you for listening," said Pierce. "You've been a good assistant these many years. How long is it you've been with us?"

"Four years as your personal assistant."

"It seems longer," Pierce reflected. "Well, you'll keep this conversation between us, won't you? I wouldn't want my family business discussed by the gossip mongers outside this office."

"Strictly confidential."

"Good man," said Pierce, dismissing him.

"There is one thing, sir."

Pierce glanced up, a hint of annoyance in his expression. "Yes?"

"This matter of the psychic. Perhaps I could help."

"Help?"

"I might contact the woman. Speak to her myself, if you know what I mean. Persuade her to leave your daughter alone."

Pierce's fingers rubbed at the gray stubble of mustache above his mouth. His eyes showed he was considering the proposal. "You'd be willing to do that?"

"Yes, sir. I'd like to help. I'm reasonably confident I can rid you of this psychic."

"Nothing illegal?"

"Of course not."

"All right, if you're willing. Why not?"

"I'll need the woman's name and address."

"Yes, I have it here somewhere." Pierce dug through his desk drawer for the slip of paper. "I scribbled it down when Diane told me. You're sure about this?"

"Sure?"

"You realize, I don't expect you to—"

"We understand each other. I'd like to help."

Harper Pierce handed Daniel the slip of paper. "I'm a man who remembers all that's done to him, good and bad. I won't forget this."

Daniel glanced at the address on the notepaper. "I'll leave for West Virginia this afternoon."

He left the office, walking fast, his mind already planning what he'd do to the psychic, Rowena Rawlings Crawford, when he found her.

"You must have something else to tell me. Please try." Diane's voice sounded small and weak.

She's almost given up, thought Rowena.

"I can't force things to come into my mind," she tried to explain to the desperate mother. "Visions are instant, like a quick touch, then they're gone."

"But you told me what was happening to Paige before. That was only a few days ago. Can't you do it again? I have to know," she said, her voice breaking.

"I can't sleep. I can't do anything but think about her. You've got to help me. If you don't, I'll—"

"Diane," Rowena quickly stopped the words she knew were coming, "it's bad luck to speak such a thought. Suicide's a terrible thing. I know. I've felt what's left inside a soul when a person's done that. You got to be strong."

"I'm not strong!"

She could hear the agony in Diane's voice, and worse, she felt the suffering. That was the dangerous part about being psychic. Sometimes, Rowena got too close to people, and then she knew their hurts as if they were her own. Right now, she felt Diane Kendall's hurt, and it was awful.

"Please don't stop helping us," Diane begged. "You're our only connection to Paige. I found her through you. I can't lose her again."

"I already told you all I know." Rowena tried to pull away—mentally, verbally, physically.

"You said she's alive," Diane insisted.

Rowena felt the suffocating memory return. The hand clasped over the baby's mouth—Rowena's mouth . . . falling into a silent dark . . . as she felt her spirit leave her body. Paige—Rowena. She had taken on the feelings of the child so strongly for those few moments, she had become that baby, dying with it.

"I'm begging you. You have to help me find her."

Rowena had felt the presence of death hovering near her since that vision. She'd dreamed about it and felt the dark shades chasing her. If she got too close, if she risked it, the next time might be her last. What if she tried to reach into the baby's spirit again and something happened, like it had the last time? Sometimes feelings were too strong. She was afraid to try, afraid she might lose her own life.

"You promised you'd do what God gives you to do," said Diane. "Please, don't stop trying. She's so little, just a baby. You're my daughter's only hope."

"I know what I said." Rowena tried to deny the woman.

"She'll die without your help. You know that. I can't believe you'd leave her there, without anyone to know or see what's happening," Diane cried. "Please, if you have any heart, you have to try again."

That was the problem, Rowena did have a heart. The fact that she was sensitive to feelings was what made her a psychic, and what made her vulnerable to Diane's desperate plea.

"All right," she yielded. "I'll look at her little things again. It might be I'll see something else this time. I can't promise."

Diane was crying, the tears muffling her voice. "I knew you'd help us. I was sure of you that first day. Sure. No one else believes you can see Paige—not my father, my husband, or Detective Walsh—but I do," she said in a stronger, determined voice. "You're Paige's angel, that's what you are. Paige's angel."

The words struck like an icy wedge between Rowena's shoulder blades. The only kind of angels she knew anything about were dead people, lost spirits lingering on earth. She didn't want to become one of them.

The bundle of things Diane Kendall had sent were in Rowena's basement. She'd put them down there to give herself a safe distance from the terrible visions. Sometimes, being in the same room with an object or clothes from a person could bring on unwanted images. For all she knew, the Kendall baby might be passed on by now. Rowena had been drawn into a dead body before . . . felt the corruption of the flesh, knew what the moment of death had been like, and felt the lingering trace of fear. If there was a hell, that was it. Could she live through doing it again?

There were four little children waiting for somebody to save them.

"I'll see about it now," Rowena told Diane. "If your baby's alive, I'll know it." And if she's dead, she didn't add, I'll know that, too. She hung up to the sound of the worried mother's tears.

Quickly, before she could give herself a chance to change her mind, Rowena started down the basement stairs.

Chapter Fifteen

Daniel rented a car at the Charleston airport. He used a credit card listed to an Aaron Pahl from Detroit for the transaction, risking no link to himself or Harper Pierce.

"Thank you for choosing Avis, Mr. Pahl," said the young woman at the desk. She handed him the keys to a blue Celica.

She was pretty, in a small town kind of way. There was nothing of sophistication about her, but she had attractive features, nice white teeth, and her smile seemed genuine. If he had more time . . .

But he didn't. Daniel took the offered keys without exchanging any unnecessary conversation. Less for her to remember about him. Not that he expected anyone to connect him with what was going to happen here. He planned to move quickly, finish the job, and be out of town before the authorities found the body. It wouldn't take a lot of effort. This psychic, and what she told Diane Kendall, could cause him trouble.

"Think fast, psychic," Daniel offered a warning, as he sped along the road to Millford.

The box holding the folded baby clothes, blanket, and single toy wasn't heavy. Rowena lifted the carton onto her lap, its brown paper wrapper sounding like the crunch of fall leaves against the tops of her thighs. She had deliberately left the paper on the package, wanting a better sense of the woman who had mailed it. Diane had written the address in a careful hand, but Rowena could feel the crushing terror of this mother. It permeated the paper, the box, and everything Diane had touched.

Rowena was positive this woman had done nothing to harm her baby. Some parents did hurt their children. This was a fact she'd learned the hard way. It had happened without warning. Two years ago, she'd picked up a piece of clothing from a missing little boy, and she'd known in that instant why the police hadn't found the child's killer—she'd known right then the boy was dead. The killer, the mother of that child, had stared into Rowena's eyes, as if watching for some sign of recognition.

"Your boy's dead," Rowena had told her bluntly, without pity, and put the little shirt back into the woman's hands. She was careful not to touch that mother's skin.

The case never came to trial, not because she hadn't reported her information to the police, but because no proof was ever found to incriminate the mother. Rowena didn't need proof. She had felt the severing of the threads of life that had bound that woman to her son. Those connections between parent and child linger beyond death, but not when the parent murders the child. That was what she'd seen—

that, and the mother's guilty fear. It wasn't proof which would convict the woman in court.

That kind of severing hadn't happened between Diane and her daughter. The threads of life were strong and constant. This didn't mean that the baby was alive, only that to its mother, this bonding with her child was still a sensory connection.

In the dim light of the basement, Rowena pulled Paige Kendall's belongings out of the cardboard box: a yellow-and-white gingham dress, a white toy lamb, and a pink crib blanket. Simply lifting the blanket from the cardboard box told Rowena it held the strongest lingering traces of the child. The baby dress, frilly and soft, held almost nothing. The plush lamb was another strong source, but much stronger when Rowena turned the key of its music box. When she'd seen the toy before, she hadn't noticed it was musical.

It was eerie, hearing the lullaby in the amber light of the basement. Four innocent babies, the beginnings of life, bound in a circumstance of kidnapping and murder. She held the toy lamb in her hands, closed her eyes, and listened to the nursery tune.

And for a moment . . . she was there.

While the music box played, Rowena saw through the eyes of the child. She saw a wide room nearly empty of furniture. A cabin. The baby was walking, moving across the stretch of wooden floor toward a wall that was knotty pine boards. Rowena-Paige could smell the nearness of fir trees through an open window.

Everything was seen at eye level, child level. A corner of something was visible just beyond the window. It looked like a street sign. She could see the words ON ROAD. The baby walked toward the window, a couple of more steps and the sign would be in full view. Rowena would be able to read it, to tell Diane the name of the street, and where to find Paige. A couple more steps . . .

Something startled them. Rowena felt a shudder run through the little body—her body—and knew it when Paige stopped moving toward the window. Stopped to suck her thumb.

Go on. A little more.

Her thoughts weren't linked to the child's. Paige couldn't know or hear what Rowena was thinking. The psychic could only feel what the baby felt, see what the baby saw. She could only watch and wait.

Paige took another step. Another letter of the sign came into view. YON ROAD.

Fear slammed into Rowena's soul, worse than before. Paige's heartbeat quickened. There was sudden tension in the child's muscles. A cry tore from Rowena, from Paige, and the baby was jerked up and turned around.

Rowena stared into the face of a man.

His eyes looked back into hers, as if he could know and could see her fear. The panic of that moment was within her spirit. Like the baby, she was trembling, and staring into the eyes of a killer.

Rowena dropped the toy and the image disappeared. Her heart struck like the blows of a fist against her chest. She gasped for air, realizing she had been holding her breath. Waves of weakness flooded through her body. She had seen the face of the man who held the kidnapped child. And she knew with a certainty as clear as his icy blue eyes, unless they found Paige and the other children soon, the babies were going to die.

Rowena pulled the pink crib blanket from the cardboard box and buried her face in the softness of it.

Other images came, swift as water spilling over rocks. Flashes of insight. Overwhelming feelings. Only the danger Rowena felt racing at her wasn't a threat to the baby, but somehow, through her strong connection to the child . . . it was death approaching, to Rowena herself.

The farm roads were empty of traffic. Daniel floored the Celica, anxious to get through this bleak countryside. He hated open fields and the cold-water shacks he saw behind the row of sagging fence posts. Hated the idea of being poor as that. He'd been running from that kind of crushing poverty all his life. The memory of it was a weight around his neck, trying to drag him down. But he wouldn't let it. Never again.

When he was little, he and his mother had lived through a kind of hell. He'd seen the gaunt lines of her face, the hollows of her cheeks, and he'd known the pain of his own hunger. That time was over, had been for years, but Daniel couldn't forget it. Never would. Poverty was a disease; money was its only cure.

He was in a hurry to get away from this. His foot pressed harder on the accelerator. He thought about how he would kill the psychic. It would be quick, uncomplicated. Ignorant woman. She had involved herself in something where she didn't belong. That was a mistake. Her fault, not his. She'd caused the problem.

That problem would be over as soon as he got to her house. Damn these West Virginia roads! The curves kept him from driving as fast as he would have liked, if he could see fifty feet ahead of him.

And then, when he passed the next curve, the road ahead became a long straight shot. He stomped on the gas pedal, and the Celica tore out. Everything was easing. Everything was coming together. Everything was—

The hay wagon nosed into the main road, wide and heavily laden with stacks of wired and bundled bales, stretching full length across both lanes, blocking all escape.

Daniel slammed his foot on the brakes, and the sound of the tires being skinned over macadam was like hot wires in his mind. There was no chance of missing the truck. He would hit, and the hay go up in a bonfire of spilled gasoline. His brakes locked and the car began to skid, pulling the Celica to the right.

Daniel's final thought as the car bumped off the paved highway and over the thick verge of grass and undergrowth bordering the road: *All that money . . .*

The Celica pitched over and rolled down the hill. The wheels were still spinning as it came to rest on its roof at the base of a narrow, wet gully. Smoke poured from under the hood, and a sound exploded like a shot from a cannon, blasting a screen of flames high into the air.

Rowena felt the sudden shock to her body. The threat racing toward her had abruptly stopped. At first, she thought she'd dropped the blanket, but looked and saw that it was still clutched in her hands. No, it wasn't anything she'd done. Something had happened. Something changed.

She stood, dropping the crib blanket to the floor. All at once, the isolation and confinement in the basement frightened her. She rushed up the steps, through the house, and outside into the light. *Hide!* But from what?

She'd never experienced anything like this before. For those few minutes when she'd held the baby's blanket, the danger had seemed so real. It was hurrying toward her, and she had seen herself—that was the part so hard to remember—she had seen herself dead.

A stretch of flat woodlands rose into thickly forested hills behind her house. Rowena stood within the shelter of the trees until the trembling stopped. She glanced behind her, and to both sides, alarmed and fearful.

One thing was clear: Paige was alive. Rowena had seen the face of the man holding the baby. She could tell Diane that much, and about the strong scent of fir trees. She knew what Diane would say. She'd plead with her to keep trying. But after what happened today, the way she felt, Rowena had to ask herself— should she?

It was almost dark when she went back into the house. The basement seemed colder. Rowena sat in the chair and picked up the small, pink blanket . . . but the feeling was gone.

Chapter Sixteen

The room was kept dimly lit as a protective measure for the eyes of the patient in 14-A. A reflexive movement could cause his eyelids to open and he might stare for a prolonged period of time into direct sunlight, or into the glare of a light bulb, which would cause damage to his corneas.

As if anyone expects him ever to use them again, thought LVN Rose Hunter. She hated working the fourth floor. This was the wing where patients in a vegetative state were put, out of sight of hospital visitors. Rose wished they were out of her sight, too.

Coma patients had to be treated as if they were expected to recover, even though they weren't. That meant they received daily care, as if they were cognitive, sensitive people. She thought of this one as a breathing corpse. He gave her the creeps.

The patient in 14-A had been comatose for over two weeks. His internal injuries had been massive: severe bruising of the liver, loss of the right kidney, perforation of the lungs by splintered rib cage, and blows to the cranium resulting in a hemorrhage of the brain. His condition on the chart was listed as critical.

LVN Hector Santos entered the room. "Okay, Rosie," he said, "let's get a move on and do this guy. I've got three more to lift and scrub after him."

His attitude irked her. "Maybe you'd like to trade places with me and do the six urine catheters for these slugheads?"

"No thanks. That kind of thing makes a guy wince, y'know?"

She knew. Staff usually gave that job to female nurses. The males had an instinctive reaction that patients could read in their eyes, if their own eyes weren't scrunched shut in discomfort.

Together, they rolled and lifted the patient. Under normal conditions, Rose could have done this by herself, but coma patients were a dead weight. Most were old and frail when they got to this stage, but the patient in 14-A was young and strong. She couldn't lift the nearly two-hundred-pound body. Hector helped her sponge bathe him, apply fresh dressings to the surgical wounds, change the bedding, and repositioned the body to prevent bedsores.

"It kind of gets you when it's somebody his age, doesn't it?" said Hector.

It didn't. "Personally, I think they should let all of them die. It would be a lot less trouble for everybody, especially me."

"Hey, don't be talking like that. What if he can hear you? Don't you ever think about that? It must be terrible, not being able to do anything for yourself, and hearing somebody talk like that about you."

"Yeah, like he's gonna wake up and complain about it. I'll worry about his feelings later, if it's all the same to you."

"Damn, but you're a heartless woman," said Hector.

"I save my pity for those who can feel something." She jabbed a hurtful finger into the patient's abdomen. The body didn't react. "This guy feels nothing."

"Remind me not to wind up under the kindness of your tender care," said Hector. "Has anyone been to see this one since he came upstairs? Any family?"

"Nobody," said Rose.

"That's weird, isn't it?" said Hector. "I mean, he probably didn't look too bad before the accident. Why would a young guy like him be all alone?"

"He was probably an asshole even before he became an unconscious asshole."

Hector left the room, muttering something to himself about female dogs and coldhearted women.

After Hector left, Rose still had the vitals to fill out on the chart. It was a fact that no one had visited the patient in 14-A, or contacted the hospital about his condition, in the week and a half since he'd been moved from critical care to the fourth floor wing of Stanton General. While that was a little unusual, it wasn't totally uncharacteristic of what happened up here. After a few dutiful visits, family members stayed away from this wing. It was too depressing.

Rose wished she could be given permission to stay away, too. Sometimes she just felt like going through the wing and turning off the ventilators. It would be a blessing to all of them. She had even dreamed of it. The dream had come again last night, and the patient's face she'd seen was this man's. Poor bastard. Why were the doctors keeping him alive? Nobody cared about this one. No one had even asked about him, not in all this time.

Rose looked at his face, really looked at it. He didn't have bad features, thick dark hair, pale skin like hers, and his body was muscular. It wasn't right that a man so young and strong should be up here with the zombie crowd—that's what she called them, the living dead.

She didn't mind it too much when the patients were old and feeble-looking. Having them on the fourth floor wing served a purpose; it paid her salary, for one. It paid the doctors' salaries, too, and kept this hospital going. They had lived their lives and this was the final stage for them, a lousy final stage, but it didn't trouble her.

The patient in 14-A troubled her. He was out of place. It hurt Rose to see him. And now, he was haunting her dreams. Only, he wasn't in a coma then.

"I saw you last night," she said to him, bending low and whispering in his ear. "You were walking toward me, your eyes open and your arms held out to fold me into them. You were awake. What do you think of that?" She nervously glanced around to see if anyone was listening.

Her hand rested on the ventilator hose. So easy to damage the unit. The patient jerked convulsively and yanked the hose out of its housing. The plastic duct tore. Or, the switch itself . . .

She thought of all these things as she stood close beside the bed. Not to hurt him. That wasn't why. It was to get him out of here. Nobody who looked the way he did deserved to be in this place. If she were him, she'd want someone to pull the plug on her. And he wasn't going to get better, they never did up here. Her hand moved toward the switch.

"Hey, Rosie! You still in here?" Hector stood in

the doorway. "They want us down on three for the lunch trays."

"Okay, be right there," she said.

Hector waited.

Reluctantly, she had to leave the patient in 14-A. It was in the elevator, between the fourth and third floors, that she realized what she'd almost done. Her legs began to tremble so badly, she felt her knees buckle, and she sat down.

"You all right?" asked Hector. "Rosie, what's the matter?"

She couldn't answer. Had to keep it to herself. The matter was, she'd almost killed a man . . . because she'd dreamed of him taking her in his arms.

"He's left us with these brats and he's gone," insisted Jack. He was swaggering drunk and acting tough.

"He's not gone," Lydia told him again. She watched him carefully for any sign of violence toward her. If Jack came too close, she was ready for him. A knife was inside her sleeve all the time, taped to her forearm. She'd gut him if he tried anything stupid. He was too stinking drunk to stop her. His reflexes moved in slow motion.

"Then why the hell hasn't he been here?" Jack raved. He drew his fingers through his greasy blond hair. "I mean it, Lydia. I'm not waiting around for the cops to come knocking at the door. Maybe things got too hot and he decided to let us take the fall."

She'd wondered about it, too. How long did Logan plan to let this game play out? It had been a month and a half since the babies were taken, and over two

146

weeks since they'd seen Logan. The scary part was, Jack was starting to make sense.

"We wait a little longer," she told him.

"How much longer? A week? Two weeks? Staying here's starting to drive me crazy. These kids never shut up. I didn't figure it would go on this long. He never told us—"

"We stay another week," she insisted, dictating to Jack about as far as she could push him.

"And what if he's not back?"

"Then we leave."

A space of silence pulsed between them. The whites of Jack's eyes were red-streaked. She could see the effort of his thinking twitching in the pupils.

"And what do we do with them?" He waved his hand in the direction of the four babies.

Lydia looked at the children, then back at Jack. She said it calmly. "I'll let you kill them."

Jack moved a threatening step closer. "Me! Why me?"

She told him the truth. "Because you'd like it."

I'll let you kill the rest, she thought, *but not Paige.*

That one was the prize worth saving. Jack didn't know anything about the baby's grandfather, or the plan Lydia had been working out. He could do what he wanted with the others. They'd never mattered in the first place. Only one child here was worth the risk. Kidnapping was a capital offense, a death penalty if she got caught. Not to mention the murder of that woman running the day care. That ought to tip the balance against a life sentence.

She didn't plan to get caught.

Jack started for the front door.

"Where are you going?" She hated it when he wasn't where she could watch him.

"Anyplace but here." He slammed the door when he left, setting off a round of crying from the babies.

"Shut up!" she shouted. "I'm warning you, shut up!"

The crying got louder.

It was all she could do—all she could do—not to take one of the shrieking little bodies and smash it against the wall.

"Goddamn you, Logan!" she cursed him. Her head was aching from the tormenting sound. "Goddamn you for leaving me with this!"

That was when the doorbell rang. All four kids were crying. Lydia was coming apart at the seams, and there was a stranger standing on the front porch, peering in the window.

The stranger was a woman. She'd seen Lydia through the window, and was waving fat little fingers at her.

Too friendly to be the police.

She couldn't avoid answering the door. The woman had seen her. Unless she was stone deaf, she'd heard the babies, too. The situation was tricky. There was only one thing good about it; Jack wasn't here.

With no choice for it, Lydia went to the door. She opened it a narrow crack. "Yes?"

"Oh, hi," said the pasty-faced blonde. "I'm your neighbor, Missy Dunbar. My husband and I live at the house on the right." She pointed an oversized arm.

"Hello." Lydia didn't open the door any wider. The babies were yelling.

"My . . . it sounds like you've got two or three little ones in there."

"It's nap time. They get fussy before they go to sleep."

"Oh, I know about that," said Missy. Her smile was so wide, it looked like the carved grin on a Halloween pumpkin. "We've got a six-month-old," she explained. "A little boy."

She was trying to peer around the door. Lydia stepped outside. "Sorry, I can't keep the door open. Don't want them catching a chill."

"No, course not." Missy's smile slipped a notch. "I couldn't help hearing them, and I wondered . . ."

Here it was, the reason she came over. Lydia didn't rush her.

"Well, you see, I'm looking for someone to watch my son when I go back to work. I thought, with so many children, this had to be a day care. Am I right?"

Lydia rewarded her with a smile. "Aren't you smart to figure that out?"

Missy tried to glance in the window again, but Lydia stepped into her way. "I thought I'd come by and meet you, and see the arrangements you have for the children. I can't afford much, but—"

Lydia cut her off. "I'm not taking any more babies. I already have my limit. My license won't allow me to take any others."

"Oh, you're licensed? I was hoping. That's rare up here. It makes a parent feel safer when they know someone from the state's checking on conditions."

Lydia nodded. She wondered if she would have to

kill this bothersome woman. "I have to go back inside," she said. "I can't leave the children alone."

"No," Missy agreed, "of course not." Her hair jiggled like the roll of fat jiggling under her chin. "How many are there?"

"Three." Lydia didn't want to give her any information that might remind Missy of the four kidnapped children she must have heard about on the news.

"Only three? I could swear I saw four little ones in there. I kind of peeked inside. Hope you don't think I'm too nosy."

Nosy, and stupid. If she killed her, would Missy's husband notice? Probably, and he'd bring the police to this house. It was too much of a risk.

"The fourth one's mine," said Lydia. "I don't count him as part of the day care. I watch five, actually. One's sick today. I really have to—"

But Missy wasn't through. "Five!" she exclaimed. "How do you do it? I go crazy with one."

"They keep me busy." She opened the door wide enough to squeeze through, and started to back inside, blocking the view as much as possible.

"Well, nice meeting you," Missy offered.

"Real nice."

The door was almost shut when she heard, "Oh, wait a minute. I didn't get your name."

It popped out before she had time to think. "Lydia." *Idiot!* She wanted to snatch the name back, but it was too late.

"Next time I come by I'll bring my little boy. He'd like to see all your babies. Bye, Lydia."

It was a close call: shut the door or kill the woman. Fortunately for Missy, she started down the porch steps at that moment. Lydia watched her walk away and realized the footprints in the snow would have led Missy's husband straight to this house. And the police.

What the hell was she supposed to do now? What if Missy came back? The whole thing was getting too dangerous. She could feel it closing in. Where was Logan? And what was she going to do about Jack? She turned around, facing the room, her head swimming with frustration.

The babies were still crying.

"Can you tell me your name?"

"Daniel."

The light was too bright, hurting his eyes. His head ached with an unrelenting ferocity, savage pain, made worse by the intrusive shards of light. He wanted to close his eyes and go back to sleep, but someone kept asking him questions.

"Do you remember anything about the accident?"

Accident? He tried to think. His brain felt drugged, as if it were wrapped in gauze, and his thoughts had to travel through layer after layer, tearing their way to the surface of his consciousness. Questions came before any answers.

"Where am I?"

"You're at Stanton General Hospital. I'm Dr. Clancy. I've been your primary physician while you're recovering from the accident."

Accident. There was that word again. Daniel felt the shock of it build in him like a fear. "What . . ." He couldn't think what to ask. The questions wouldn't come together into sentences.

"It's all right," said Dr. Clancy. "Don't be concerned if you're having trouble concentrating. That will improve. Your body's struggling to fully wake up. You've been in a coma."

A coma. Panic buckled through him like the wild arc of his heartbeat. The overwhelming sense of it flooded all reason. He jerked forward. Tried to sit up. Agony hit the muscles of his neck and back like a crushing hand. His body fell back against the mattress, and he heard his own cry tear through him.

"What you just felt is a far more effective lesson than any warning I could have given about why you shouldn't move around too much. You've had some serious injuries. It's going to take time for your body, and your mind, to recover. Take it slow."

There wasn't any choice.

"Do you remember driving?" asked Dr. Clancy.

He did remember something about renting a car. The girl was pretty. Driving along country roads, and
. . .

"I swerved to miss something, a truck I think, and the car rolled." He remembered that moment of terror when the truck was suddenly there before him. No way to avoid it.

"That's right. The car rolled, but you were thrown clear before it exploded into flames."

Flames. The sound of that explosion was something he remembered.

"You're doing fine," said Dr. Clancy. There was kindness in the doctor's eyes, sympathy, and a world of prying questions. "Where were you going? Do you remember that?"

Daniel struggled with the memory. The answer lay

beneath some layer of his mind his thoughts couldn't reach.

"I—there was—I don't know," said Daniel. Perspiration beaded his upper lip, and he could feel the throb of his pulse drumming at his temples.

"It takes a little time," said Dr. Clancy. "Don't try to force things. Let yourself heal. You don't know how lucky you are to be alive. An accident like the one you had doesn't usually leave survivors. What you need is rest. I'll be back later and we'll talk again."

Daniel nodded. He wanted the doctor to leave. He wanted to be alone.

When the door to his room closed, he shut his eyes and let his thoughts drift. The flash of consciousness came without warning. It was like an instant projection, large screen and vivid . . . a close-up on a small, severed fingertip.

Daniel opened his eyes and stared at the wall, afraid to go to sleep. His breath came in rapid gasps. He had to remember. There was something important. And he had to remember it soon.

Chapter Seventeen

John Tripp had a theory about witnesses: You could believe them, as long as they weren't lying to you. That just about excluded everyone. Alix Cole wasn't exactly a witness to the actual crime—the murder of Christine Campbell and the kidnapping of the four babies from the Campbell day care—but she was a parent and an attestant with valuable information about one of the leading suspects in the case, namely her ex-husband, Rick Cole.

Tripp tried not to let the fact that he was sleeping with the woman interfere with his judgment. He was convinced that she had lied to him about not knowing how to reach the South American drug lord. The fact that Tripp's house had been ransacked told him Cole still maintained contact with his ex-wife, if only that he was having her watched.

Following up on the few leads in the case had brought Tripp little success. If he'd stumbled over any obvious clues or damning evidence, he'd missed noticing them. At this point, his only new evidence was the severed fingertip of a child, and that was something he'd promised Alix not to disclose to the sheriff's investigation.

Detective Jessa Walsh was keeping tight reins on any information she'd uncovered in the case. Tripp had tried coming through back door sources, asking a few buddies in the department, but he was locked out on this one. Nobody was talking. He could only assume that Walsh was responsible for the freeze. Whatever she knew, she wasn't playing nice and sharing.

Tripp's boss, Maxwell Grodin, now frowned every time he saw him. He had always frowned, but this was worse. "Anything solid on that case yet?" Grodin kept asking.

"Working on it," Tripp told him.

Working on it. Yeah, like watching cheese age. He was stuck in the center of the problem, and flat out of answers—not to mention sleeping with one of the suspects. Grodin would probably fire him if he knew that. But hell, life was full of risks. Chances were good that Rick Cole might kill him first.

As much to protect his life as to investigate the prime suspect in the case, Tripp started watching Alix. If his hunch was right and she knew how to contact Cole, he wanted to know it. His kept his relationship with Alix separate in his mind. What she was to him in bed had nothing to do with how she was involved in the case. At least, that's what he told himself. Sometimes, he believed it.

There was only one problem: watching Alix gave him more questions than answers. For a woman who claimed to be afraid of her ex-husband, she was remarkably casual about home security. Her door locks were minimal, and she didn't own a weapon—at least, none she'd shown him. If she'd left Rick because he'd killed a man, then why didn't Alix behave as if she was afraid? The questions got tougher. If Cole and Alix were through, why had he trashed Tripp's house, as if in a jealous rage? Something didn't add up.

With dogged determination, Tripp staked out Alix's house. He parked the van PIC used for stake-outs a few doors down from her address, and set up surveillance. On one of his visits to her house, he'd planted a bug on the bedroom phone. It was illegal, and he couldn't use any evidence he received this way in court, but it might save his life. The surveillance van was set up with telephone and recording equipment.

Now, it was a matter of waiting until something happened.

Diane picked up the phone on the first ring. She'd been expecting a call from Rowena. The psychic had given her some information about Paige over two weeks ago, frightening news, but then had been impossible to reach ever since, as if deliberately avoiding her.

To Diane, the idea of actually seeing Paige's kidnapper was a major breakthrough. She'd convinced Detective Walsh to arrange for a police illustrator near Millford to come to the Crawford house. The drawing which came back was limited, at best. Diane had studied the face of the man, needing to know his identity, to recognize him, but it had proved useless. A stranger stared back at her, a stranger with a killer's eyes.

"Hello," she answered the phone.

"Mrs. Kendall?"

The voice surprised her. She hadn't expected it to be a man.

"Yes, this is Diane Kendall."

"I've got your kid."

Breath left her body. She'd been staring at the drawing, and now ... she was speaking to the man whose pen-and-ink image was before her on the table.

"D'you hear me?" he asked. His words rolled together, slurred into a line of sound without breaks, like someone who'd been drinking. "I'm talking to you!"

When he shouted, she gasped. That gave her air enough to speak. "Where's my daughter? Where is she?"

He laughed, and she felt the chill of that sound run through her.

"You want her back?" He coughed, like a smoker.

"Yes." Every detail, every nuance, registered in her mind. She held the drawing before her and tried to connect the image to the voice. The result was terrifying. This man had her child.

"Please," she tried desperately, "tell me what you want. If it's money—"

"Shut up! Did I say anything about money? Did I?" he yelled.

"No. No, I'm sorry. I ... I thought—"

"Quit talking and listen to me! Are you listening?"

She was shivering. Her heart felt solid and unmoving. "Yes, I'm listening." She stared into the sketched eyes of the drawing.

"Your kid's alive, but only because of me. You hear that?"

"Yes."

"I almost killed her once. Tried to shut her up with a hand over her trap, but he stopped me."

Rowena had been right. That terrible vision. She'd seen it happen, felt Paige smothering . . . felt her start to die. There was no doubt in Diane's mind. This was the man who had her daughter.

"I want her back." The words were pulled from her by a force greater than her fear, a force of love for her child.

"Do you? You want her back," he mocked in a singsong voice. Another spasm of coughing held him. "I'm sick of her anyhow. Can't decide what would give me more pleasure, killing the brat, or going ahead with the plan."

"Don't hurt her."

"You warning me, lady?"

"No." She couldn't risk making him angry.

"You threatening me? Cause if you are—"

"No, I'm not threatening you, I'm asking. Please, don't hurt her."

There was a long pause. She was afraid he'd left the phone. "Are you still there?" she asked. "Hello?"

"Did I tell you he cut off a piece of one kid's finger? D'you know that, lady? He chopped it off with his pocketknife. What do you think of that?"

It felt as if a fist had hit her stomach. She tried not to believe him, tried, but the image stayed. "Paige . . ."

"Not her. One of the other ones—Chelsea. He took that fingertip and mailed it to her mama, like a present. She didn't tell you?"

"No." Diane knew it was true, knew it with absolute certainty—the same way she knew that Rowena was a real psychic, and that this man was Paige's kidnapper.

"It was a real sweet idea. We've been thinking of sending out some more little gifts."

Diane felt a cry rise up within her, but it was strangled into silence at her throat.

"I don't hear you talking. Maybe you want me to send you one of those presents?"

"I—" She tried to think, tried to push past her fear. "My father's a rich man. If you give Paige back to me, he'll pay you whatever you want."

"Is that right?"

"He's the CEO of a major banking conglomerate. Whatever you ask. He'd do it if I tell him. I can make him do it."

"Hold on, I'm thinking. I don't know . . ."

A wild courage came from somewhere she couldn't claim as her own nerve. It was like a will outside herself, pure terror speaking. "If you hurt her, he won't pay you a cent."

"Did I say I was gonna hurt her? Relax. Hang tight a second. I gotta think this through."

She waited.

"Yeah," he said at last. "Maybe that's not such a bad idea. I'll work out the details."

"Make it soon," she said.

He laughed. "You anxious? I like that. I don't think your kid likes it here. She's always crying. One of these days, one of us is bound to shut her up. You got a noisy kid, lady. Did I tell you I tried to smother her?"

"You told me."

"Yeah, well . . ."

"I don't care what's happened, or what any of you have done," she told him. "I'll make sure you get the money from my father, as long as you give Paige back to me, and she's not hurt. When could you—"

"I gotta go. You play games with me lady, I'll send your kid back in pieces."

"Wait! You said—"

A click sounded as the line disconnected.

Diane crumpled, head to knees, as if all life had gone out of her body. Her arms hung slack. All she could think of was the face of the killer Rowena had described, and the image of his cold blue eyes leaning over her child.

The call to Diane Kendall was exactly what Jessa had been waiting for. Each phone of the families involved in the case had been tapped since the beginning of the investigation, including the one at the home of homicide victim, Christine Campbell. If the caller was the kidnapper, he'd made some serious slips of information.

"The voice print's the same as the one from the earlier call to Carin Sayers," said Dillon, Jessa's partner. "His speech is slurred, but the boys in Tech identified it as a match. Probably drunk."

Jessa shook her head. "Why would he risk this? It doesn't make sense. It's a stupid thing to do." She paced the floor of the office, drumming her fingernails on the mug of hot tea in her hands. "Dammit!" she swore, banging the mug onto the desk. "This was not the same person who took the babies from the Campbell home. It wasn't."

"What makes you so sure? For God's sake, Jessa, what's the matter with you? We haven't had many breaks in this case."

"We haven't had *any* breaks. That's my point. It's been too clean so far. No mistakes."

"Now you're complaining about the doer's mistakes? Christ! We had the call to Carin Sayers. What about that?"

She nodded, admitting this. She heard what Dillon said, but he didn't have her total attention. The larger part of it was drawn to the map she'd set up on her office wall. Colored pins marked the sites of evidence, or investigation in the case. Blue and green pins marked the babies' homes and the Campbell day care, encompassing the cities of La Cañada and Glendale. Red pins identified areas of leads they were following.

Until today, there had been only one red pin on the map. The point of origin for the first call was Highland, a suburb of San Bernardino County. The call had been placed from a phone booth in the parking lot outside a Circle-K.

Now, there were two red pins on the map. The second marked area was Palmdale. The doer apparently liked convenience stores. He'd made this call from a phone booth outside a 7-Eleven on Palmdale Boulevard.

Two red pins. The package they'd heard about would mean a third point on the map. Where? Jessa took a yellow highlighter pen and drew a line from Highland to Palmdale. Where would the next line go? She was drawing in the noose.

"You should be thrilled," said Dillon. "How do you know he didn't start drinking and screw up? People do stupid things when they're drunk. I've done some pretty—"

"He's not the same one," said Jessa. "The kidnapper—the one who took the kids—he wouldn't give away information. That person was careful, thorough, and planned everything out to the last detail. Look what we've found so far—nothing. No, this is someone else. I'm sure of it."

Dillon leaned across the desk, picked up the mug, and put it back into Jessa's hands. "Drink this. Ease back a minute."

She took a sip of the tea.

"Okay," he said, "let's assume the caller is one of a team, all right?"

She nodded.

"All right. Now, maybe the one who took the kids is out of the picture."

She gave him a doubtful glance.

"Hey, maybe he's dead for all I know. Maybe he got scared and cut out. We haven't received any ransom letters. Nothing. Nada."

"What are you saying?" She was impatient, anxious.

"I'm saying, maybe the great plan fell through. Things might have changed. Maybe this jerk's in charge."

"God, I hope not." The thought was like the point of a needle jabbing her brain. "You heard what he said. He tried to kill one of them."

"I heard," said Dillon. He didn't sound as excited as he had a few minutes earlier.

Jessa held the side of the mug against her lips, letting the heat penetrate her skin. "Why is he doing this? Making these calls?"

"For the thrill," said Dillon. "I think the guy gets off listening to the fear in the mothers' voices. Remember him making Carin Sayers say she wanted him?"

Jessa nodded. That was what she thought, too. This was a cruel game the caller was playing with the mothers of the babies. "That's why he told her about cutting off a piece of Chelsea's finger, to hear the fear in Diane Kendall's voice."

"The baby's fingertip," said Dillon, "you knew about it before?"

"No."

"But you think he's telling the truth?"

"I don't know," she said. "Maybe. Yes, I think it's true."

He let out his breath in a hard rush. "If it is," he said slowly, as if still trying to figure the whole thing out, "why would Alix Cole keep it a secret?"

Jessa drank the last of the tea, then placed the mug down carefully. "That's what we're going to find out."

"Uh-huh," said Dillon, not looking convinced. He had frown creases in his forehead, and he was leaning back in his chair.

"C'mon," she said, shoving his chair upright. "We've got work to do. I'm going to pay a surprise visit to Alix Cole. You call that PI, John Tripp. He's been wanting to talk. I think it's time we gave the man his opportunity."

She was out the door before Dillon could pick up the phone. Things had changed. She'd almost given up, but now, there might be a chance to save the children.

Chelsea Cole's fingertip had been cut off. The

monster who did it sent a piece of the child through the mail to her mother. And now, one of the kidnappers—it seemed likely there were more than one—had called Diane Kendall. For what? For kicks.

Someone was slipping up, making mistakes, and that was exactly what Jessa wanted. The thought of that poor baby being mutilated burned in her mind. She could imagine it, picture the scene. She could feel what it must have been like to be held down, have your hand spread open, and a knife cut into your flesh.

If it took everything she had, she was going to get those bastards.

Chapter Eighteen

"Rowena, you have to come out here," begged Diane. Emotion and desperation came through the voice on the phone.

"Oh, I couldn't do that." Leave this house, these woods? She had avoided close contact with people for a long time, and especially now, when the visions she'd seen involved danger to her life.

"But you have to!" Diane insisted. "He called me."

"Who did?"

"The kidnapper. It was him, the man in the drawing. I had his picture right in my hands. He called me. It was him, I know it."

Rowena remembered the cruel eyes of the man she'd seen. It didn't take much imagination to know what it must have been like, talking to him.

"You carry this news to the police," she told Diane. That would be the best thing, let the police handle it. They were trained for such work. They carried guns and knew how to use them. They weren't short, easily winded, and scared.

"Detective Walsh already knows. She's had a tap on my line since the babies were taken."

"Wait, you mean someone's listening to every word we're saying right now?"

"Yes."

"Oh."

"It's all right," said Diane. "Don't worry about them. I need you to come to California, Rowena. He may call again, and if he does, you should be here."

"What earthly good would that do?" She couldn't get the idea out of her mind, someone listening to their call. It made her nervous.

"I don't know what good." Diane's voice was breaking up, as if she were crying, not sobs, but pitiful, broken-spirited tears.

"Don't take on like that," Rowena said. "Stop it now." It was hurtful to hear the pain in Diane's voice, as if nothing would ever help it. "I mean it. I can't think what good it would do, me being out there. Honestly."

She didn't want to go to California. She was comfortable here. People left her alone. In California, she'd be lost in a sea of strangers. She wouldn't know anyone, except Diane, and Diane was on the edge of a breakdown. It would be difficult, and maybe dangerous.

And she knew that other things would happen. In large groups of people, Rowena's senses and precognition worked on overload. It was an unpleasant experience she'd experienced too often in the past, with images flashing through her mind so quickly she didn't have time to identify the source. Terrible images. Threatening. That was why she lived in privacy, in the back hills of West Virginia, to close herself off as much as possible from the rest of the conscious world.

166

"If you don't help me, my baby's going to die. I'm her mother," Diane said softly. "I know it."

Rowena felt pulled by the woman's need, felt it dragging her away from safety. She didn't have children of her own, but she responded to Diane's maternal emotions. They were genuine, and as much as Rowena wanted to deny it, she thought what Diane had said might be true.

There was an audible pause, like a catch of breath. "You should have heard his voice," Diane told her. "He said he might send me pieces of my daughter."

Dear God. Rowena didn't want to hear any more.

"I'll give you anything I have, if you'll help me. Please." The word was drawn out, and heartbreakingly sad. "Please."

"I don't want your money. It's not that," Rowena tried to explain. How could she tell her that it was her own life she was worried about?

"I can't do this alone," said Diane. "I can't find her by myself. You're Paige's angel. You're all she's got. Help her."

Rowena almost said yes right then, but barely managed to hold back. "I'll have to think on it. I'll let you know soon."

"Rowena—" The voice was high and sharp, losing it.

"I'll call you in a day or two," she said, cutting off whatever words might have followed. "All right?"

"All right," said Diane, giving in. Giving up?

She couldn't leave her like that. "You remember something. Paige was okay when I saw her. I would have felt it if there had been anything . . ."—she searched for the right word—"terrible."

"Is that supposed to comfort me?"

"It's something," said Rowena. And then, with more determination, "It's all I have."

"I know. I'm sorry. I don't mean to take this out on you. Really. It's just . . . there's nowhere else to turn."

That struck home, harder than anything else she might have said.

"I'll be calling you," Rowena assured her, and said goodbye.

When she was off the phone and completely alone, Diane's words came back to haunt her.

There's nowhere else to turn.

The flashbacks were getting worse. At first, Daniel had tried to ignore them, but now, they were constant. Memories surfaced as if rising out of deep water: faces of people he was sure he knew, a mountain road, an office in a high building with a window overlooking the city. But what city?

"I don't know where I belong," he admitted, and felt the anger of that statement strike back at him like a heavy fist.

"I know it's frustrating," said Dr. Clancy. "Actually, you're fortunate to have so much of your memory come back in so little time. Don't try to force it. The mind doesn't work that way.

"You're recovering from severe physical injuries. Your body, and your memories, will come back slowly. You can't make a broken arm heal any faster than it takes for the cells to reknit themselves in the bone. Trying to force that arm to work sooner would only cripple it. The mind works the same way. You see what I mean?"

Daniel nodded. He was tired of listening.

"Physically, you're much improved," said Dr. Clancy. "I'm going to be able to release you in a few days."

Daniel didn't react.

"I thought you'd be pleased with the news," said Clancy.

"I might be, if I knew where to go when you put me out of here."

Clancy stood. "Nothing's definite yet. We'll re-evaluate your condition in two or three days. Meanwhile, I'm going to have one of our social workers come and speak with you. It's possible that she can set up some kind of temporary housing and financial assistance for a few weeks."

"I'm not an indigent." Daniel said it with more heat than was necessary. He was furious, and for some reason, his anger was focused on this doctor.

"I'm sure you're not," said Clancy. "We found a single credit card in your possession, listed to an Aaron Pahl. The police have been trying to trace it for us, but there's been a problem."

"What kind of problem?"

Dr. Clancy didn't look at him. "They can't find a record of anyone by that name—at least, not a living person."

"What's that supposed to mean?"

"I'm sure I don't know. I leave all such details to the police. They're checking into it. In the meantime, our social worker might be able to arrange something for you. It would only be temporary of course, until you or someone you know fills in the blank spaces of your life." Clancy left the room.

The turmoil was still seething for Daniel. He thought, *Who do I know?*

He closed his eyes, and in that unguarded instant, he saw again the face of a baby. A little girl. His child? Her name was there, close to his consciousness. He could see her clearly, as if he were holding her, the blue eyes, the straight blond hair like a little Dutch girl . . . and the red marks on her neck.

"Paige." He said it aloud, and suddenly he knew so much more than the child's name. He knew who he was, where he belonged, and why he had come to West Virginia. And he knew he wasn't Paige Kendall's father. He was her kidnapper.

The answers were before him; now the questions came.

How long have I been here? What's happened since I left? And the biggest question of all: *How can I get out of this hospital before I'm accused of murder?*

There was no way for them to connect him to the murder of Christine Campbell, or the kidnapping of the four babies—at least, he hoped there wasn't. He had to make sure that didn't happen.

It was painful, but he forced himself out of the bed and walked to the small closet of the hospital room. It was time to get out of here. Except for an extra pillow on the top shelf, the closet was empty.

"Going somewhere?"

Daniel turned his head sharply toward the unexpected voice. LVN Rose Hunter stood inside the doorway.

"Where are my clothes?" he asked.

"They're in hospital storage. When you were on the fourth floor, we didn't think you'd be needing them. Coma patients rarely need a change of outfits. Then you surprised everyone and woke up."

She stepped all the way into the room. There was something about her expression that told Daniel she was interested in him, and more than in her capacity as a nurse. Was she flirting? The smile was beyond friendly. It was provocative.

She closed the door.

"I could get your things for you, if you want. I'll bring them here tonight, after my shift."

"I'd appreciate the favor."

"Would you?" She moved a little closer. "It's funny to see you standing up. When I bathed you, I could see you were a big man, but you're taller than I imagined."

He let that remark go without response.

"I used to think what a waste it was for someone so young and good-looking to be stuck on the fourth floor with all the slugheads."

"Did you?"

"Um-hmm." She moved in close and put her hand on his face. "I even dreamed about you."

He touched her wrist. No more than that. Not overplaying his role. Give her enough to keep her interested, so she'd do what he wanted.

"Maybe if you'd send my clothes here this afternoon, you and I could get out of here for a couple of hours tonight."

She laughed. "Are you kidding? I'd be fired."

"No one would have to know."

He watched her eyes. He could see she was considering it.

"Where would we go?"

"Your place." He gave her wrist a small squeeze.

"Oh, my God. I can't believe I'm even thinking of this."

He waited. It would be wrong to push her. Too much pressure could scare her away. And he needed those clothes.

"Do you promise not to say anything about us," she asked, "even if you get caught coming back?"

"You're safe with me."

She ran the palm of her hand from his face, down to his chest. "Okay," she said. "I'll put my address in the pocket of your shirt. About eight?"

He reached across and unfastened the top button of her uniform. "Eight's fine. Send the clothes this afternoon."

"Okay." Her voice was husky.

When she left, Daniel washed his face, brushed his teeth, and combed his hair. He stared at his reflection in the mirror and realized that if he was wearing regular clothes no one would notice him as being different from anyone else. He had scars and bruises on his body, but they would be hidden under a long sleeve shirt, a bulky sweater, and pants. He still had a bump on his forehead, but it wasn't discolored. He could take a cab to the airport and get a seat on the first plane to Los Angeles. It was going to happen, thanks to Rose. He could get away with it.

But first, there was a little unfinished business with a lady psychic.

Chapter Nineteen

Detective Walsh didn't give an inch when she laid it out before Alix Cole. The woman had kept evidence from the police, and probably had damaged the case.

"Why didn't you contact me immediately?"

"I told you."

"Tell me again." Jessa had little sympathy for a mother who suppressed crucial evidence which might help to save her child's life, especially this kind of evidence.

"It was because of Rick. I thought my ex-husband might have been the one who'd done it. If I went to you with the"—she was having trouble with the word—"with the evidence," she used the term Jessa had called it, "I thought he might kill her. She's my daughter, the most important thing in my life. I wouldn't do anything to hurt her."

Alix looked and sounded convincing, the grieving mother, but Jessa wasn't so sure. How many other mothers in similar circumstances would have done what she had? It was a bizarre choice, hiding this grisly evidence, which meant Jessa suspected Alix of either being more involved in the crime than any of them had believed, or being atypical in the way she reacted to terror. Looking at her, Jessa couldn't see the fear in this woman, and that scared her.

She remembered Amy Peterson's father.

"Did you ever work with your ex-husband on any of his drug deals?"

An adamant, "No."

"Have you had any contact with him since the day of the kidnapping?"

There was hesitation.

"Mrs. Cole?"

"I—I'm not sure."

"What does that mean?"

"It means, if Rick sent me this—"

"Any other contact," Jessa specified. She was impatient, annoyed by the cautiousness of the woman, and suspicious of her motives.

"Maybe."

Jessa started to say something more, but Alix seemed to reach a decision, and said, "Yes, I think I have had contact with him."

"What do you mean 'think'? Don't you know?" She waited for a beat, then pushed a little. "Would you like to share it with me?"

Alix's dark eyes stared in a look of undisguised contempt. "I know Rick's been spying on me."

Jessa wanted to jump all over this woman with everything she had, but she let the scene play itself out, let the words come at Alix's pace. This was a second piece of information that had been concealed, but she wanted to hear it, so she shut up and waited.

"Something happened."

The vagueness was setting Jessa's teeth on edge. "What?"

"I was with another man recently"—she didn't look Jessa in the eyes when she said this—"here, in this house. You know what I mean?"

Jessa nodded. She didn't trust herself to speak.

"After, when he went home, his place had been broken into and trashed."

"Robbery?" Jessa needed to get the image straight in her mind.

"No. Rick doesn't need to steal. He was sending a message, that's all."

"What message?" She wanted her to say it.

Alix glared at her. "He was saying, 'Stay away from my wife.' Is that what you wanted to hear?"

Jessa didn't react to the obvious challenge. "When did this happen?"

The body language said it all. Alix glanced away. She hugged her arms to her chest, and crossed her legs. When the answer came, it was spoken so softly, Jessa couldn't hear.

"When? I couldn't—"

"It was the day the package . . . It was the day when he sent Chelsea's . . ." She started to cry.

The picture didn't make sense. Jessa tried to imagine the scene. The mother gets a package in the mail. She opens it and finds a piece of her daughter's finger. How does she react? She hops into bed with someone. It was too weird to be believed, and yet the tears seemed genuine.

Sex could be a lot of things, a sign of love, a moment of passion, an act of aggression. Some people used it like a drug, to release tension. And some people hid behind it, never willing to face their fears. Cops did that sometimes.

"I need a name," she told Alix.

"What difference does it—"

"I need the name," Jessa interrupted the protest. "I won't know what's important, or isn't, until I check it out. Who was with you that day?"

To her credit, Alix had the decency to look embarrassed when she answered, "John Tripp."

"The private investigator?"

She nodded.

I shouldn't be shocked, Jessa kept telling herself. I shouldn't be shocked. But she was.

John Tripp needed a break in this case. Even with the information he'd concealed from the sheriff's investigation, and from his boss, Maxwell Grodin of PIC, he had about as much possibility of finding the four missing babies as a dead gambler did of winning a ticket out of hell. The kids had been missing for two months. What were the odds they were still alive?

He didn't want to think about it.

Tripp poured another cup of coffee from the thermos at his feet. Since he began the stakeout, his car had become a veritable snack palace, carrying everything from Aztec blue corn chips, to the still pungent leftovers of almond duck in one of those small white cartons with a handle. The back seat of the Mazda was the cluttered afterlife of Tripp's snack world.

He'd stopped using the company's surveillance van after a couple days, realizing it would become too noticeable in this stranger-wary neighborhood. His

Mazda RX-7 looked less out of place. Besides, Grodin said he needed the van for "more productive investigations."

The rule was never stay too long. Best not to alarm the neighbors. Every couple of hours he drove to a different location. Some locations along the block were better than others. This morning, he'd had a really good view of who was coming toward Alix's house, a little too good.

He'd seen Detective Walsh arrive, hours ago, and he hadn't seen her leave. That fact was making him nervous. When he was nervous, he couldn't keep his hands still, so he filled them with corn chips, a thermos mug of coffee, and two-day-old donuts that tasted like a baked version of waxy, chocolate-flavored dust.

His attention was completely focused on Alix's front door. That was why he never saw it coming. The passenger door of his car opened, and while Tripp's hands were full of hot coffee, a dark-haired man with a gun slipped into the seat beside him. The nose of the Browning 9mm was pointed in Tripp's direction.

To his credit and self-respect, he didn't spill the coffee.

"Are you here to kill me, or just hungry?" he asked the gunman. Tough. Very tough. Except his knees were shaking. He hoped the guy with the pistol didn't notice.

"You've been watching that house up the street."

"Maybe," said Tripp. This had to be a cop, maybe an undercover detective from Foothill Division?

"My wife's house," said the man.

Oh, shit. Not a cop.

It was time to think fast. "If you're Alix's *ex*-husband"—he emphasized the prefix—"I've been hoping to talk to you. What's the matter, Rick? Did you forget my address?"

"I never forget." Cole's eyes were slashes of dark blue, like the sea at night, and just as cold.

"It's a comfort to know you've been watching over Alix," said Tripp. "If you're keeping such good track of me, then you must know who else is keeping track, and who's in the house with her right this minute."

"I'm not here to see Walsh. I don't talk to cops."

Tripp could feel the hard knot that was his heart ease up a little, and start to unclench. He even felt it beat once or twice.

"Why are you here?" It was the obvious question. The man was a killer, Alix had confirmed that, and if he was the one who'd sent Chelsea's fingertip to her mother, a sadistic psychopath, too.

"If Chelsea hadn't been kidnapped," said Cole, "you'd be dead right now." There was hate in the man's eyes. Hate, and something more. Jealousy?

"If Chelsea hadn't been kidnapped," said Tripp, "I wouldn't be here."

It was a verbal standoff of machismo. Of course, there was the matter of the gun pointed in Tripp's direction. That swayed things a little in Rick's favor.

"I came here to tell you something," said Rick. "You're looking for the wrong person."

"What's that supposed to mean?" Tripp's adrenaline rush was turning from fear to anger. "You're telling me you didn't trash my house? You didn't come here today wanting to kill me?"

"I didn't take my daughter."

178

He didn't know whether to believe him.

"And I sure as hell didn't cut off her finger and send it to Alix."

Tripp watched in horrified fascination as Cole's finger on the pistol tightened and released against the trigger. The man's hand was shaking with rage.

"I never did that to my kid. And if I ever find out who—"

"Take it easy," Tripp warned him. "Want to point that thing someplace else?"

The Browning stayed aimed at Tripp's chest, but Cole lifted his finger a breathing space off the trigger.

In his five years of PI work, Tripp had learned something about human nature. People lied, but reactions didn't. What he'd witnessed convinced him that Rick Cole hadn't taken his daughter, and he hadn't cut off her finger and sent a piece of it back to her mother.

"Okay, if you didn't do it, why are you here, and pointing that gun at me?"

"Could we have had this little talk without it?"

Yeah, with you behind bars. "Sure," Tripp said. "Why don't we try it right now?" He nodded toward the weapon.

A slow smile pulled at the corners of Rick's mouth. There was something fanatical and a little crazy in the way he looked. It was a power thing, about control. "I sell drugs," Rick said, "I don't take them. And I'm not stupid."

"I didn't say you—"

"I came here to give you something."

Tripp was sure he didn't want anything Rick had to give him.

As it turned out, he was wrong.

Rick pulled a slip of folded paper out of his pocket and passed it across the car seat. On it was a phone number.

"What's this?"

"It's a way to reach me. There may be something I can do," Rick paused, and then added, "Something not quite legal."

He thought about what was happening here. It didn't make any sense. "I don't get it. Why would you risk giving me a phone number that could be traced?"

"That bastard took something that was mine."

The double message wasn't lost on him. *So have I,* thought Tripp. He was feeling his heart clutch again, when Rick added, "Chelsea's my kid. I want her back, whatever it takes."

He didn't know what to say, so he didn't say anything.

"You call me if there's something." Rick opened the passenger door and put one leg out. With the gun still pointed at Tripp's chest, he added, "You find my daughter, I might forget about you fucking my wife . . . and let you live."

Tripp didn't move. He heard the car door shut softly when Rick left. He didn't turn to watch him walk away. A hard grunt of expelled air forced its way past his mouth, as if he'd been holding his breath and his lungs were bursting.

For a minute, nothing was real. He stared blindly at the road ahead, then realized that Detective Walsh's car was gone. Thoughts shivered through his mind like ice needles.

If Rick didn't do it, who did?

Alix had said she couldn't get in touch with her

ex-husband, but here he was, as if summoned, knowing about the two of them, and knowing about Chelsea's fingertip.

How could he know that, unless—

Tripp's arm jerked in reflex to three sharp bangs against the driver's side window.

Rick . . .

A leather-encased sheriff's ID was slapped against the window. Tripp scrutinized the rank and name—Detective Second Dillon Rhys—before cranking open the window.

"Detective Walsh would like to see you," said Rhys. He was leaning in, staring at the scattered remains of blue corn chips, open take-out boxes of Chinese food, and an empty bag of Dunkin' Donuts.

"You want something?" Tripp snapped at him. He was in no mood to put up with an inspection from this junior cop. The kid looked about twenty-two, but Tripp knew better. Right now, he resented the cop's age, his boyish good looks, and his curiosity.

"In Walsh's office," said Rhys, stepping back. "Now."

Swell, thought Tripp. He'd see Walsh, but he had to stop at home first to get a change of pants. His hands had jerked when the cop had rapped at the window, and the spilled coffee had soaked right through.

Chapter Twenty

Daniel's clothes and belongings were brought to his room at three that afternoon by an apple-cheeked, white-haired, hospital volunteer. Her white dress and candy-striped apron covered an ample bosom, broad waist, and generous hips, a body lived in for so many years, the owner looked comfortable with it.

"I hear you're tired of hospital gowns," said the woman. "Can't imagine why." She put the suitcase on the floor inside the closet. "Want me to put your things away for you?"

"No, I'll do it. Thank you, Alice." He read the name from her badge.

"Anything else I can get for you? A magazine? A book? The high school volunteers bring a cart to the rooms around four, but I could—"

"No. I don't need anything."

She was looking at him—of course she would be—but Daniel felt it was more than that. She was staring. The paper-thin folds of skin above her eyes creased into serious wedges. "I know you."

Daniel felt an added pace quicken his heart. He

heard the rushing of the blood in his veins, and the stillness of his mind as he *completely* listened.

"You're that one I saw on TV."

How much did she know? About the murder? About the kidnapped children? What had happened while he was hospitalized? Daniel stepped closer. "You're a clever woman, Alice."

"I never forget a face. You were in the papers, too. I remember."

He would have to kill her with his bare hands, there was nothing else. She knew too much, and if she talked . . . It would be simple and quick, his hands around her neck. One step closer to the closet, and—

"They were asking for anyone with information about the man in the coma," said Alice. She wasn't smiling now. Her eyes were touched with fear. "You know, they were looking for your family, I guess."

His body was tensed, absolutely still. He drew one quick breath.

"Are you all right?" The flesh above her mouth had paled, circling her brightly painted lips with a pallid ring. "I could get someone, or—"

"No," he managed. "I'm fine. Just felt a little dizzy for a minute." He took a step back. "Really, I'm feeling better now."

She made an effort at a smile, then backed toward the door. "I—I have to take a book to one of the other patients."

"Thank you for the clothes, Alice."

She didn't stay. When she had gone, he had to sit for a moment, because the fade-away feeling after the rush of adrenaline had made his legs weak.

He might have killed her, and that would have

been a serious mistake. She didn't know anything about the murder, or the kidnapping. Killing her would have led the police right to him. His fingerprints were all over this room. It wouldn't have taken them long to find out that the driver's license and credit card were under an assumed name. They would have known his real identity before he arrived back in California, and the game would have been up.

Such a close thing. A risk.

Daniel would have felt no remorse over the woman's death, only regret that he had made a mistake. Her murder could have complicated things.

He was hurting when he tried to stand. His body hadn't healed from the trauma inflicted during the accident. Surgery had saved his life, but he'd lost a kidney, suffered a punctured lung, and a bruised liver. Right now, his head throbbed with a savageness that reminded him he'd had a concussion, too, one that had put him into a coma.

It was time go home.

Daniel changed into the clothes from his suitcase—a white shirt, gray sweater, dress pants, black socks, and Italian soft leather loafers. He didn't rush, but took the extra time to shave and carefully comb his hair over the still-visible bump on his forehead.

It was better to leave the suitcase behind. It might draw too much attention as he walked through the hospital corridors. He wanted anyone who saw him to assume he was a visitor, not a patient.

Only, he needed some things from the suitcase. With a spoon from his hospital tray, he pried apart the inside lid of the case. The fabric was glued to a

184

false lining held together by Velcro strips. He peeled back the lining. Behind it was a new set of credit cards, driver's license, and identification. It was different from the set he'd used to pay for the one-way airline ticket to West Virginia, and the rental car. He would need the new set of cards and ID to get back to Los Angeles.

Taped into the lining was a sealed plastic envelope containing ten thousand dollars in cash. He'd withdrawn it from his account before he left Los Angeles, as a precaution. It was all the money he had in the world, not much, but enough to get him out of the country if there was trouble.

Daniel slipped the envelope of money inside his shirt, against his skin, and put the new credit cards and ID into his wallet, replacing the other ones. He glanced into the hallway. It was clear.

To his left, he could hear laughter from the nurse's station, someone telling a joke.

Not that way.

To his right, he heard the sound of elevator doors opening on this floor.

Go, he told himself. *Go, now.*

He wished he could steal a bottle of Dilaudid before he left. The ache in his side was growing to feel a lot worse without the pills they'd been giving him. His head throbbed.

Walking for any distance was out of the question. What he needed was a way out of here, before anyone noticed. He stood beside the front entrance of the hospital, trying to decide what to do.

"Making your escape a little early, aren't you?"

Daniel turned toward the exit of the hospital's underground parking structure, at the side of the building. Leaning out the car window and grinning like a schoolgirl playing hooky, was LVN Rose Hunter. She had changed out of her nurse's uniform, and was wearing a clinging, pale pink sweater.

"You're a little anxious, huh? C'mon, get in here before somebody sees you."

Daniel crossed the distance between them, opened the passenger side door, and eased into the seat beside her. "I was needing a good luck piece," he said, "and there you were."

"A good luck piece?" She laughed. "I've been called a lot of things, but never that. Are you a superstitious type?"

"Only when luck coincides with what I want."

"That's honest," she said. "I like that. You're a pretty interesting guy." She stopped at the next light. "Since we're being honest, I guess I was a little anxious, too. I managed to get off work early."

He knew what the next line ought to be, understood his role, that he was supposed to flirt with her, but his head wouldn't let him concentrate on anything but pain, intense, worsening pain.

"So, where do we go?" she asked. Her mouth was pretty, holding the shape of the final O longer than necessary. "You hungry? Want to go to dinner? A movie? What's your pleasure?" She was leaning toward him, as if she expected a kiss.

"Your place," he said.

That brought a smile. "I like a man who knows what he wants."

She drove, and Daniel closed his eyes. What he really wanted right now was a place to rest, a way to drop out of sight for a while and get away from this hospital. Rose Hunter provided him with both.

"You rest," she said. "I'll take it from here."

His eyes closed, and his body rested, but his mind was working out the details. She could be helpful. He would use her car to drive to the psychic's house—later, when his head felt better. That would save him the trouble of going to a rental agency, and one less tie to connect him to the crime.

Of course, there would be the problem of what to do with Rose Hunter's corpse. He was under no illusion that she would willingly give him her car, and he couldn't trust her not to go to the police. Killing her would buy her silence. It might be days before anyone found her.

No ... A better idea came to him. The nurse's body would fit into the trunk of the car. Better still, two bodies—Rose Hunter's and Rowena Crawford's. After he took care of the psychic, he would find an isolated place to dump their bodies. The back roads of West Virginia were full of isolated canyons. It might be months before anyone found them. By then, he would be out of the country, and safe.

The car slowed and he felt it when she turned into a driveway. He opened his eyes and stared at her.

"You were so quiet," said Rose. "I thought you fell asleep."

"No, but I was dreaming," he said, and reached for her hand, "about you and me."

She leaned nearer. He took her face between his hands and kissed her. Her mouth was warm, yielding, and eager. It had been a long time since he'd been with a woman. Remembered feelings stirred in him.

"You've got nice, strong hands," she said, "but gentle. I like a man with gentle hands."

He wondered if she'd think so, later.

They walked to the door and Rose let him in. Her house was cluttered, magazines and books littered every tabletop, amid overflowing ashtrays and lipstick-stained coffee mugs. The living room rug was coated with white cat hair, and a layer of dust powdered all flat surfaces. The stale air of the house smelled of cat, cigarettes, and Pine Sol.

"Didn't know I'd be having company." She reached for the coffee cups on the table.

He grabbed her hand. "Don't bother. It's fine."

"Guess I'm kind of a slob."

He smiled.

She looked nervous. "Do you wanna . . . ? I mean, do you feel like . . . The bed's made."

He nodded.

She leaned close and kissed him. The tip of her tongue touched his lips. The softness of her breasts pushed against him. He could feel her hand exploring, its open palm stroking his chest, his thigh, holding him.

"I'll only be a minute," she said, walking toward the bathroom. "Why don't you get comfortable, under the covers."

He took off his clothes, folded them neatly, and laid them on a chair. He was standing in the center of the room when she opened the bathroom door. It was dark in her bedroom, the window covered by the kind of heavy drape used by people who worked nights and slept in the daytime. Her naked body was silhouetted by the light of the bathroom window, as she moved toward him.

"I dreamed about this," she said.

So had he.

"I have some . . . you know, in the drawer." She

pulled the drawer open, and he could see a folded track of condoms inside. "I keep a few around for unexpected visitors." She tore off one of the packets and held it out to him.

He reached for her wrist and tipped her hand, sliding the condom packet back into the drawer. He hadn't touched it.

"Not yet," he whispered.

Excitement stirred in him, but not at the thought of sex. His hands moved up her bare arms, to her neck, fingers locking around her throat. "Kiss me," he said, and touched his lips to hers.

It was only when his fingers began to press hard that she started to struggle. His mouth crushed over hers, smothering her cries. His hands squeezed with brutal force, choking the life from her.

She was strong and young. After a startled reaction of panic, she fought him. Her fingers pried at his hands. Clawing. Striking at him. He felt the blows to his face and arms, felt them, but as if they were to someone else. He was outside pain, knowing only the strength in his hands as his grip tightened around her throat . . . tightened.

A savage thrust of her knee caught him in the groin, and he drew back his head to gasp in sudden recognition of hurt. And fury.

She tried to scream, but her voice was lost beneath the pressure of his hands. Strangled. Her knee came up again, but he twisted to avoid most of the impact. His fingers loosened, slipping in that instant, and she gasped a single breath. Enough to hold on to life. Gaining strength to fight him.

The struggle was costing him. His body was weakened by the surgery and damage inflicted during the car accident. She wouldn't die easily. Rose was a big woman. It was all he could do to—

Her finger stabbed at his eye.

Jesus! The pain was excruciating. Couldn't ignore it. *Couldn't stand it.* She'd blind him if he didn't stop her . . . if he didn't let go and stop her . . . if he didn't *kill the bitch.*

The instant his hands let go, she screamed. Not loud. Her voice crackled like tin foil, high pitched as wire threads. Weak. The neighbors couldn't hear, but he did. Like a noise heightening his senses, the thin, desperate cry punctuated his fist smashing into her face and knocking her back against the wall. Blood poured from her shattered nose.

Her eyes, fixed with fright, gaped at him like open wounds, as he grabbed her by the sides of her head, twisted the long, dark hair in his fists, and smashed her head on the hardwood corner of the dresser. Again. And again. Smashed it until his hands were covered in blood, and the lifeless, staring eyes saw nothing more.

Daniel's head throbbed viciously as he stepped into Rose Hunter's shower to wash away her blood. A violent pressure pounded in his ears. He stood for a long while under the warm spray, letting the water soothe him. A trail of red slipped down the drain. The water washed him clean.

His arms and legs were trembling when he got out of the shower, stood waiting until his body dried, and dressed in his clothes. He looked at himself in the mirror. His pants and shirt didn't show any evidence of violence. He only had one set of clothes, and he couldn't have risked a tear or a bloodstain. That was why he'd taken them off.

Daniel combed his damp hair, parting it carefully and making himself presentable. His left eye was red and sore, the only visible sign of what had happened here. With Kleenex covering his fingerprints, he opened the medicine cabinet and found a bottle of Visine. The drops felt good. He pocketed the bottle, taking it with him.

He also found a large plastic vial containing a prescription of Demerol. The prescription was for a James Fenton, Stanton General Hospital. It was dated that month. Daniel wondered if James Fenton had died before Rose helped herself to his medicine, or if she had stolen the drugs from a living patient. Either way, Daniel was grateful.

He used the same Kleenex to turn on the bathroom faucet, cup water in his palms, and swallow two of the Demerol tablets. With the Kleenex still in his fingers he flushed the toilet, then threw the tissue into the swirling water.

Avoiding stepping in the spattered blood, he picked up Rose Hunter's keys from where she'd left them on the living room table. Someone would find the body, but it might be days before anyone checked her house. There was no reason for the local police to connect Daniel with her death. Even if they found out that he'd left the hospital without authorization—if the hospital staff who was already busy and overworked bothered to report him as missing—the man they'd be looking for would be Aaron Pahl from Detroit. Aaron Pahl wouldn't have much to say, even if they dug him out of his grave at the Illinois cemetery. The dead didn't talk.

All that was left to take care of was the psychic, then get back to California. He couldn't call. Jack and Lydia didn't have a phone. He didn't want to risk putting a call through to Harper Pierce. All that could wait. First things first.

He had come to West Virginia to kill Rowena Crawford. Now, finally, that was what he was going to do.

Chapter Twenty-one

"You're a PI with Pasadena Investigative Consultants." Detective Walsh made the statement sound like a question. She'd made this whole meeting sound like a formal questioning. It wasn't, being strictly legal, but when a thing has the eyes, hair, teeth, and claws of a cat, it's probably looking for kitty chow.

"I'd say you know my background pretty well." Tripp was uncomfortable with this setup. The day had been weird enough, meeting Rick Cole, and now this. All he wanted to do was take a few deep sighs, curl up in a blanket, and sleep for about twelve hours. Make the world go away. Unfortunately, this cop wasn't going anywhere.

"I want to know more."

She waited, but he didn't offer anything. If this was the way they were going to play the game, they were going to be here a long time. He knew the rules: don't tell them anything they don't ask. It usually applied to suspects. Right now, it applied to him.

"Why was Alix Cole under surveillance?" asked Detective Walsh.

"For her own protection."

"Do you suspect her of criminal involvement in the kidnapping?"

That was a loaded question. If he said no, he was lying. If he said yes, he was guilty of criminal negligence, withholding information from an investigation. Given the choice . . .

"No."

Walsh stared at him, unblinking. "You knew about the package Mrs. Cole received in the mail?"

Shit.

She waited for an answer.

"Yes."

"And you saw the contents of that box?"

"Yes."

"What was in it?"

"A mutilated piece of a child's finger."

She got up from her chair, came around the corner, and sat on the desk, close to him. "What the hell's going on? I want to know."

He'd expected her to throw legal threats his way. This was something else. "I was hired by my clients to locate their children. I've been trying to do that."

"By sleeping with one of the mothers?"

There were no secrets; that was a lesson taught to rookie investigators. Walsh had proved the truth of it. "That was something unplanned. It—"

"Unplanned!" Walsh was on her feet again, and the smooth-as-linoleum expression gone. She was storming.

"Yes, unplanned," he jumped in before she got a chance to start, "like my unexpected meeting today with her husband, Rick Cole." That ought to stop her in her tracks.

It did.

"You saw Rick Cole?"

"This afternoon."

"And you didn't tell me?"

"I just did."

Whatever she'd been planning to say about him sleeping with Alix was lost on the greater issue. Walsh was moving around the room. Not pacing. Only a step or two, standing for a couple of minutes, then another step. Not talking.

Sweat trickled down Tripp's back.

She went back to her chair behind the desk. The body language was subtle, but clear. They were back to a business level. He had something to offer, and she was interested in buying.

"Why did Rick Cole meet with you?"

"He wanted to scare me."

"Is that all?"

"No, he wanted to tell me he didn't take his kid."

"Why would he bother?"

"So I wouldn't waste time looking for him. He knows what happened to Chelsea, about her finger, and he wants whoever did it to be caught."

"How would he know about that?"

"He watches his ex-wife, or keeps track of her through his people. He knew about the package."

"And he knew about you?"

Tripp nodded. "I got a calling card from him, the night Alix and I . . ."

She waited to let him finish the statement, but he didn't. "I'm surprised you're still among us. From what I hear, Cole is a dangerous man. He's wanted for questioning in a murder case. Did you know that?"

"I knew." This was starting to get to him. "Look, can we stop playing hot foot with each other?"

"Meaning?"

"Meaning I want to get those kids back as badly as you do. Maybe I had a decent reason for withholding information."

"Such as?"

"Such as, maybe Alix Cole thought her ex-husband was the one who took the babies, and the one who cut off Chelsea's fingertip. Maybe she convinced me that if I told you, he'd kill the kid. You said it yourself—the man's dangerous. If I'd told you what I knew, I thought maybe he wouldn't stop at mutilating her finger. Maybe he'd kill her and the other three children. I had to make that decision, that choice."

When Walsh looked away and glanced down at the papers on her desk, Tripp knew she wasn't going to charge him with anything. She was a good cop, a by-the-book detective, but she was a human being first.

"I want to be informed about everything you learn about this case from here on out. Understand?"

"Got it."

"I'm committing about five separate violations of my position by letting you walk out of this office uncharged. Not for you, not because you're a PI and I'm a sheriff's detective, and not because I admire your style. I don't. I'm doing this for the good of those children."

He felt the burning in his gut begin to ease. He was off the hook.

"Tripp, you fuck with me again, Rick Cole and his men won't have to search very hard for you. You'll be easy to find. In jail."

The burning was back at work, and so was he. Detective Walsh turned him out of her office with that final message, and an imperative, "Call me."

She wasn't flirting.

It was an attached garage, easier for carrying the body to the car. Daniel wrapped Rose in sheets, careful to keep her blood from getting on his clothing. She fit in the wide trunk of the Oldsmobile Ciera with room to spare. That was good. He would need space for the psychic.

Inside the house, the bloodstains on the rug, dresser, and walls were unmistakable. He thought about trying to clean up the mess, in case someone came looking. It would take a long time, and with scrubbing the walls and rug, he'd be likely to leave incriminating evidence of his own, fingerprints, hair, flaked skin cells. The forensics team would love that.

In the end, he left everything as it was.

The Demerol was making him groggy. He had to fight to stay alert while driving. Several times, he went over the double yellow line, and once almost ran head-on into a green Chevrolet. If its driver, a round-faced dark-haired woman, hadn't honked her horn, he wouldn't have seen her and they would have hit. She glared at him as she drove past. The surge of adrenaline made him more alert after that.

Once off the main highway, the backroads became rougher, sometimes no more than narrow dirt stretches with deep, axle-breaking potholes. Every one of these jarred his insides and felt like hammer-blows to his head.

All the way there he thought about how he was going to kill the psychic. A gun would have been easiest, but he'd decided against bringing one on the plane. Carrying guns on airplanes invited trouble, and questions. As things had turned out, a gun would have been difficult to explain to the hospital staff, too. No, he was better off without an obvious weapon. But the struggle with Rose Hunter had cost him strength.

What if the psychic turned out to be a two-hundred-and-fifty-pound farm woman who was all muscle? He'd never seen a picture of her. He only had her name and address. Considering the way he felt right now, if there was much of a fight, she'd win.

To kill her, to get her out of the way so that she could never lead the police to him, he needed something simple and quick. He drove deeper into the back country, thinking. What did every farmhouse provide?

A butcher knife.

He'd get her to let him into the house, work his way into the kitchen, and then, when she wasn't expecting it, shove the blade into the back of her neck. That would bring her down. The rest would be easy.

He was so involved in the planning, he almost drove past the road sign. It was a small marker placed atop a stand of stones. Burned into a wooden shingle was the name CRAWFORD. Daniel turned left and headed up the dirt and gravel access road.

It was twilight when he pulled up to the front drive of the wood and stone house. A curving driveway of gravel crunched beneath his tires, and he could hear the sound of quarreling birds in the woods nearby.

The house was isolated, and apart from the noise of the birds, disturbingly still.

He got out and went to the door. No lights showed through the glass panel. No one answered his knock. He moved to the side of the porch and peered in the windows. The rooms were encased in darkness. No one home?

The doorknob twisted easily in Daniel's grasp. Unlocked. It didn't surprise him, people in the country left their houses unlocked. Inside, he roamed silently from space to space. In the kitchen, he found the knife. It was long, wide-bladed, and sharp. With this in hand, he was ready to meet Rowena Crawford.

He searched the house, dark room by dark room, and the earthen-walled basement. It smelled of damp soil, like the roots of a potted plant. He waited. But the psychic was gone.

Had she known that he was coming here? Had something happened to warn her? Or, had she seen it in the vision of her mind?

He felt some connection to this place, a kind of link to the woman, this psychic. Part of him wanted to leave her a message, to say *I was here*. He didn't. That would be a risk, and Daniel disliked risks.

He rubbed a dishtowel over the handle of the knife, and put it back into the rack. With the towel, he wiped his fingerprints from the doorknob, too. The only evidence that he'd been here were his tire tracks in the road.

Coming to West Virginia had been a mistake—an accident that nearly cost him his life, time lost in arrangements he needed to make for disposing of the children, and another murder, one which might lead the police right to him. All of it, a mistake. He couldn't afford to make any more. And after all that, the psychic wasn't even here. Angry, he drove away, the body of Rose Hunter still in the trunk of the car.

It was a strange, dark-spirited day. On the way to the airport, Rowena had almost been killed by another car. The driver had been on the wrong side of the yellow lines. She'd seen him as she came around the corner, and honked. He swerved seconds before they would have hit.

The near accident had left her feeling shaky. Everything about this trip was worrisome. She'd finally decided to leave only two hours ago. She had resisted the idea of leaving her home, but late this afternoon, without a speck of warning, she had found herself packing suitcases and hurrying toward this very uncertain future.

The truth was, she was scared to stay alone in the house. She'd never been scared to live there, before. Her house by the woods had always seemed safe and comfortable, till now. It was a jittery feeling, as if something were stalking her. Or someone. For now, being away from home was best.

Diane had promised to meet the plane in Los Angeles. Rowena had refused to stay with the Kendalls. There was more heartache in that house than she could bear. Diane would take her to a hotel.

The airline terminal was small, uncrowded. Rowena waited at gate 7, the jumpiness she'd been aware of all day beginning to close in around her. Something was wrong; she knew that, and she was running from it. But would it be any safer where she was going?

At the last minute, when the flight was called and the passengers began to file onto the plane, Rowena almost didn't go. She stood wavering, unsure and afraid. All of the other passengers boarded, and still she stood. Waiting.

What's wrong with me? Fear had driven her from her house and brought her here. Now, fear was keeping her from getting on the plane.

"Final call for flight 617," announced the young flight attendant at the desk.

It was either get on the plane, or go back to the foreboding she'd felt in the house. With trembling legs, unsure of every step, Rowena walked onto the plane which would lead her to Los Angeles, and all that waited for her there.

Another passenger, a tall, dark-haired man, was the last to board flight 617. Rowena was already on board and buckled into her seat. She glanced up as the man approached. She noticed that one of his eyes was swollen and blood red, as if recently injured.

We're all wounded, she thought, *one way or another. Only with some of us the scars don't show.* She closed her eyes, tried to make herself relax, and settled back for takeoff.

For Daniel, it was after midnight when flight 617 arrived, but nine o'clock Los Angeles time. The Demerol had allowed him to sleep, but it had given him weird dreams. Children with their hands mutilated. A woman calling to him, but with no voice, no sound. And a car in flames, with him trapped inside. The fire touched his bare leg, and he woke with a start so sudden, the passenger in the seat beside him moved to another section of the plane.

A bell announced the fasten-seat belt sign, and the captain's disembodied voice reported that they would be landing at LAX in five minutes. Two smiling stewards and a leggy stewardess came through the cabin collecting cups and cans of soda, and requesting passengers to raise their seatbacks to their fully upright position.

Daniel hated landings. He hated touchdowns, and he hated the sound of the brakes trying to stop the powerful thrust of the engines. He always imagined that the plane would tilt, catch a wing, tumble down the runway, and burst into flames. It was the flames that frightened him, especially after that dream. He had a terror of being burned alive, trapped in the wreckage, his life out of his control.

He gripped the armrests—a white knuckle flyer— and felt the first bump of touchdown. The brakes grabbed, slowing the plane's speed. Slowing, screaming like the tires on the car before it turned over and exploded. He saw it again. Felt the fear. Heard the scream of the brakes.

But they were safe. The 747 moved from the main landing strip to a long network of secondary lanes leading to the terminal. The engines shut down, and the passengers crowded the aisles to deplane. Except Daniel. He didn't try to move. He couldn't stand. His leg muscles were locked.

It took time. Passengers struggled with pulling their luggage from overhead bins. Businessmen and women forced their way into the forefront of the crowd, briefcases in hand. Tourists, and Angelinos coming home made up the bulk of the other passengers. Mothers waited until the crowd had thinned to exit with their small children. Elderly people, slower in their movements, followed next.

Daniel pulled himself up by the backrest of the seat in front of him. His legs were shaky. The stewardess asked, "Are you all right, sir?"

"Yes."

He wasn't all right. He was trembling so badly he could barely stand. By sheer willpower, he made himself stagger down the aisle.

"How many did he have?" Daniel overheard one of the stewards ask the other.

They thought he was drunk. Good. Maybe it was the bloodshot eye, or maybe he looked so unsteady, they just assumed. Either way, he was glad. Now, they would remember a drunk, not a man who was so badly hurt, he could barely get off the plane.

He kept his head down as he passed them, and as he moved through the connecting tunnel to the terminal gate. Most of the passengers of flight 617 had dispersed to the baggage claim area, or the gates of connecting flights. A few still remained, those obviously waiting for someone to meet them.

One woman, seated in the waiting area a few rows ahead of him, kept glancing right and left, noticeable in her manner of searching the hall. She looked confused and vulnerable, a backwoods sort, out of place in an airport terminal the size of LAX.

Daniel was feeling stronger. His legs had stopped shaking. He sat for a moment to gather his strength. Then, out of the milling stream of humanity within the airport hallway, came a surprise he wasn't ready for. He was stunned.

The blonde who walked up to the backwoods woman said, "Rowena? I'm Diane Kendall."

Chapter Twenty-two

I can't believe I was late," said Diane, "not for this. I'm so sorry. I was stuck in traffic."

Daniel tried not to stare, tried not to draw any attention to himself, but couldn't help repeatedly glancing in their direction. This was the psychic. The woman he should have killed. All this time, they'd been on the same plane!

He overheard snatches of their conversation. Diane Kendall's voice was slightly shrill, easy to understand, but Rowena Crawford spoke softly. Some of her words were lost to the sound of airline announcements.

Diane didn't act as if she recognized him. She might have seen him once or twice at the office, but they'd never spoken to each other. He was sure she wouldn't remember him as her father's assistant. Still, he kept his head lowered and avoided eye contact. Anything might have happened while he was away. Harper Pierce might have mentioned Daniel's disappearance to his daughter, since Daniel was supposed to have paid a visit to the psychic.

"Would you come to the house with me now, see

Paige's room?" Diane asked. There was a pleading quality to her voice.

"In the morning. I'm not a good flyer. Remember, it's three hours later for me. I'm all worn out."

"Oh." There was clear disappointment in the way she said it. "Of course. I understand. I'll take you to the hotel. I've arranged for a room at the Doubletree in Pasadena. That's near us."

"Sounds fine."

"But tomorrow, could you—"

"Don't you worry. We'll get started in the morning. I wake earlier than the birds. I'll see Paige's room then, hold her little things, and we'll see what happens. All right, honey?"

"Oh yes, please." If Diane wasn't crying, she was close to it. Daniel could hear the strain in her voice.

"Now, I told you. I can't promise anything," the psychic warned.

"Don't try to prepare me for failure. I'm desperate," said Diane. "I want my daughter back. She's alive. I know it."

"I think you're right about that," said Rowena.

"You do? You really think—"

"Not now," she stopped Diane. "I'm worn right through."

Daniel risked another glance at the psychic. She looked like an acorn, round and smooth, bigger at the top and smaller at the bottom where her body narrowed to toothpick-size legs. Her hair was pulled into a topknot, a little nub like an acorn's stem. She was comfortable-looking, down home, like somebody's aunt.

He would regret killing her.

They left the terminal, stopping first at the baggage

claim area for two travel-worn suitcases, then crossing to the parking structure. He followed them as far as Diane Kendall's gray Volvo station wagon, watched as they drove away, then turned around and retraced his steps to the terminal, where he rented a Hertz car to drive himself home.

He was back. Tomorrow, he'd see the children—find out what had happened while he'd been away. Were they still alive? He wondered what he'd find. It had been so long without any word from him. Jack and Lydia might have abandoned them. At least, he knew the police hadn't broken the case. Diane Kendall had told him that.

He opened the windows of the car and let the night air blow its chill breath against his skin as he drove to the Los Feliz apartment complex that was his home. Traffic was busy on this street, no matter what time of day or night. He pulled into the underground garage, parked in one of the visitor's spaces—his own car was already parked in his assigned space—and turned off the engine. It was dark, silent, and still. For the first time that day, Daniel took a deep breath.

He was home.

"Oh *shit!*" said Jack.

Lydia was seated in front of the high chair, spooning morning oatmeal into Sydney's mouth. All the babies were hungry and hollering to be fed. She'd started with Sydney. "What's wrong?"

"Look for yourself."

She stood and craned her neck to see through the crack of light above the curtain of the living room window. It was Logan. He had parked out front and was walking across the dirt and gravel yard toward the house.

For a second she panicked like Jack, then made herself calm down. "It's all right," she said, trying to believe it. "Don't get into an argument with him," she warned Jack. There wasn't time to say anything else. Logan was at the door.

He used his key. That was good. Jack might not have let him inside, and Lydia's legs were suddenly too shaky for her to cross the room to the front door. Where had Logan been all this time? What did he know about the plans she'd made? She felt the knife strapped to her forearm, underneath her sleeve. If she had to, she'd use it. She'd never let anyone beat her again.

"Where the hell have you been?" Jack demanded as soon as Logan shut the door.

"There were problems," Logan said, as if that were enough of an answer.

"Problems!" yelled Jack. "You left us sitting here all this time, not knowing if you'd cut out."

Lydia was nervous, but Logan didn't seem to be reacting to Jack's outburst of temper. "I'm here now," he said. He didn't look well, pallid and thin. There were deep circles beneath his eyes, and a grim set to his lips, as if . . .

"Are you in pain, Logan?" She wanted to put him off guard, and her question seemed to do that. He glanced in her direction, a quick, hard stare, and then avoided her eyes.

"Let's talk about the children," he said, ignoring her question. "It's time we begin to set events into motion."

"Finally!" said Jack. "I've been about to go out of my mind, keeping watch on this goddamned nursery."

As if you've done anything, thought Lydia, but kept the resentment to herself. There would be time for recrimination later. Time to pay back all debts, to Jack, and to Logan. She had to wait for the right moment. A little longer. Soon, she'd be ready to make her move, if Logan didn't get in the way. If he did, she might have to remove him earlier than planned.

"Until now, we've been warehousing these babies for a black market adoption ring."

"No shit?" Jack looked surprised and pleased.

"It takes time to place children, and negotiate over price and means of payment. I've taken care of those details."

Lydia wasn't buying this. She knew the value of one of the children, and it wasn't because of some high-priced adoption. Paige Kendall was worth a lot more to her family. They had access to big money, the only thing worth risking a capital punishment crime. Logan was lying, had to be. He wasn't stupid enough to risk his freedom for anything less than a big payoff.

"I'll begin placing the children this week," he said, "one at a time, starting today."

Jack gave a loud whoop. "Here, take this one," he said, grabbing the nearest child. He shoved Paige into Logan's arms.

Lydia could feel her skin prickle, tiny pinpoint bumps surfacing on arms and legs. Her hands went ice cold, too, all in the space of a single heartbeat.

"No, not this one," said Logan. He put Paige back on the floor. "It's the youngest one they want." He walked to the high chair and nodded toward Sydney. "Get her out of there and clean her up. I'll be taking her with me when I leave."

"Hold on," said Jack. "What do we get out of this? We're the ones doing all the work. How do we know you're coming back? You got a deal with these baby sellers? I want my share. I want something now, today."

Lydia stayed out of it. Let the two of them kill each other. She had her own plans. As far as she was concerned, if Logan wanted Sydney, let him have her. It would mean less work. As if Jack ever did anything for these babies.

"The money's turned over after the child is placed. That's the way it works," said Logan. "We'll have to wait, all of us."

"Hell no!" said Jack. He was facing away from Lydia, but she could see the back of his neck. It was fiery red. "I'm not waiting another minute. You've been lying to us, Logan, using us and making your own deals. Leaving us out. I'm not having it. Not anymore."

Logan's eyes narrowed. "What are you going to do about it, Jack?" The tone of his voice hadn't changed, not one notch higher or lower. That fact chilled Lydia, but Jack seemed unaware of any subtle warning.

"You're not telling me what to do anymore, that's what," said Jack. His hand reached under his loose shirttail, and pulled a .38 from beneath the waistband of his pants.

It happened fast. Lydia wanted to get out of the way but Logan's hand was in his coat pocket. The next thing she knew he was holding a gun, one with a silencer on it, his arm straight out, the weapon pointing at Jack's head.

"You get away from here!" Jack shouted. "Get the—"

He didn't finish the sentence. Logan fired a bullet into Jack's throat. Blood, and the meat of Jack's neck splattered on the floor behind him. Jack grabbed his throat, as if his fingers could stop the gushing blood. He turned and stared at Lydia, as if he wanted her to help him. His mouth fell open. He tried to make a sound, but nothing came out. And then there was blood, more blood than she'd ever seen. He looked at her . . . pleading. The second bullet went straight into the braincase of Jack's head. She heard a muffled sound, and Jack fell back, nearly landing on top of her, a stunned look in his unseeing eyes.

"You need a payoff, too?" Logan was still holding the gun. Now it was trained on her.

"No," she said. Her voice was tinny with fear, but she figured it didn't matter. If he was going to kill her, he would have done it by now.

"Get the baby ready."

She said, "Okay."

She tried to stand, tried to do what Logan wanted, but her legs wouldn't work. They were too weak to hold her weight. Jack had pushed it. That's what caused this to happen. His fault.

"I'm glad you killed him," she said. "I never liked Jack. He's always been a mean drunk, and made everything harder here. I mean it, Logan. If you hadn't done it, I might have killed the bastard myself." She cried. Hot tears ran down her cheeks and she couldn't stop. Not for Jack. For herself.

"Stand up, Lydia. I'm not going to shoot you."

She stood, holding Sydney, clutching the baby close against her chest as if this small body could somehow protect her from whatever Logan might do.

"Go on, get her ready to leave. I'll take her with me. I'll take Jack, too."

There was a thick red puddle on the floor behind Jack's head. Chelsea crawled toward it. She reached out her hand and—

"No!" Lydia screamed at the baby. "Don't let her . . . oh God! Don't let her touch that."

Logan moved Chelsea out of the way. He put her in the playpen, and put the other two babies with her. "It's all right," he said to Lydia. "Take Sydney upstairs. Wash and dress her. Pack me a bag with a couple of bottles and some diapers. By the time you have her ready, I'll have this cleaned up. Go on," he said. "Do it now."

She walked upstairs and didn't look back, even when she could hear Logan dragging Jack's body across the pinewood floor. He dragged him toward the attached garage. She didn't know what Logan did with Jack after that. Didn't want to know.

Instead, she concentrated on bathing Sydney, washing the child's straight blond hair, and finding warm clothes for her. She could hear the children crying downstairs, wanting out of the playpen. Jennifer and Paige were big enough to climb over the rail. They could get out, toddle over to the red smear on the floor, walk in it, touch it. . . .

Lydia pushed that thought away.

It didn't take long to get the baby ready to leave with Logan, maybe fifteen minutes. Lydia pulled six disposable diapers from the economy-size box, tucked Sydney into one arm, the diaper bundle under the other, and started downstairs.

Jack's body was gone. The red smear on the floor was gone. For an instant, it seemed like a terrible dream. It hadn't really happened. Jack was in bed, drunk or asleep. She was tired. So tired.

And then, Logan was there. He came in from the garage. He stood at the foot of the stairs, looking up at her. "That's fine, Lydia," he said in that calm voice of his. "Bring me the baby."

Her legs were trembling again, but she came down the stairs and handed Sydney to Logan.

"She looks fine," he told her, like a compliment.

"I'll get the bottles," she said.

She went to the kitchen and grabbed the first two she could find from the refrigerator, put the diapers and the bottles in a plastic sack, and handed the sack to Logan.

"You've done well," he told her. "I won't forget that."

She wondered if it would be possible to kill him while his arms were full. Would he reach the gun before she could plunge the knife into his heart? Into his throat? If she stabbed him, would he bend down to put the baby on the floor, exposing his neck?

No. He'd drop Sydney like a rock.

She'd have to find a chance to settle with him later. It wasn't that she hated him for killing Jack. Jack needed killing. It was because he'd done this in front of her. Terrified her. She feared Logan. Lydia understood for the first time, when this was over, Logan would kill her, too.

"I'll be back for the others," he said. "Maybe tomorrow. Maybe next week. You've played it smart so far, Lydia. Don't do anything stupid. Our deal is the same as it was before. Nothing has changed."

He was wrong. Something had changed. She'd seen what was waiting for her at the end of the road. She'd seen the look on Logan's face when he shot Jack. And in a bizarre way, she had felt the bullets that killed Jack enter her brain, and stay there . . . waiting to explode.

Logan buckled Sydney into her car seat. The baby didn't struggle. He put a crib blanket over the passenger window in the back of the rental car. No one would see her from the road. Even if someone did, she was simply a child in the back seat of a car. Nothing out of the ordinary.

"You'll be all right?" Logan asked solicitously.

What was she supposed to say to that? She nodded.

"I'll have the money for you when I come back. Jack had become dangerous. You understand?"

She didn't trust herself to speak, or to do anything more than nod again.

"I won't be long." He got in the car and drove away.

It was after he left, after she took a deep breath for the first time since Logan had entered the house, that Lydia finally allowed herself to be scared. There was no solace, no strong arms to reach out and surround her in consoling embrace. She was alone. God had abandoned her. Logan would kill her. There was no one to help her . . . no one but herself.

"I'm afraid," she cried, and crossed her thin arms

over her chest and rocked back and forth as if comforting one of the babies. "Don't let him hurt me. Please, God. I'm afraid."

Chapter Twenty-three

Rowena had been restless and awake for two hours before the phone rang in her room at the Doubletree. She'd woken up on West Virginia time, and had always been an early riser. She'd gone for a walk at daylight, around six, to get her bearings and clear the cotton out of her head. The night's sleep had been stuffy, trying to breathe in a room without windows she could open.

"Rowena?" said the caller. "It's Diane. Did I wake you? I could call back later if you—"

She had known who it would be. Who else? "I've been up a good while. Saw the sunrise."

"Oh, the time difference. I should have realized. You must be hungry. Could I take you to breakfast?"

"That would be good. I've always got an appetite. You can tell that by looking at me. I tried the restaurant at six, but it wasn't open yet. You can't get so much as coffee here till half the day's gone."

"You could have it delivered to your room," said Diane.

"Oh, I figured I'd wait till they opened, or till I heard from you."

"Could I come by now and pick you up?" Diane sounded eager.

"Honey, I've been waiting for you to call."

"I'll be there in fifteen minutes," said Diane, and hung up the phone.

While Rowena waited, she took the baby blanket out of the suitcase, sat on the edge of the bed, holding the blanket loosely between her fingers, and closed her eyes. She didn't want Diane to be with her at first, in case she saw something bad.

The images came, cold as water poured over her skin.

She saw the moment through Paige's eyes. A sound, loud enough to startle the child. A single glimpse, still as a photograph. Bare wooden floor, a chill that made Rowena pull the blanket closer, and a dead man lying in a pool of blood.

It was him, the one she'd seen before, long angular face, dirty blond hair, and the cold blue eyes of a killer—now staring, but seeing nothing.

The stolen glimpse was over in an instant, but in the shimmering memory of it, Rowena had seen enough to know and be afraid. If the kidnapper was dead, what would happen to the babies?

The question burned itself into her heart and mind.

It was morning in Pasadena. A new day. The sun had climbed like a mountaineer up the side of the San Gabriels. A steady stream of cars moved along Walnut Boulevard. People were on the street. And somewhere in those mountains close to this place, the babies waited to be found.

If they were still alive.

She believed the connection was over, stood to put the blanket away, then another wave hit her. Impressions were like that, crashing waves overwhelming all of her senses. She felt this one like a hit to her body.

He sent a message.

There was no doubt. The thought was clear and certain. Before he died, the man she'd seen lying in a pool of blood had sent a message to someone about the children.

Rowena clutched the baby's blanket to her, needing the comfort of its answers, but the images were gone. She was left with only questions.

Who? And *why?*

A whole lot of things were coming into play. John Tripp sat hunched over his coffee table. On it was a spread of three-by-five index cards, of what he termed *linkability,* how an action in a case was connected to a person, and how that person was connected to the crime. At the moment, the cards looked like a game of Solitaire.

Cat was curled onto the sofa cushion beside Tripp. Well fed. Warm. Comfortable. Not a worry troubling his furry head. Tripp was jealous of such peace. Had to resist the urge to push the tom onto the floor. Instead, he put his hand on the cat and felt the thudding purr rising up from it. The noise calmed him, and the warmth of Cat's luxuriant coat, and the sleepy one-eyed stare Cat aimed in his direction.

"You sure you're comfortable?" Tripp asked sarcastically. "Anything I can get you? A saucer of milk? A few Kit-Nips? Maybe a blanket?"

Cat, lying on his side, stretched all four legs then curled into a snug circle, head resting on his forepaws, tail curving around his back feet and resting against his nose.

If Tripp had a tail, he'd have curled up, too.

Damn, but the pieces weren't coming together. He stared at the names on the index cards. Where was the motive? Where was the kidnapper? And where were the children?

They weren't dead. He didn't buy that. Why would the kidnapper send a piece of Chelsea's finger to Alix if the babies were dead? It didn't make sense, or maybe he simply didn't want to believe it. Not yet.

Under Alix's name was a long trail of cards. The first three read: *Divorcee, Inheritance, Seducer*—there was a question mark after that one. Had she seduced him? Or had they seduced each other? A few more followed into a line of seven. The final card bore the single, horrifying word, *Finger.*

On the table arrangement, the name next to Alix's was Rick. He had a long track of three-by-fives under that one. They started with: *Drugs, South America, Murder, Jealousy,* included a second *Finger* card, and a final card marked, *Phone.* Tripp reached into his pocket and retrieved the folded slip of paper bearing the contact number for Rick Cole.

Why would the man give him his private phone number if he'd been the one to send a grisly piece of his daughter back to her mother? No, he didn't think Cole had been the one who had done it. Tripp removed the *Finger* card from Rick's track. He didn't know where to place it, but not with the drug lord. Rick Cole had killed his wife's lover, and Tripp had no doubt Cole would have killed him, too, but he didn't believe the man would have butchered his own daughter. For now, he pocketed the card. It didn't belong anywhere else on the table.

Cat stood and arched his tawny back. His white hind legs crouched low. He was still purring. When Tripp realized what was about to happen, it was too late. Before he could do anything to prevent the action, the tom sprang from the sofa cushion to the coffee table, landing with all four paws on the slippery surface of the cards, scattering Tripp's neatly ordered rows. Over the side of the table and onto the floor slid the three-by-fives, creating a new mix of *linkability* words.

Cat, a feline of uncommon good sense, ran for his life.

Tripp, deciding words were getting him about as far as words would get him, tried out a few good ones he hadn't used in a while. They didn't make him feel any better. After a quick sulk, he scooped up the cards, dropped them in a drawer, and left the house.

Two minutes later he came back, shooting unhappy glances around the room at any wisely hiding animal, and filled the feeding dishes with cat chow and fresh water.

"Remember I did this," he said to the unseen presence of the cat.

Tripp left the house a second time, consoling himself with the thought that someday, if some ex-husband killed him and his skinny soul was dangling over the fires of hell, this might be the one kind act on his roll card to pull his carcass out of the slow cooker.

As comforts went, it wasn't much. Still, it followed the adage, always cover your ass.

Daniel drove through the exclusive Bel Air neighborhood and parked in the driveway of the house on Sunset Plaza at a quarter to noon. Dr. Walker Reinhard's green Jaguar wasn't there yet. Daniel wasn't surprised. He hadn't given Reinhard much time to drive from his office to home. That had been deliberate. The less time Reinhard had to think about his plans, the better.

The baby had fallen asleep in her car seat sometime during the ride along the curving Angeles Crest Highway from Wrightwood. The drive had been slow, but the scenery beautiful, overlooking the foothill communities, the San Gabriel Valley, and the unique high-rise vista of downtown Los Angeles.

The throaty rumble of Reinhard's Jag pulled in behind him. Daniel stayed in the car. An unfamiliar car in a driveway was one thing; a stranger standing in that driveway might be noticed. One hand stayed at the side of Daniel's seat. It was holding a gun. If things went down wrong, Reinhard wouldn't walk away from this.

"What do you think you're doing?" Reinhard's words were forced through nearly clenched teeth. Anger stood out in cords along his neck and forehead. "You brought one of them here? This is my home, for Christ's sake!"

"Get in, and stop making a scene," said Daniel. He lifted the gun so Reinhard could see it. "Now."

Seconds went by while Reinhard seemed to be deciding what to do. Finally, he came around to the passenger side of the car and got in.

"We're making the first exchange today," said Daniel.

"That's impossible. This is not the way I do business, in broad daylight and from the front yard of my home."

"These are my arrangements," said Daniel. "We do it my way."

Reinhard's pale skin deepened with anger to a red wine tone. "Are you insane? Do you think I have the money with me? I'm not a bank, Gage. It takes time to prepare for these things."

"You've had plenty of time. The deal is today."

"And where have you been? For all I knew, you might have backed out of the whole thing. I haven't heard from you for weeks."

"I'm here now. Keep your voice down," Daniel warned. "You'll wake the baby."

"You don't honestly expect me to pay you right now?"

He lifted the gun to the level of Reinhard's heart.

"The money is always paid after the child is received by the adoptive parents."

Daniel knew better. He'd studied Dr. Reinhard's practice, the patients on the books, and the patients off the record. He knew that Walker Reinhard always got his money for private adoptions up front. That way, if a deal fell through—as it often did—he was still paid.

"Get the money, Reinhard. Fifteen thousand. Cash."

"We agreed on ten! What is this? I'm not paying—"

"Now it's twenty. You want to keep negotiating?" asked Daniel. "What's your life worth?"

Reinhard had to swallow down whatever else he might have said. A twitch started at the left corner of his mouth. He stared straight ahead, not looking at Daniel or the baby. Fury rose off the man like a cloud of dark, angry heat.

"I'll have to go inside the house," Reinhard said finally, and got out.

Sydney woke and started crying when the car door slammed.

Daniel watched Reinhard walk to the front door and enter the house. The drapes were drawn over the windows. It was impossible to see inside.

The baby cried louder. Daniel glanced toward the back. She was trying to get out of the car seat. Someone would hear and notice.

He glanced back at the house. He was locked in by the other car. Reinhard was an uncertain risk, capable of any sort of treachery. Would he come back with the money, or a gun? Would he disappear out the back door? Was he calling someone? Daniel didn't trust the man, but needed him to dispose of the babies. Otherwise, he'd have to get rid of them himself.

If he could have explained her options to Sydney, maybe she would have shut up.

He was thinking that, and about how he'd do it, staring at the baby, when Reinhard came back to the car. The jarring movement of the door opening startled Daniel. He brought the gun up, aiming it at Reinhard's head as he leaned down to get inside.

"What the—" Reinhard started, then choked on the words.

"You're damned slow."

"I had to open the safe. It's a timed lock."

"Where's the money?"

Reinhard moved his hand toward the inside breast pocket of his suit.

"Hands on the seat!" Daniel directed.

Reinhard obeyed the instruction instantly. With his left hand, Daniel reached into Reinhard's jacket. He felt a bulge in the pocket and pulled out an envelope stuffed with money. He didn't count it. If the agreed amount wasn't there, he knew where the doctor lived and worked. The envelope dropped to the floor under his seat.

"It's all there," said Reinhard, "exactly what you said."

Daniel made no comment.

The doctor was squirming in his seat, twisting around to glance out the windows, look at the baby, then glance back at Daniel. "What do you want me to do?" he asked finally, his voice betraying his fear.

"Take her, and get out."

Daniel's head was cracking. He felt pain from the base of his skull to the crown of his head, pain that split his vision and seamed his mind into red weals of agony. It had come on with the tension, with the waiting, and the baby's shrill cries.

Reinhard struggled with the door handle before getting out. He had to reach back inside the car to unlock the rear door. Sydney was screaming and Reinhard was fumbling with the buckles of the car seat, trying to remove the car seat with the baby still in it. At that moment, Daniel thought about killing him. He wanted to shoot both Reinhard and the baby. Would have, but the noise from the gun . . . his head would burst open.

The doctor finally pulled the car seat free and started walking toward the house, carrying the screaming baby.

"Reinhard!" Daniel called after him. "Not to the house. To your car. Drive out of here."

Reinhard looked bewildered, and then recognized that Daniel was trapped by the Jaguar. "Oh, I didn't realize . . . I understand." He got in the Jag, put the car seat beside him, not bothering to strap it in, and backed out of the driveway. He waited at the curb, engine running.

Daniel backed out and pulled alongside him. The car seat was tipped to the side and Sydney was facedown on the seat. He shifted the car into park, set the parking brake and got out.

"Wait! What are you doing?" cried Reinhard. "I paid you the—"

"Shut up!" Daniel told him when he opened the passenger side of the Jag. He leaned in and secured the baby's car seat, slipping the metal brace under the back of the seat, and fastening it with both lap belt and shoulder straps.

"Deliver this baby to the adoptive parents today," he told Reinhard. "Understand?"

"That's impossible. Arrangements have to be made. It's never done this suddenly. It could be dangerous for us," he whispered, his tone and manner conspiratorial.

Daniel didn't think Sydney would live through more than a few hours in Reinhard's keeping. For the business Reinhard dealt in, the man was surprisingly ignorant about the care of babies. Or, maybe that shouldn't be surprising at all. The doctor didn't take care of children; he simply sold them.

Daniel was exhausted, hurting, and angry. "I want this child out of your care before six o'clock tonight.

If that isn't done, I'll find you, and we'll discuss it."
It was an idle threat, but Reinhard didn't know that.

"You're endangering both of us," Reinhard said, "but I'll do it. I'll place her this afternoon."

Daniel thrust the baby bottles and diapers onto the seat beside Reinhard, then got into his own car, released the brake, and shifted to drive. He glanced once at Sydney, who had stopped crying finally, then he drove away.

He drove toward the mountains, where he would find an isolated canyon, count the money in the envelope, and dump Jack's body.

Chapter Twenty-four

In the two-story cabin in Wrightwood, Lydia Spencer waited for Logan to return. She listened for the sound of his car, knowing he would come back for the other children, and wondering if this was the time she should leave. Go someplace, anyplace, where Logan could never find her.

He had killed Jack. Would he kill her, too?

She had to get away, but should she take Paige? The thought teased her like the lure of sweets to a hungry child. *Take Paige and run.* Maybe she could make her own deal with Harper Pierce for the money. Wasn't she as smart as Logan? Smarter? Hadn't she figured out Logan's real plan? He wouldn't be expecting that.

She tried to believe it would work, that she could ransom Paige to her grandfather and beat Logan at his own game. She tried, but the problem with ransom was that you could never collect the money without getting caught. That's why kidnapping never worked.

Besides, if she took Paige and left, what would she do with the other two babies? Take them with her?

Impossible. One child she could hide; three would be conspicuous. Abandon them? She didn't like to think of herself as cruel, vicious like Jack, or without a conscience like Logan. She could phone the police from somewhere far away and say where to find the children, but that was stupid. Calls could be traced. It was too much of a risk.

There was one other alternative. Kidnapping was a capital offense. Jack would have killed them.

She couldn't do that. She wasn't a monster. The idea of smothering the babies wrapped itself around Lydia's thoughts like a soft blanket. It would be so quick and easy. They were so small. . . .

No. The best thing was to leave, to get out before Daniel came back. *He killed Jack.* She ran upstairs for her purse and car keys.

All that money!

The babies were staring at her, following her with their eyes. She ought to give them a bottle, or something, but felt time touching her with a cold and pressing breath.

Hurry. If Logan came back, it might be too late. He'd see her with the car keys, know she was leaving. Like Jack. He wouldn't let her go. She knew too much. The money didn't matter. What was her life worth?

She put the babies in their cribs. "Bye," she said to them, then walked downstairs, out the front door, and left.

The garage door was heavy. She had to pull hard to raise it. If Logan drove up now . . . She kept glancing over her shoulder, afraid of what she'd see. Would there be a warning, or would he slip up behind her without a sound? Opening the garage door seemed loud, its rusty hinges whined in strident, metal squeals.

The car started at the first turn of the key in the ignition. Lydia backed into the driveway, got out, and closed the garage door. Better to let Logan think she was here. He'd search the house before going into the garage. That would buy her time.

Lydia drove along Lone Pine Canyon Road until she reached Park Avenue, then headed toward the main section of town. She nervously watched the streets, not for the traffic lights, but for who might be driving alongside her, or following behind.

Would she recognize Logan's car? He'd been careful not to come to the house more than once in the same vehicle. She never knew what he'd be driving, and had to strain her eyes to look for the faces behind the windshields.

Traffic moved slowly through the central part of Wrightwood Village. This merchant hub of town was a place where pedestrians claimed right of way at any crossing point. Traffic waited for a steady stream of women and children, free-roaming dogs, and long-haired, bearded men in blue jeans and plaid wool shirts rolled up to their elbows.

All this time for nothing. The frustrating thought kept drumming in Lydia's mind. She'd done the hard work, kept the babies alive, not Logan. He was going to get everything. Anger boiled inside her at the unfairness of it.

You're alive, common sense argued. It was more than she could say for Jack.

Leaving was the only safe choice. If she'd had more time to figure out a way to use her knowledge of Paige's grandfather, if she knew Logan's plan, how he figured to collect the money, she'd have killed him and finished the deal herself. It occurred to Lydia, she wouldn't mind killing Logan.

Being stalled for so long at the center of town made her nervous. People could see into her car. They might remember her face, or something about the car. She'd have to lose the car when she got to Los Angeles. Logan would recognize it. That was something she couldn't risk. Leave town. Make herself small somewhere. If he could, Logan would find her and pay her for what she'd done.

You need your payoff, too? The expression on his face hadn't changed after he shot Jack, but there was a harder edge to his voice. She didn't want or need that payoff. Fear of it was why she was running.

The jam of cars finally moved, and Lydia was speeding along the mountain road, surrounded by green walls of tall coniferous pine. Her ceiling was a blue sky washed with feathering clouds, her floor, a dark highway leading to a place called AWAY.

A tremble of hopeful exhilaration started in Lydia's chest. It spread in tingling currents up her spine and to her arms and neck. Free. Down from the mountain on Angeles Crest Highway, take the 210 freeway to the Valley, and from there, a world of choices about where'd she go, and how she'd stay alive. Away from Logan. God, she could feel the adrenaline pumping through her legs and—

A California Highway Patrol roadblock barred entrance to Angeles Crest. Two wide wooden barriers were braced at the entrance, standing sentinel, and three CHP units—one car and two motorcycles—framed the rim of the road.

A tight band of panic stretched itself around

Lydia's throat. For an instant, she couldn't breathe. The air swelled around her, pressing close. A patrolman stopped each car. He leaned in the windows, saying something. Asking questions? Looking for her? She focused on the gun holstered at the man's hip, imagined the feel of that gun pointed at her back.

The only turnaround was where the CHP units were parked. Where she was, the road was too narrow to pull out of line, hang a U-turn, and speed away. Even if there had been enough room, such an act would draw unwanted attention.

Couldn't avoid it. Couldn't run.

She waited, car engine thrumming at the delay. Her foot pressed harder on the brake. She hadn't shifted out of drive. Slow. Why was it taking so long? The Check Engine panel lighted on the dash. Christ! The car was going to die. The whole line of traffic would be held up because of her. The CHP officer would walk over and check it out, and when he saw her, she'd be the one the roadblock was meant for. He'd pull her out of the car and the nose of his gun would line up with her spine.

If she got out and ran, would they shoot?

She shifted gears into neutral, revved the engine a couple of times, and the Check Engine light faded. Why were the CHP here? Did they know about the kidnapping? Had they caught Logan? Had he given up her name and description for a plea bargain?

The cars moved forward, inching closer. The patrolman who kept leaning in the cars wore sunglasses and a motorcycle helmet. She couldn't see his eyes, didn't know if he was looking at her. She had to force her fingers from the steering wheel to shift into drive. Her hands were slick with fear.

One more car.

Moving up.

The sunglasses leaned in close. "Make a U-turn, ma'am. This road's been closed because of a rock-slide on the Crest, about two miles down. Steer your car to the right. There's room to circle back."

She nodded, afraid to speak.

He didn't step back, his face still inches from her own.

"Hope you don't need to be out at Wrightwood today. We heard over the radio that the San Bernardino exit is blocked, too."

"What? How could both, I mean . . ."

"We've been directing traffic that way all afternoon, but an eighteen wheeler overturned along the On ramp about ten minutes ago. Chemical spill," he added. "Hazardous material. EPA has closed both the On and Off ramp due to exposure to toxic gas. Cleanup crews expect to be working at it till around eight tonight."

"What kind of toxic gas?"

"They don't tell us, lady." He waved her through.

She couldn't believe it—both roads closed. Why had this happened now? Then she realized something else. If she couldn't get out of Wrightwood, Logan couldn't get back in. He hadn't had enough time to make a round trip. For the moment, she was safe. She could go back to the house and get Paige. These accidents, they'd bought her time. Why should she lose out on everything because of Logan? She'd worked too hard.

"Thank you," she told the patrolman, meaning it, and pulled forward, hanging a wide U before the roadblocks. She was feeling better, as if she'd been given a last minute reprieve.

Returning traffic was backed up for miles, moving in slow inches. Fifteen minutes crept by. A half an hour. With her car windows rolled up, she screamed in frustration. If anyone heard or noticed, they didn't react.

It was like this until two blocks outside of the village. By then, enough cars had turned off the main road for side streets, and traffic was easier. She looked at her watch. Since the time she left, she'd been gone about an hour.

Maybe it would be all right.

No, it *would* be all right.

Nothing had happened.

The words sang in her mind, repeating over and over like a mantra. Her car whipped past columns of road-bordering trees, and a Mercurochrome sky bled sunset beyond the dirt glaze of the windshield. She turned up Lone Pine Canyon Road and felt the presence of the houses on the street, their open windows like staring eyes, watching her.

She approached the house with caution. Looking for Logan's car. It wasn't there. The garage door was closed, exactly as she'd left it. She hadn't wanted anyone to know she was gone. It was dusk, no kids on the street, no neighbors standing in their yards talking. No Logan.

She pulled into the driveway, got out, opened the garage door, and got back in. Then she drove inside and parked. Her hands were shaking when she pulled the garage door shut from inside. She switched on the light and tried to get it together before she went in the house.

No one would know. It was as if she'd never left. Lydia opened the door and walked into the house.

Missy Dunbar was sitting on the couch, holding a baby.

Chapter Twenty-five

"You left these kids alone." Missy's lips pooched out with the final word, holding that pouty-mouth look. "I can't believe you'd do that."

"I didn't mean to. I thought I'd only be gone for a few minutes." Lydia was caught off guard by Missy's presence in the house. Questions were flailing like drowning swimmers in Lydia's mind: *How had Missy gotten in? Why was she here?* And *What now?*

"A few minutes! I've been here almost an hour. Do you realize what could have happened to these babies in a solid hour?" Missy looked ludicrous when angry. Her face mottled to unflattering blotches of ruby wine and slab gray. Her eyes widened and bulged, like a mad-eyed cow, and her nostrils flared.

"You didn't call the—"

"I should have. I should have called the police when I first got here and found these babies alone." Lydia's chest hurt, her heart was beating so hard. "I know it looks bad ... like I abandoned them or something, but I had to make a call about my little boy—he's in a hospital—and I got stuck in traffic. We don't have a phone and ... it should have just taken a minute, but cars were backed up all along the road because of the accidents. I tried, but I couldn't get back here any sooner."

"What accidents?"

"You don't know? There's been a rockslide on Angeles Crest. The highway's blocked, and somebody told me the freeway ramps are closed, too, because of toxic gas from an overturned tanker, some kind of chemical spill."

"Oh, my Lord!" Missy sniffed, as if fumes from the gas were leaking into the house at that moment.

"My little boy's having an operation," Lydia padded the lie. "I had to call."

"What's wrong with him?"

She had to think fast. "His heart, it's a valve on his heart—doesn't work right."

"Oh, poor little thing." Missy's corpulent face relaxed, double chins sagging to her chest, sausage-lipped mouth easing into a slack, passive droop. "You could have come next door. I would have let you use my phone. Leaving these children was—"

"Stupid, plain stupid," said Lydia. "I know now, and I wish I hadn't done it."

"I was going to say dangerous."

"That, too. It was wrong, but I was desperate. My little boy's so sick," she said, and willed her eyes to fill up with tears. "If you tell anybody about this, I'll lose my license, and then all the children will be taken away from me, and I don't know what'll happen to my boy, how I'll pay for—"

"Now, don't fall apart. I won't say anything. I guess you've learned your lesson about how foolish it is to take chances like this. You probably wouldn't have done it if you hadn't been so worried about your

236

little boy. I know how I'd feel if my son were in the hospital and I couldn't be there with him." Missy heaved her body off the couch and walked over to where Lydia stood. She patted her bare arm.

"Your boy's all right?"

"I think so."

"Good, I'm glad. I'm going home now. Don't want to be here when the parents arrive. That wouldn't look right. I know how parents think. You shouldn't be visiting with a neighbor; you should be watching their children. I'm right, huh?"

"I guess."

Missy got as far as the front door, then called back over her shoulder, "Next time, you come to me. Okay? That's what neighbors are for."

"I will, thanks."

"You know, I haven't seen that man coming by lately. You know, that tall, thin one. Blond hair. Is he one of the parents?"

She was talking about Jack. When had she seen him?

"He's one of the parents, separated from the mother. He doesn't come here much."

"Drinking problem? Drugs? He looked the type."

Lydia nodded. "Both."

"Good riddance, I say. That kind of thing leads to trouble."

Trouble, thought Lydia. Jack's troubles were over.

Missy's hand lingered on the doorknob. "You know, I never see the parents come and pick these babies up at night."

For an instant, Lydia panicked. What could she say? If Missy suspected that something was wrong, she'd never leave it alone. She'd keep poking her nose in until she knew everything.

The excuse came in a rush. "These are my foster children. They're placed here by an agency."

"Foster children? That's not what you told me. You said—"

"I don't like most people to know. Sometimes people make it hard on children who are in a bad situation. Not everybody understands. These kids come from broken homes, fathers like the one you saw, mothers doing anything for the next heroin fix. It can be pretty bad."

"Oh, the poor things."

"I'm a little cautious about who I tell," confided Lydia. "Actually, I didn't lie to you. It was you who guessed that I ran a day care, remember?"

Missy nodded. "You're right."

"I can trust you?" asked Lydia.

"Of course. Yes. I won't say a word to anyone. Oh, it breaks my heart. Sweet babies. How could anyone . . . the world makes me sick sometimes. I can't tolerate people who would hurt a child. There's such evil in this world, don't you think?"

Lydia nodded. It had gone amazingly well. Missy believed everything. She was feeling the power and excitement of the lie running through her, roiling in her blood, tasting it on her tongue, loving the high it gave her.

"Good luck to your boy," Missy said, leaving. She walked out the door. "What's his name?"

Nothing came to Lydia's mind. She drew a complete blank. The muscles of her throat squeezed hard.

Missy was staring at her, waiting, those cow eyes

subtly changing from sympathy to a question. "Lydia?"

"Huh?"

"Did you hear what I said?"

"No. I didn't."

"Your mind's on that hospital. I asked what's your boy's name."

"Brian . . . his name's Brian."

"Hmm," Missy nodded approval. "My son's Clayton. You like that name? It's Old English. I thought it sounded nice."

"Clayton," repeated Lydia. "I like it."

Missy smiled hugely. "We're going to be friends, you and me, I know it."

The door closed gently, a quiet exit for such a large woman. Lydia made it to the sofa before her knees gave away.

Diane Kendall called Tripp, told him what the psychic had said about a message, and begged him to talk to all the parents again. He hadn't known she was working with a psychic. The paranormal wasn't a field in which Tripp put a great deal of faith. Or maybe faith was required in order to see. Either way, he'd never had any working experience with a psychic investigator. The words amused him. He guessed she was a PI, too.

Because the Kendalls, like the other parents, were paying him to do the job, he had to take the request seriously. It wasn't a bad idea. Review the case. Maybe there was something he'd missed.

He hadn't been to the Richards' home since the first round of interviewing all the parents. After some false starts, the focus of his investigation had centered around Alix and Rich Cole. Too much of that time had been spent with Alix, and Tripp now started to wonder if his relationship with her had hindered his judgment. Detective Walsh thought so, and maybe it was true.

Alix had called this morning and wanted to see him, but he'd made excuses, determined to put some distance between them for a while. After his surprise visit with her ex, he wasn't sure about anything. He had always trusted her instincts. That had changed. He didn't know what, or who, to trust. Right now, he didn't trust himself very much, either. How long could he hold out before seeing Alix again and telling her all he knew?

The babies had been missing for too long. If the kidnapping had been committed for ransom, why hadn't the parents or the sheriff's investigation been contacted by now? The call to Carin Sayers and the package sent to Alix weren't acts motivated by someone wanting ransom. They were acts motivated by someone who liked hurting the mothers. The thought struck Tripp cold. Whoever had these children—if the four babies were still alive—was a person who drew pleasure from hurting others.

The babies were probably dead. That was the truth Tripp had been avoiding. Did Detective Walsh know it? Had she come to the same depressing conclusion?

It was afternoon when Tripp arranged to meet Susan Richards at her home in La Cañada. All of his previous assumptions about the case had to be set aside. He had believed Alix's fear that Rich was behind the kidnapping. Following that lead had gotten his house ransacked, his life in danger, and a threat of imprisonment from Detective Walsh. He was back to square one, looking for clues to the babies' whereabouts. To please Diane Kendall he would start with questioning Susan Richards again.

He rang the bell. He could hear footsteps shuffling toward him. Slippers? It was two in the afternoon.

"Mrs. Richards?"

The change in her appearance astonished him. The Susan Richards he remembered had been a pretty young woman of barely twenty. The person standing before him seemed much older, some indefinable age that was more about appearance than number of years.

"Mr. Tripp," she said, pulling back the screen door and inviting him inside the small house. "Bark your toe again?"

He remembered the sprinkler head and smiled. Any other time he might have laughed, but he didn't feel like laughing. There was such a sense of oppression about this woman, both physical and mental. It was shocking, what stress and worry had done to her. She looked like someone who hadn't slept in days; her hair lusterless and uncombed, no makeup, and a dullness to her eyes that bore witness to the life dying with her.

He sat on the sofa in the living room, acutely uncomfortable within the air of quiet desperation in this house. The living room hadn't been cleaned in a long time, not even when she'd known he was coming to see her, he realized. Things left undone. What else had been neglected or forgotten? Meals? Sleep?

"You found my baby?"

He hadn't expected the question. Of course, it was

what she would have thought. He hadn't been here in a long time.

"No. I'm sorry, not yet."

She didn't sit on the straight-backed chair or the sofa, but moved around the room in a slow methodical dance of distraction: stopping at the table full of plants, touching each green leaf; across to the window, her narrow hand pressed against the pane of glass; to the center of the room, standing, weaving slightly.

She seemed unbearably vulnerable.

"My investigation has taken a new direction." Tripp thought this sounded positive. "I'd like to review the information taken from you and your husband in our first interview."

"Doesn't matter."

He thought he'd misheard. "I'm sorry, did you say—"

"I never told it. I kept it quiet, but the one who's got my baby didn't give her back." The weaving became rocking on her feet, back and forth, her body leaning in, leaning out, arms clutched around her middle.

The psychic's words were on his lips. He could have, but didn't ask the question: *A message?* If there was something, let Susan say it on her own. He didn't want to introduce the thought.

"What didn't you tell, Susan?"

She stopped rocking, turned her attention completely on him, her eyes dark and haunting. When she spoke, it was a whisper he could barely hear. "About the letter. If I told anyone, the letter said he'd . . . send me back her eyes."

Tripp was shocked by her words. It knocked the

wind from him and left him breathless and rubbing at a place on his chest, a spot just over his heart, where a dull pain bloomed like blood roses.

It was a minute before he could think what to say. Finally, he asked, "Could I see the letter, Susan?"

She looked unsure. He could see fear balled up as tight as clenched fists behind her eyes. "I don't know. It said—"

"I know you're afraid, but everything's going to be all right. I promise." He never promised a client anything, that was one of the first things he'd learned as a PI, but Tripp was making this promise to her. He was losing himself to this case, first with Alix, then with keeping information from Detective Walsh—including the fact that he had a phone number to reach Rick Cole—and now this, promising an emotionally fragile young woman that he would help her. Could he?

"My husband will be so angry. He doesn't know." Her face assumed a childlike quality.

Tripp couldn't believe she'd kept this horror to herself for so long. No wonder she was coming apart. "Why didn't you tell him?"

"Mike would have given the letter to the sheriff. No matter what I said, he would have done it. Jennifer's my baby. I gave birth to her; he didn't. Every day I waited for the mail to come, wondering if it would be another letter, or . . ."

She didn't need to finish. Tripp had seen what kind of package could come through the mail, the grisly stump of a child's finger.

I'll send you back her eyes.

"Go get the letter, Susan. You want me to find Jennifer and bring her back, don't you?"

243

She nodded, her brown eyes wide. She looked lost and alone.

"The letter's going to help me. Go get it."

She out of the room and into the kitchen. He didn't follow, not wanting to frighten her. He listened, heard a drawer open, the dry rattle of papers, and the drawer shut again. In a moment she returned to the room holding a corner of the envelope by two fingers, as if touching it could hurt her. She handed it to him.

He guessed that all the fingerprints on the envelope would have been smudged by the letter being shoved among other papers in the drawer. He slipped his pen under the envelope flap and held it up to the light. The first thing he noticed was the address. It was a different handwriting from the one on the package mailed to Alix. He didn't take the letter out of the envelope. Not yet.

The postmark was stamped Phelan, 2:00 p.m., March 12.

"Where the hell is Phelan?"

"It's between San Bernardino and the mountains," said Susan. "I looked it up."

Of course she had. Maybe she'd even driven there, looking for her baby. No desperate act would have surprised him.

"Do you still have that map?" Tripp had the county maps at home, but if she had this one with her, it would be quicker. He wanted to check places Phelan was near. He didn't believe the kidnapper had been stupid enough to mail the letter from the town where the children were being kept—if this letter wasn't some kind of cruel joke.

Susan brought him an Automobile Club map of

244

San Bernardino County. Tripp spread it open on the coffee table and searched for a minute.

"There it is," said Susan, touching her finger to a tiny dot. She had circled the name in blue ink.

He saw it now. Phelan was in the foothills of the San Gabriels. It was near a lot of places, the mountain communities of Big Bear, Arrowhead, and Wrightwood; the desert communities of Apple Valley, Victorville, and Palmdale; and the urban areas of San Bernardino and Riverside.

He remembered the pins on the map in Detective Walsh's office. Tripp got out a red pen and circled the places where the two calls, the letter, and the package had come from: Palmdale, Highland, Phelan, and downtown Los Angeles. Then he circled the places where the babies had lived, and the day care from where they had been taken: Glendale and La Cañada.

He stared at the map for another minute, then drew a line connecting the dots. The result looked like a bloody arrowhead, with the corners being Palmdale and Los Angeles, and the point being the city of Highland.

The babies, he figured, were somewhere in between.

Chapter Twenty-six

Tripp should have taken the letter to Detective Walsh. He should have. That was the deal he'd made. So why was he driving to Diane Kendall's home, to show this letter to a psychic he'd never met?

Rowena Crawford had known about the message. Lucky guess? Or could it be she was the genuine article? Tripp had no experience with psychics, he'd never even had his palm read. He couldn't tell Tarot cards from a trump, and he didn't know his birth sign. But dammit, she had known about the message, the letter.

The landscaping was a restful sight along the 210 freeway from Pasadena to La Cañada. It was a blue sky kind of day, with light traffic. Orange California poppies bloomed along the side of the freeway. Pink and yellow iceplant flowers looked like Easter eggs hidden in the lush ground cover. Green like this only happened in Southern California in the spring. It was too beautiful a day to be thinking about work, especially work involving kidnapping and death.

Tripp pulled off the freeway at Foothill Boulevard

and headed north. La Cañada was a city where trees outnumbered people, and both thrived. Diane Kendall's home was situated near the top of a winding road leading from Foothill Boulevard, up through the moneyed estates of Flintridge, and to a hillside lot with a view overlooking Arroyo Seco Canyon.

Diane Kendall's blue Volvo was in the driveway. Tripp parked his Mazda beside it, and set the hand brake so he wouldn't roll off the side of the cliff and drop into the canyon. A spectacular view was nice, but there was such a thing as being too much on the edge. He preferred his home on the flatland.

The front door opened before he had a chance to ring the bell. He'd been expecting to see Diane. There was an awkward moment of surprise when it was obviously someone else. His reaction to the woman standing before him was one of amusement as well as surprise. This had to be Rowena Crawford, the psychic, and she wasn't at all what he'd expected.

"I'm John Tripp," he said finally, realizing he'd been staring. Normally, he wasn't rude, but this short, pincushion of a woman looked like Humpty Dumpty in heels.

"Come in," said Rowena. "We've been waiting for you."

Tripp stepped inside the doorway.

"Did you bring it?" she asked.

"It?"

"The message. You found it, didn't you?"

Now, how the hell had she known that? He'd only found out about the letter an hour ago. Susan could have called here, but he didn't think she would have. This was getting stranger and stranger.

Diane walked into the living room. "Oh, John. I'm glad you're here. You've met Rowena?"

"Well, sort of."

"She told me you'd be bringing us something today," said Diane. "Is that right?"

He pulled the plastic specimen bag out of his coat pocket.

"Oh God, a letter," said Diane.

"It came sometime ago," Tripp explained. "I'll have to give it to the sheriff's investigation." He didn't know who he was saying that for, himself or the psychic.

"You knew it was coming. You were right about the message," said Diane, staring at Rowena in amazement.

Yeah, that part was getting to him, too.

"Why don't you give it to me, Mr. Tripp," said the psychic.

Tripp held the sealed plastic bag closer to her. She could look but not—

"I need to touch it," she said, as if reading his thoughts. She held out her hand.

This was not good. "I don't think I'd better let you do that."

"Go on," said Diane. "Let her hold the letter. She was right about the message. Please, let her try."

Oh man, thought Tripp, *this is nuts.*

"I might be able to help you find the babies, if you let me," said Rowena.

He didn't know why the hell he'd come here. This was like some fifty-cent ticket to a spook show in a circus. Shouldn't have come here. Plain stupid. He'd done this on impulse and now he was sorry. He'd have to explain to them about—

"If you're worried about fingerprints, I'll put a tissue in my hand. Rest the letter on it. Would that be all right?"

Damn, she'd done it again. Read his thoughts as if they were written on her eyes. She made him nervous, this mind-reading woman.

"All right, all right," Tripp gave in, wanting out of here.

Diane put a tissue across Rowena's open palm. Tripp used his pen to hook the letter beneath its envelope flap and pull it from the plastic bag. It was a tricky maneuver, but he managed to hold the letter, still inside its envelope, an inch above the tissue in Rowena's hand.

"You can't open it," he warned.

"I won't need to," she said.

He believed that, and let the letter drop.

Rowena took one sharp breath as the letter touched her. "Oh," she said, then closed her eyes.

"What?" Diane reached for the envelope, but Tripp was faster. He grabbed her arm.

"Leave it," he said.

They were glaring at each other, Tripp and Diane, and he wondered for the second time since he'd arrived, how the devil he'd made such a stupid move as to bring the letter here. What if Diane grabbed it? Detective Walsh would have his license for this one.

A horrified cry broke his concentration on Diane. He turned to Rowena. Her face was wide-eyed with panic, or fear.

"Take it away. Take it away!" Rowena yelled.

Her hand shook with such force it looked palsied, and the envelope nearly slid to the floor. Tripp hooked the envelope with his pen just in time, and slid it back into the plastic bag.

Rowena slapped at her face and arms. "Get them off me! No, no! Get them off!"

"What's wrong?" cried Diane. "Stop it! Make her stop. What does she see? What's happening?"

Tripp didn't know, but could see the terror in Rowena's eyes. Hearing her voice, he could sense her fear. She opened her mouth to scream . . . and he grabbed her.

"Take it easy," he said. "You're all right. You're here with us. Look at me," he told her.

Her eyes didn't focus.

"Look at me!"

She stared. Slowly, he saw the recognition come into her eyes. A deep shudder ran through her body. It touched him as he held her.

"Oh, sweet Jesus," Rowena said. "He's dead. His body . . . it's wet with corruption. Dirt and leaves piled on him. I was trapped inside . . . maggots," she said.

Tripp felt the woman slide from his grasp. He kept her from hitting her head, but she slipped to the floor. In the background he heard Diane stumbling through the house, saying something that he couldn't understand. She was over the edge with this. They all were. Susan, Diane, Carin, and Alix. *And me,* thought Tripp. *I'm over the edge, too.*

Maggots. The thought sickened him. Another thought made it worse: If the psychic's right, and the kidnapper was dead and moldering in some shallow grave, then what about the children?

He sat beside Rowena, waiting until she was calm

and breathing normally. Her face was pasty. Shock, he guessed.

"If you've got any whiskey in the house," he said to Diane, "get her some."

Rowena struggled to sit. "I don't drink."

"Until today. After this, we could all use a shot." Diane brought a decanter and three glasses.

"Bourbon?" Tripp asked hopefully.

She shook her head. "Scotch."

He'd suffer. He poured two fingers into each glass and handed one to Rowena. Her skin looked ghostly and damp. Tripp didn't want her to die on him, especially now that he believed she was for real. Not that he had a good reason to believe. He didn't have proof. It was more that he believed she believed.

"Come on, drink it," he urged.

She tasted the scotch and made a face. "People pay money for this? Smells like rubbing alcohol."

"Don't smell. Drink it."

She stopped arguing and gulped it down like medicine. That was what he intended it to be, medicine to bring her back from the dead.

When Rowena's color was better, and they had moved to the sofa, Tripp asked, "Do you have anything else you want to tell me about this case? Anything I should know?"

She looked as if she didn't want to talk about it, but told him anyway. "There were two wounds in the body, one bullet in the throat and one in the head."

Tripp's gut clenched. This psychic had left him wrung out and twisted dry. The whole story might not be true. Probably wasn't true. But if it was ...

The next step was to take the letter to Detective

Walsh. He would drive to the sheriff's department after leaving here.

He remembered the white-and-yellow nursery at Alix's house, the brightly colored stuffed animals on shelves along the walls, and the brass and porcelain crib in the center of the room. It stood empty now, waiting for the child.

And he thought of Christine Campbell, murdered on the day the babies were taken. A single bullet hole in her forehead. Was it possible? If the man who wrote the letter to Susan Richards was now dead, as Rowena claimed, could whoever have killed him also be Christine Campbell's murderer?

It was possible, but the proof was hidden in a psychic's dream.

Daniel went home with the money.

He'd intended to give Lydia the money and smooth things over with her, but Angeles Crest Highway was closed. The only other way into Wrightwood was through San Bernardino, a much longer drive. The prospect was overwhelming.

The struggle with Jack—arguing with him, killing him, and dumping his body in a shallow grave—had left Daniel exhausted. He's pushed himself too hard. His body felt the strain of muscles forced long past their strength. Taking Sydney to Reinhard had been strictly to get the money for Lydia. Her soul was counted in dollars. Now, she'd have to wait. There was no way to contact her.

His chest ached from his still healing ribs and lung. And his head . . . most of the time it was bad. Now it was worse. He was taking the Demerol too often. How many today? He'd lost count. That was dangerous. Sloppy. It couldn't be allowed.

Daniel took the remaining pills and flushed them down the toilet. Pain would keep him alert. Alert would keep him alive.

There was one last thing to do before he could rest. He picked up the phone and pressed the top memory button, Harper Pierce's private listing.

Daniel felt the ringing in his head. One. Two. Three.

Pierce answered.

"Hello, sir. It's Daniel."

He could hear a sharp intake of breath.

"Where the hell have you been?"

"It's complicated, a personal problem."

"Personal problem! In three weeks you couldn't have found a goddamn phone?"

"Sir, did you know Rowena Crawford is in Pasadena?"

That shut him up.

"She arrived last night."

There was a deep sigh. "What's she doing here? Why didn't you stop her?"

"I'll explain that when I see you." He didn't want to go into details of the car accident over the phone. He wasn't thinking clearly. His head throbbed with unrelenting pressure.

"My daughter knows this Crawford woman's here?"

"She sent for her."

"Dammit, Daniel! How could you let this happen? What were you doing all this time, sitting on your hands?"

The heat of Daniel's anger welled like blood to a wound. "You need to know right now? Right now? Fine. I was in a car accident. It was nearly fatal. I've been in the hospital."

"Hospital? Why didn't you let us know?"

"I was in a coma for the first two weeks."

"A coma . . . good God. But the doctor," said Pierce, "the staff, someone should have told us."

"I didn't travel to West Virginia as Daniel Cantrell. I assumed you didn't want any connection linking my actions to you or Trans-Continental Bank."

There was a beat of hesitation before Pierce said, "I don't know what you mean by that." The man hadn't become CEO without some common sense. He was being careful, structuring his response to protect his interests from anything illegal, in case someone else were listening.

"I'll be at the office tomorrow afternoon," said Daniel.

"Afternoon! I need you there before then. You know how important this is to me."

The room shifted. Daniel felt sick. He clenched his eyes shut, trying to regain his balance, but stumbled as if the floor had tilted beneath him. Everything was off center.

"I can't be there in the morning, a doctor's appointment. I can't break it. I'll be at the office by early afternoon."

"Fine," said Pierce, and hung up.

Daniel wanted to shout at Pierce, "I'm the one who's got your granddaughter!" But he didn't. The anger stayed within him, fused and cored into his soul. The day was coming when Harper Pierce would give Daniel everything he wanted. On that day, Daniel would bring all the pain of his anger into the open for everyone to see.

Chapter Twenty-seven

Detective Walsh skimmed through the multipage report detailing what the team at Tech had concluded about Alix Cole's package. She had read it carefully the first time. Now, her gaze followed the point of her finger down the page as she searched for the part about ... yes, there it was.

Analysis confirms the handwriting sample taken from the package wrapping was not executed by the same individual as the sample examined on the second document.

Not the same as the writing in the letter John Tripp had brought them. She'd known that. Had the caller been the letter writer, or the package sender? There was no means of matching voice print with handwriting. The boys at the lab were sharp, but not that good.

Jessa sat in her office that night, long past her scheduled hours on duty. She wished she could be outside, wished she was off this case. It stayed with her like a flu, night and day, an ache in her muscles, a coldness in her bones. She couldn't get it out of her mind.

Now, they had two postmarks. The package had been mailed from Los Angeles, a different handwriting from the letter mailed to Susan Richards. Not the same individual. Islands of thought surfaced in Jessa's consciousness. If she could bring it together, pull the net closed.

The letter had been written in a childish scrawl. The address slanted high to the right hand corner of the envelope, and in such large letters, it almost ran out of space. By contrast, the package had been addressed in an easy-to-read and meticulous hand. The handwriting seemed . . . professional. It was the word that came to mind. Someone who used this skill every day. The thought was logged at the back of her mind. She went on.

The first call had come from Highland, near San Bernardino. Jessa closed her eyes and remembered the sound of the man's voice, bullying, loud, abusive, the way his words slipped together. *I saw you on TV. You gotta nice shape.* Ignorant.

The kidnapper was neither ignorant nor abusive. The kidnapper, in a calm, premeditated act, had taken the baby bottles out of the refrigerator, brought the childrens' diaper bags and the pacifier. The kidnapper had made so few mistakes, the only things the police had to go on were the phone calls, the letter, and the package.

The second call had come from Palmdale. Same voice, same man. Jessa drew a mental line between the pinpoints on her office map. These two were connected.

The letter had come from Phelan. The language of

the letter, the elementary-school handwriting, the crude violence of the threat . . . it had to be the same man as the caller. She'd bet on it.

Mentally, she connected the three places: Palmdale, Phelan, Highland. She went to the map and circled the connected areas, then enlarged the circle to include La Cañada, the place where the babies had been abducted. She connected this larger circle to Los Angeles, where the package had been mailed, but stopped, her pen poised above the map, and knew—suddenly knew—the one from Los Angeles was the kidnapper.

It was a warm spring day, but Jessa's thoughts filled her with the numbing cold of winter. This one was the planner, the brains behind it all. This one never made mistakes. Jessa tried to take a deep breath, but couldn't. The certainty was so strong. It held her in its grip.

She knew the kidnapper. Not who it was, but the kind of person who'd done this.

Without a name, her hunch didn't mean much. The excitement of the moment was brief. The drama had been visceral, as if she had somehow touched consciousness with the kidnapper, with the killer of Christine Campbell.

There was a soft knock on her door. "Yes?"

"You're going to love me for this one." Dillon stepped into her office. He looked and sounded happy.

"What is it?"

"The boys at Tech found a fingerprint."

She couldn't believe it. The kidnapper wouldn't have made such an amateur's mistake. "On the package?"

"No, on the letter. They lifted a print off the stamp—can you believe it?—from when he pressed it to the envelope."

"That's wonderful." She felt a weakness in her legs, as if she'd been on a powerful high. "Why are we getting this now? It's after hours. I thought they'd checked the letter and found nothing."

"They had, but I convinced them to stay late and check it again, in case something slipped by the first time."

"You did?" She was amazed.

"That's right, and you want to know something else?"

She did.

"The print led to a name. I brought you a present, Jess. We have the identity of the man who sent the letter."

And who made the calls, she added silently.

"His name's Jack Kordera. He's a small-time thief who served time for breaking and entering, and car jacking. He spent three months in Mama California's summer camp for baby burglars, picking trash off the highways. He was arrested after that for drunk driving. Lost his license. The judge gave him four months in County. He was released on the 21st of December."

The kidnapping had taken place January 20th. It was possible. This man could be working with the kidnapper, and he'd screwed up.

"Dillon, I could kiss you."

"I'd hoped you'd do better than that."

She smiled. Their sex life had been nonexistent since this case had taken over her days and nights. The news about Jack Kordera wouldn't change that.

If anything, she'd be more driven, now that they had something to work with. There wouldn't be time for anything else, Still, she appreciated being wanted.

She was tempted to come around the desk and kiss that boyish grin on his face, but someone might walk into her office. Kissing your assistant wasn't considered professional behavior, at least, not in the workplace.

Oh, the hell with it. Jessa gave him the kiss he deserved, and a promise of more.

Lydia waited until well after dark. It was a quarter to eight. If she drove away without headlights, maybe Missy wouldn't notice. The woman was nosy, but she also had a family. Lydia hoped she'd be too busy with them to be peeking out the windows and spying on her neighbors.

There wasn't much choice. The Highway Patrol had said the road would be closed until eight. Logan could be back any minute. She had to get out of here before then.

This time, the babies were asleep when she left. That made it easier. She lifted the garage door, put Paige in front with her, and strapped the belts of the Dodge's bucket seat over and through the car seat's frame.

The old Dodge Colt was noisy. There wasn't anything Lydia could do about that. If she started the engine, it might draw Missy's attention. She released the brake, shifted gear, coasted down the driveway in the dark, and onto Lone Pine Canyon Road. Two blocks away from the house, she turned the key in the ignition.

Through it all, Paige never made a sound. The baby watched Lydia with passive interest.

"Maybe you'll get home after all," Lydia said to the kid. She was feeling optimistic. "You're luckier than the rest of them. Worth more. That's why I'm taking you with me."

Paige stuck her fist in her mouth and chewed on it. She was teething.

The night sky was alive with light. In a gap between the curtain of trees along the road, Lydia saw the stars. They were brighter than she'd ever seen before. She pulled onto the verge and started through the windshield, then opened the window and looked up at the heavens. A perfect wedge of beauty.

Nothing of beauty had ever touched Lydia's life. Such things had never been for her. They were for the rich, the educated, for other people. But now, with the kind of money this baby might bring, her world could change.

She looked back at the baby beside her. Paige held out her wet fist to Lydia, like an offering. Lydia touched the tiny fist with one finger. Paige's hand opened and curled around it.

"You help me; I'll help you. Deal?"

The only answer was in Lydia's head. It was in a dream of beauty. She saw it before her as she drove, like the millions of stars in the sky—a new world, open and shining with unlimited possibility.

She drove into the desert following the lonely stretch of Highway 15, past Hesperia, Victorville, and Apple Valley, to Daggett, a town just outside Barstow. The road branched off the main highway. She passed a fenced off area of brightly lit concrete runways and long stretches of open hangers, a small airport or flight museum. Floodlights distinguished one parked fuselage from another, like a ghost town for planes. She drove on.

Two green lights later, the Dodge nosed into a narrow parking spot and shuddered to a stop beside the pink office of the Desert Flower Motel.

Lydia got out and stretched her back. Her muscles ached with more than tiredness from the drive. Stress had put knots of tension into her shoulders. Her legs trembled as she tried to stand on them after the cramped hours in the car.

Paige was asleep. Lydia closed the door. The fewer people who saw her with the baby, the better. She was almost at the office door when she turned and hurried back. What if some jerk stole the kid out of the car, now, when her luck was about to change? The dream would be ruined.

She released the clasp of the seat buckle and lifted a sleepy Paige out of the car, wrapping a knit blanket around her. The baby's face was warm against Lydia's neck. She could feel the rise and fall of Paige's breathing as she carried her, resting on her shoulder like a limp stuffed doll.

The noise of a TV commercial blasted when she opened the office door, loud and intrusive. The lobby looked vacant, no one sitting behind the desk, but she could see a light from the open doorway of an adjoining room. She walked to it. A boy of not more than sixteen was stretched out on a couch, his long legs propped on the back of a chair.

"You got a room vacant?"

He didn't hear.

"Hey kid!" she said louder.

"Oh, gosh. Sorry. I didn't hear you come in." He

muted the volume on the set. Assistant manager, Matt Parker. His badge was on crooked. "You been standing there long?"

"Long enough."

He was leaning over, scrabbling for his shoes. "Be right there," he said. "Sign-in sheet's on the desk in front of you."

But Lydia was staring over the boy's back at the TV monitor, and the eleven o'clock news. There was no sound, but the picture was louder than spoken words. Staring at her from the screen, like a body resurrected from the dead, was a picture of Jack.

The boy straightened, ran spread fingers like a wide-tooth comb through the lengths of his brown hair, pushing it off his forehead. "You'll be staying more than one night?"

Lydia had to swallow hard before she could speak. "I—maybe, I'm not sure. Do you have something kind of isolated? The baby sometimes cries at night. I don't want to disturb anyone."

"We've got the cabins. They're always vacant this time of year." He pulled a map from a drawer, showing a side road leading to a set of four cabins a half of a mile from the main building. "You might not like it. You'd be the only one in the area right now. Kind of scary place for a woman alone."

"I'll take it," said Lydia.

"Okay by me." He turned away and typed the information into the computer file.

The news was showing pictures of the kidnapped babies . . . Sydney, Chelsea, Jennifer. And Paige.

Come on, Lydia silently urged the boy. *Give me the damn key!*

If somebody saw the baby, recognized her from the

picture on the news, the police would be here in no time. She covered Paige's face with the blanket.

"Here you are. Cabin 4, it's the nicest." He handed her a key slipped into a folded paper sleeve. Follow the paved road to where it veers onto a dirt track. Cabin's about a half mile from there. Number 4's the last one."

She turned to go.

"Wait a minute."

Had he seen the news? Fear lay like a writhing snake along Lydia's back.

"You need a crib for the baby?" Matt Parker asked.

"No," she told him, not turning around, "he can sleep with me." Let him think the baby's a boy. Better yet, let him not think about the baby at all.

"You need anything," he called, "I'll be here."

She nodded, and hurried out the door. Walked until she was out of sight of the motel window, then ran to the car. Her hand shook so hard, she couldn't fit the car key into the door.

"Open, damn you," she whispered, cursing the Dodge and her fate. The point of the key finally slid into the notch. She turned it, opened the door, and slipped inside the shelter of the car.

"Jesus!" Her breath fogged the air. How did they know about Jack?

She shoved Paige back into the car seat. The gentle dream of a better life was shattered. It was always that way. Every time Lydia tried to help herself, something or somebody came along and stomped on her. This time it was Jack.

"God damn his shitty soul to hell!"

What else did the police know?

She drove. The road was dark as Lydia's thoughts.

264

She found the cabin, parked in the space in front, and went inside. Matt Parker, assistant manager, had been right. The cabin, and this lonely night ... it was a scary place for a woman alone.

Chapter Twenty-eight

"Quit complaining and eat."

Tripp forked the mushy contents of the can of "mostly trout" into Cat's dish, but the tom was still letting him know how late it was for dinner. Small glistening bits stared back at Tripp from the bowl. He wondered what they put in after mostly trout. Then he decided he didn't want to know. Definitely.

It had been a long day. First the meeting with Susan Richards, then seeing Diane and the psychic, then taking the letter to Walsh. His legs ached, his back hurt, and his neck felt kinked. He did a general survey, twisting and turning to assess the damage. There wasn't a part of him that didn't feel worn out. Well, maybe one, but sex was out of the picture, for now. He didn't have the energy, or maybe the desire.

He'd been thinking about Alix, wondering if what they'd been to each other wasn't a kind of pressure valve for letting off steam. They had steamed, but it wasn't more than that. And wouldn't be. Alix had reacted out of hurt, fear, and loneliness. Not much of a reason to build anything longer than a one-night stand.

Love wasn't part of their relationship, Tripp knew that. And Rick Cole was still in love with his wife. Cole had told him by his actions, not his words.

Cat hunkered down and furiously lapped at the wet stuff in the bowl. The white point of his tail twitched.

Tripp pulled himself a bottle of Harp beer out of the fridge, uncapped it, took a long cold drink, and sank into the deep cushions of the chair. His legs hooked over the padded arm of the sofa. His head slipped back, breathing slowed, eyes closed, easing into peaceful—

The phone rang.

"Whatever it is, I don't want any."

"John, it's Alix. Why haven't you called?" Her voice didn't sound lost and scared like Susan's, or Diane's. It was accusatory, angry, brittle.

"I've been working."

"I pay you. Remember?"

That didn't sit well. "You're one of the people who pays me, yes."

"I want to know what's happening. What are you doing about finding my daughter?" He could hear an edge to her voice. Emotion? Alix didn't break down easily.

He told her about the letter, and the psychic. He told her about his meeting with Rick, and that he didn't think Chelsea's father was the one who took the babies.

"Which leaves us where?" she asked. "If Rick didn't take my daughter, then who did?"

He couldn't tell her that; he didn't know.

The tone of her voice changed sometime during their conversation, softened. Weakened? He could feel the weight of her fear wash over him like an ice bath, wash into him, into his thinking and purpose. She was locked into this kind of feeling, but he wasn't. He couldn't be, not if he expected to find the children. This kind of thinking was numbing, crippling, and contagious. He needed to set up a distance between them, so he could do his job.

"John, could you come here tonight?" He knew what she was asking. It wasn't to see her as a client.

"I don't think that's a good idea."

There was a pause. That was the way things ended sometimes, with only an extra beat of silence. "All right. Let me know if you find anything."

"I will," he promised, and they both hung up.

There was a lot left unsaid between them. Recriminations. Lost dreams. Nightmares. He'd been so tired before she called. Now, he was awake and restless.

He switched on the TV and turned to the news. Cat settled himself on Tripp's lap, a purr of contentment reverberating through the solid warmth of feline flesh and fur, rising from him like sacred smoke, or prayers.

Tripp drained the bottle of Harp, and would have gone to the kitchen for another, but moving Cat seemed like too much trouble. He stayed put and stared at the TV, not really watching. Not listening. Until photos of the missing babies appeared on the screen. He turned up the volume.

"The Sheriff's Department has issued this photo to the news media, and is asking for assistance from the public in locating a possible suspect in the case of the four children kidnapped from a La Cañada day care nearly two months ago, and in the murder of the day care provider, Christine Campbell.

"The suspect's name is Jack Kordera. The Sheriff's Department would not disclose in what way Kordera might be involved in the case, but said the suspect has a history of being in trouble with the law. Jack Kordera is described as being tall and thin, with blond hair and blue eyes. The Sheriff's Department suggests that if anyone knows Kordera's whereabouts, they should contact their local authorities immediately."

Tripp lunged to his feet, dumping Cat to the floor. For a few seconds he stood without taking another breath, staring at the face of the man who had the children. Was it him? The high-angled cheeks, pointed chin, the eyes that showed nothing of caring or human kindness. Was he the one?

The program went on to other news. For some people, there was other news. For Tripp, nothing else mattered. The phone rang again, and he answered it quickly, thinking it must be Detective Walsh.

"Mr. Tripp," said the very recognizable voice of Rowena Crawford, "that man they showed on the news—"

"Yes," he interrupted, "I saw him."

"He's the one."

"The one?" Tripp asked, unsure of what she meant.

"He's the one I saw trying to smother Paige, the man who wrote the letter."

Tripp sat back down, feeling the weight of her words.

The night was going to be a long one.

Unable to sleep, Daniel turned on the television.

Watching a few minutes of an old movie or a talk show sometimes made him drowsy enough to shut down his senses and allow him to rest. It was too early for the talk shows. The late news was on, finishing the last few minutes of its broadcast.

His mind was on Pierce, the money, and Lydia. Each in his or her own way was a problem Daniel could worry like a sore tooth. He thought about how to deal with them, carefully listing in his mind the steps he needed to take. Focusing on the goal. Letting nothing interfere or distract. Focus.

He was focusing hard when he saw Jack's picture on TV. All his attention shifted, centering on the weasel-like face before him, and the words of the reporter detailing this "late breaking story." He listened, and heard the clang of steel bars threatening in the prison of his mind. Every word mattered, things they said, and things they didn't say. He listened.

They didn't say the babies had been found.

Maybe, if he hurried, there might still be time.

Daniel left immediately, not bothering to lock the apartment. If the police knew about him, a locked door wouldn't stop them.

On the drive to Wrightwood, his exhaustion vanished. He was running on pure energy, chasing the lure of excitement. He wasn't afraid. Never was. He had only three moods: Excitement, thinking, and anger. Maybe only two. Anger was what excitement became when it got too high. Like it had with Jack.

What had Jack done to be found out? And what had he done to Daniel's plan? The thought was the center of Daniel's mind as he drove. Not the aching in his chest, back, and legs. Not the stars above him in the night sky. His mind worked at the immediate problem: Jack.

He was glad he'd killed him.

Traffic was light. Most people were home in bed. Lydia would be, he assumed.

Lydia. What to do about her?

He could take Paige and leave, but if Jack had done something stupid, if that something might lead the police to the cabin in Wrightwood ... It was better that Daniel settle with Lydia now.

He was ready. The gun was with him.

Missy Dunbar pulled at the polyester knit top. It was stuck on her head, the neck opening too narrow for her wide skull to pass through. She had to tug hard to get it off.

The action left her puffing for breath. She sat on the edge of her bed and unfastened the hooks of her bra. "Ooh," she sighed. That was better. Darn things never fit. She had to cut the metal stays out of them as soon as she brought them home from the store. They'd poke into her flesh, those jabbing metal stays, rubbing a raw spot under each breast. Missy's breasts were heavy, especially since Clayton, but satin soft. She let her hands slide over them now, freeing them from their confinement.

With her big toe, she punched on the TV. The set was close to her bed. She bent over, struggling to remove her pink socks, listening to another report about crime in America. They didn't have to tell her. It was sky high. That was why she and her husband moved to a small mountain community, to get away from the violence of the cities.

"Ed?" She turned to remind him of this fact, but he was asleep. More often than not, Ed was asleep before she came to bed. She wondered about that. Was he really so tired, or was he avoiding being intimate? She had been the one to avoid being touched for the first few weeks after Clayton was born. She'd been sore from those stitches, and the memory of childbirth was too strong in her mind. But now, it was Ed who didn't seem to have any interest.

Fleetingly, she wondered if Ed was having an affair. She'd have to watch him, look through his pockets, and maybe she'd lose some weight, too. She wasn't pregnant anymore, but her body didn't look much different. The bulge that had been baby was now just fat. Was that why Ed turned away and slept?

Oh, well. She crawled in beside him, plumped the pillows, and studied the anchorwoman on TV. That woman was pregnant, and look at all the money she was making. Her face looked puffy, like Missy's. Ed didn't understand how having a baby could change you. If a man had to carry a baby for nine months, and go through hours of labor, he'd—

A face came on the television screen that shut down Missy's nightly act of self-contrition and absolution. She sucked in her breath, stayed quiet holding it, and scrutinized the lank blond hair, blue eyes, and gaunt angles of the man in the photo.

"His name is Jack Kordera," said the anchorwoman, "and authorities want to question him for his possible involvement in the kidnapping of four infants from a La Cañada home day care, and the murder of the day care provider. The Sheriff's Department is asking for the public's help in locating this man."

The Sheriff's Department was asking for her help!

"Ed!" she yelled, shoving her sleeping husband with the well-padded butt of one meaty hand. "Ed, wake up. It's him! That's the man I saw next door."

She was so excited, her lungs wheezed when she drew in her next breath. "Why, that liar! I believed her story, and all the time I was right there with them. Ed, wake up, I tell you," she yelled, poking him harder. "Call the police. I found those kidnapped babies!"

It was after midnight when Daniel turned off the San Bernardino freeway to Highway 138, leading to Wrightwood. His car raced through the night-quiet streets. Dark houses stood back from the borders of trees and roads like faceless shadows. He felt their presence, and the unseen eyes of the watchers within them. The rest of the world was still . . . and Daniel was moving.

This night, he was rushing toward his future. His freedom.

When the money was his and he was safe in Bolivia, he would take a long rest, let his body grow strong again. There would be time for healing when all of this was over.

Pain stabbed at a point behind his left eye. Agonizing. He could smell it, a heat of burning metal, and taste the flavor of pain on his tongue—a lick of pure silver. He needed the pills, Demerol, but he'd thrown them away. Couldn't use them tonight. His mind needed to be clear. The pain would work for him, keep him alert.

He turned onto Lone Pine Canyon Road. Headlights off, furtive as the night . . . and saw the cordon of police, ambulance, and sheriff vehicles. The windows of the house shone with brightness. Every room.

They'd been found.

Keeping the car's headlights off, Daniel shifted into reverse, backed around the corner to the main road, and escaped into the covering dark.

Chapter Twenty-nine

Bedspread, blankets and pillows were kicked to the floor. A single sheet covered them. Jessa stared into the dark, watching the slow rise and fall of Dillon's chest, neck, and chin as he moved above her. His face was a blur, and his eyes, but she felt the warm brush of his kiss on her mouth, and the hard muscles of his back, where her hands touched.

He had asked to come home with her, and she had let him. Knowing what would happen. Wanting it.

Sex was a pleasure she'd learned to love. A need. Not for the sake of the man, but for herself. She'd learned that before she met Dillon. It didn't control and cage her, as it did many women, but she didn't deny it, either.

Her strength was that she knew her weaknesses.

"Touch me," she said to Dillon, "there."

He did.

And all of her flowed like rushing water to that point. Urgent. Shuddering. A heat cored within a heat, needing to break free. And the burst of it within her body, washing through muscles and flesh, a warmth spreading over her legs, belly, and arms.

Dillon pressed himself closer to her. Steadily, deliberately, his body moving in purposeful concentration.

The phone rang.

His breath was warm against her ear. "Don't."

She didn't.

It rang again, and the machine picked up, playing her recorded message.

They waited, like hovering wings, waited . . .

Until the jarring *beep,* and the intrusive voice of Detective Victor Raimondo from Desk Watch. "Jessa, pick up, dammit. We've got a lead on the missing babies. The caller says she recognized Jack Kordera from the news."

Jessa pushed herself free of Dillon and sat up, listening intently to every word. She grabbed for the phone.

"What else?" she asked. Hoping.

"Christ, Jessa. You've got to get down here. It's all coming together. The caller says she's seen the kids."

"What? She's seen them? Alive?" It was too much to believe without proof.

"Four babies," Raimondo repeated what the caller had told him, "matching the description of the kidnapped kids, and the pictures she saw on the news. They're living right next door to her."

"Be there in five minutes," Jessa said, hanging up.

She started pulling on her clothes.

"Hey," said Dillon. "Didn't you forget something?"

She looked back at him as she shoved her feet into her shoes. "Sorry," she said, running for the door. "I owe you. C'mon, let's go."

Her blood was up, her mind chasing down dark alleys, and there was a prize waiting at the end. *Four babies!* Alive.

God, could it really be true?

It had been two hours since the siege in front of the house on Lone Pine Canyon Road had begun. Police directives over loudspeakers gave clear instructions. "Put down your weapons and step out of the door in single file, hands above your head."

This request had met with no response from anyone inside the residence.

"You sure somebody's in there?" asked Detective Third Randall Boyd. He was on loan from Riverside County.

"I'm not sure of anything," said Jessa, "but I'm not taking a chance of hurting those babies."

Fifty armed officers, special units, and rescue vehicles waited until the S.W.A.T. Team maneuvered one of their men into a rear second-story bedroom window. A few minutes later, he called an "all-clear" from inside.

That was when they found the babies.

Jessa entered the house with a caution learned from a school of hard lessons. She'd seen cops shoot when everything seemed safe. Good cops. Men with wives and kids. When it came to her job, it wasn't part of her nature to be reckless, and she was careful now. Her weapon was drawn and held before her, safety off.

She went through the house slowly, assessing the security of each room by its level of danger: To her, to her team, to the babies. From upstairs, the sound of crying.

When she was positive the ground floor was secure, she moved to the second level. Others were behind her, officers in flak jackets, strung with the same cold wire of tension she felt. Scared.

The officer from the S.W.A.T. Team stood at the head of the stairway. "Over there," he said, pointing.

Jessa saw him, heard the words he told her, but looked beyond the man. Her attention was focused on the room at the end of the hall, where crying could be heard.

Please, God. Please, God. Please, God. She didn't say the words, but her thoughts were a litany. She was a cop, and had stopped believing in prayer when Amy Peterson died. Stopped wanting there to be a God. And yet . . .

She stepped into the bedroom, looked, and knew them at once. Chelsea Cole and Jennifer Richards.

Jessa crossed the room to Chelsea, lifted the baby's hand, and saw where the tip of her first finger had been severed. It wasn't the action of a tough, hard-bitten cop, or a detached, dispassionate professional; she leaned close and kissed the baby's hand.

The S.W.A.T. Team officer came into the room.

"The other two?" she asked. "Sydney? Paige?"

"Only them." He nodded at the babies in the cribs. "There's nobody else."

That denial was hard to bear. She'd wanted them all. Dreamed of giving these children back to their mothers, their families. Still dreamed of little Amy Peterson, and needed to assuage the guilt she felt— the guilt she'd always feel—with the act of saving these babies. All four.

Dillon came up beside her. One look at her face, and he seemed to know what she was thinking. "Don't be so hard on yourself, Jess. Whatever else happened here, we got two of them back. After so long, it's more than I'd dared hope for. We got two."

It wasn't good enough. She wanted all four.

The children were taken to Verdugo Hills Hospital in La Cañada. Reporters, and a bevy of the simply curious, gathered outside the emergency room doorway, waiting for information. Two officers stationed at the door kept them out of the main building.

Inside the emergency room, Jessa waited for the parents to arrive. They hadn't been notified until the children had reached the security of the hospital. Medical exams indicated that other than the damage to Chelsea Cole's finger, both babies appeared to be in good health.

Jessa had made the calls, first to Alix Cole, then to Susan and Mike Richards. She'd been able to tell each of them, "We found your baby. She's safe." Being able to do that was the second best thing that had happened in Jessa's life—the first being finding the babies.

Then, she'd had to make two more calls. She didn't want the parents of the other children, the ones still missing, to hear about this on the news. They had a right to hear the truth from her. Telling them had been hard. It was like saying their children were dead.

"But you found Chelsea and Jennifer," Diane Kendall had cried. "Where's Paige?"

"I'm sorry, I don't know."

A sound followed, like terrible pain that started deep in the gut and worked its way up to the throat. A sound Jessa would never forget, not if she lived forever and saw a hundred thousand deaths. It was the mourning cry of a mother keening for her child.

Carin Sayers hadn't been able to speak. She'd given the phone to her husband. While they were talking, Jessa had heard Zack shout, "No!" and then heard Carin Sayers scream.

"What happened? What was it?" she asked when Zack returned to the phone.

"What you heard was my wife trying to kill herself. She had a knife at her wrist, and she almost used it. If our daughter isn't found soon, I'm going to lose my whole family."

"Get her to a doctor," Jessa told him. "Tonight."

"I will," he promised.

But it didn't make Jessa's fear go away. Zack Sayers was right. If the other two babies weren't found soon, the loss would be more than the children. It would be the destruction of entire families, the marriages, and the weight of guilt Jessa would have to carry for the rest of her life. The nightmares. Like the ones of Amy Peterson.

She was lost in these dark thoughts when she heard a loud noise, looked up, and saw Alix Cole running down the hospital corridor. For once, Alix wore no makeup. Her hair wasn't combed. She was dressed in jeans, a faded sweatshirt, and tennis shoes. She looked vulnerable, real, and never better.

She grabbed Jessa's hand when she saw her. Alix's was ice cold. "Where is she?"

"In there." Jessa pointed toward the examination room.

"She's—is she all right?" It was clear that Alix had rushed here, uncaring or unaware of how she looked, but now she was hesitating before going into the room.

"You know about her hand," Jessa reminded her.

Alix nodded.

"Other than that injury, she's fine."

"I don't know what's wrong with me. Suddenly, I'm scared to see her."

"Come on," Jessa told her, "I'll go with you."

This woman had been through hell, Jessa thought, maybe even more than the others, because she'd been alone. Out of fear, she'd kept secrets, even from the investigators. Carin Sayers had become suicidal, but her husband had stopped her. All this time, Alix had been alone. Was that why she'd turned to the comforting arms of John Tripp?

The thought made Jessa feel sorry for the way she'd treated her. The woman had been hurting, exactly like the rest of them, but she had dealt with that hurt in a different way.

They walked through the double doors. A woman officer was holding eight-month-old Chelsea. Alix let go of Jessa's hand. She took a single step toward her daughter.

"She's grown so much. Look at her. Chelsea? Chelsea, honey . . . do you know me? It's Mama, baby. It's Mama."

Chelsea looked confused, as if she didn't know, didn't remember.

And then Alix rushed across the room and took her daughter into her arms. Hugging her. Kissing the baby's face, and the small maimed hand. Laughing. Crying.

Jessa cried, too, watching their reunion. Couldn't

help it. This moment was the most beautiful thing she had ever seen.

A few minutes later, Susan and Mike Richards joined them at the hospital, and the emergency room rang with the joyous sounds of happiness, relief, and love.

Chapter Thirty

John Tripp leaned back in his chair in Rowena's room at the Doubletree. The chair was balanced and rocking on two spindly legs.

"You keep doing that," she warned, "you'll pitch backwards."

He brought the chair level. "That's what my sixth-grade teacher used to tell me."

"Should have listened. Might not have cracked your head so much over the years."

Tripp had been in this room for the last two hours, learning what Rowena had seen, felt, and thought about the missing babies. He wasn't sure he believed in psychic ability—anybody's—but he liked this woman. She was a good sounding board for talking about the case. Everyone else was either too close to the circumstances, like the parents, or professionally involved, like Detective Walsh, or Max Grodin, Tripp's boss at PIC. Technically, Rowena could be said to be professionally involved, too, but he thought of her as different.

Different was the word. Not many people could make Tripp dismiss the main lead in a case and follow another, but Rowena had done it. All of the facts in the investigation pointed to Jack Kordera. He'd been identified by the next door neighbor in Wrightwood, Missy Dunbar. His picture was on the news. Walsh saw Kordera as the main suspect in the case.

Rowena didn't.

"That one's part of it, oh sure, but he's not the one who made it happen."

"How do you know that?" he challenged her.

"When he was smothering the baby, somebody pulled him away. Somebody stronger."

It made sense. "Not the woman," said Tripp, referring to Lydia, the suspect Missy Dunbar had described to the sheriff.

"Not her. Wouldn't be strong enough. There's somebody else. He's the one I've been seeing in my mind. Not his face, can't see that, but him—his presence." She moved her hands in quick, short, waving motions.

"Like ectoplasm?" asked Tripp. She amused the hell out of him.

"Like spirit," said Rowena, and she wasn't smiling.

"You expect me to look for a spirit?"

"He's flesh and blood."

"Not much of a lead."

"It's my job to find the spirit, yours to find the man."

She was actually serious. He'd heard enough. "Have you ever worked on a missing child investigation before?"

She nodded.

"And? You found the kid?"

"No, he was dead. I found the body."

Tripp felt like something stuck to the heel of a shoe.

"Okay," he gave in. "Tell me about the suspect."

The road crew found the corpse. While clearing the landslide debris from Angeles Crest Highway, one of the workers spotted something blue in the underbrush. A shirt. Rescue Unit brought up the body.

That was how Jessa learned Jack Kordera was dead.

She was at home, soft music playing on the stereo, the smell of roasting chicken and new potatoes coming from the kitchen. Dillon cooking. A cool breeze drifted from the open window. It was a quiet night, a nice evening away from work for them both, a reward to themselves for finding two of the babies.

It should have been wonderful, but Jessa couldn't relax.

"Jack Kordera's dead," she called into the kitchen, where Dillon was opening a bottle of wine. "Why?"

"Why not?" he hollered back. "What's the problem?"

"Kordera was the letter writer, the voice on the phone."

"Yeah?"

It didn't fit with how she imagined the kidnapper. "Who sent the package? The woman? The neighbor said the woman—Lydia Spencer—was small, thin, and pretty. Did she kill Kordera? Or was there someone else?"

That *someone else* lingered in Jessa's senses, like

the aroma of the roasting chicken and the sound of the music. It was her take on what happened.

"I don't believe Lydia killed Kordera."

"Why not?" yelled Dillon. "A woman can't pull a trigger as easily as a man? Come on."

"She could, but I don't buy it."

"Because?"

"Because I don't believe she's the kidnapper. That's the point."

Dillon thumped the wine bottle onto the counter. "You won't let it go, will you, Jess? This is the first night in nearly two months that we've got something to celebrate, and instead of being thrilled that we've got two kids back, and Kordera's dead, you're telling me we've been going after the wrong person. You want me to sit here and pick it apart. Is that it?"

"Lydia isn't smart enough, not from the way the neighbor described her. 'Not educated,' Missy Dunbar said."

"How smart do you have to be to steal a kid? You're looking for trouble that isn't there."

"Smart enough not to get caught. What about the package? Whoever sent it didn't leave a single fingerprint. Lydia's prints are all over the house. She's either dead, like Kordera, or she left damn suddenly, abandoning two babies, as if something, or someone, scared her."

Dillon came into the room. "What makes you think she didn't kill Kordera? She could have shot him and dumped the body when she left the house that afternoon. The neighbor said the woman was gone for at least an hour."

"That's just it," said Jessa. "The M.E.'s report claims Kordera died between 5 and 9 A.M. on the day the babies were found. Missy Dunbar's testimony placed Lydia at the residence until early evening, except for the period of time that afternoon when she was away from the house and Missy was with the children—from three till four o'clock. The landslide took place around 9:30 that morning. By 10:30, Angeles Crest Highway was closed to traffic. She couldn't have dumped the body that afternoon."

"Dammit, Jessa!"

"What's wrong?"

"This was supposed to be a celebration, remember? You're not ready to quit, even for a night, and celebrate anything. You're so tied up with this case, there's no room for anybody. I'm tired of trying to distract you."

She was hurt by his attitude. He was a cop; he should understand. "I don't want to be distracted, or stop thinking about them, not till they're all back."

"Right." He nodded. "I guess that's it." He walked toward the door.

"You're leaving?" she called.

"Yeah," he said, pausing at the open doorway. "The party's dead here. See you at work, Jessa. Maybe that's the only place we belong together."

She heard the soft click of the door shutting as he left.

And she wondered . . . if Lydia didn't kill Kordera, who did?

"Two of the babies kidnapped from the Campbell Day Care were discovered by the Sheriff's Department late last evening in an abandoned cabin in Wrightwood," said the correspondent on the morning news program. "A neighbor, Mrs. Missy Dunbar, recognized the television photo of suspect Jack Kordera, and notified authorities. The two remaining kidnapped children are still missing."

Two remaining! Where was Paige? And where was Lydia?

It didn't take Daniel long to understand what happened. Lydia had Paige. Somehow, she'd figured out that this child was the important one, the reason for it all. But how?

That didn't matter. There wasn't a damn thing he could do about it. She was gone, and so were all his plans.

"In an added twist to the story, workers from a road maintenance crew clearing Angeles Crest Highway yesterday uncovered the corpse of Jack Kordera, the primary suspect in the case. Kordera had been shot. Anyone with information concerning the two missing children, or the murder of Jack Kordera, is asked to please contact local authorities."

Daniel left the house and drove to work. It was important that everything seem normal. He wasn't concerned that Jack's body had been found. Jack had a criminal record, unlike Daniel. It would keep investigators busy for a long time.

Lydia was the real problem. She had Paige.

Without the baby, the game was over.

Consumed with thoughts of how to find her, Daniel pulled into the parking garage of Trans-Continental Bank. He drove to the eighth-floor level. His space was vacant. Pierce hadn't replaced him.

There would be questions from coworkers, some he couldn't answer. The main thing was to satisfy their curiosity. They didn't honestly care what had happened to him, but they would ask. Before he stepped out of his car and went inside the building, he formulated a story. By the time he walked through the office door, he believed it.

"Mr. Cantrell, you're back!"

"Hello, Ginny," he addressed the secretary in the outeroffice. She was young enough to make spring look faded, one of the temps who'd stayed on because Pierce liked being around pretty women. Pierce had never strayed from his marriage as far as Daniel knew, and Daniel was sure he knew everything about the man, but Pierce admired beauty.

"I've been so worried about you, I mean . . . we all have." Since her first week of employment at Trans-Continental, Ginny had made her infatuation with Daniel known to everyone in the office, but he continued his pretense of not noticing. Even if she had been his type, which she wasn't, he wouldn't have allowed a relationship to develop with anyone in the workplace. The area was too crucial to his plans.

"I'm all right, Ginny. Is Mr. Pierce in?"

"He is," she confided, "but he's in a terrible mood. You might want to wait until—"

"Ask if he'll see me now, will you?"

She looked unsure about this. "Oh, I wish you wouldn't. You heard about two of the kidnapped babies being found last night? His granddaughter wasn't one of them. He's been taking it out on everybody."

"Buzz him for me."

"Okay, but I warned you."

As Daniel had anticipated, Pierce told him to come in.

"Thank you, Ginny."

He walked through the double doors to the corridor and past his office to Harper Pierce's suite. The richly carved oak door was closed. He knocked.

He hadn't expected Pierce to yank open the door.

"Daniel, thank God! I've been waiting for you all morning. Come in quickly. We have to talk. And for God's sake, shut the door."

"Mr. Pierce, is something wrong?"

"What I'm about to tell you is strictly between us."

"Yes, sir. Of course."

Pierce's color was bad. He was pale, sweaty, and looked on the verge of a heart attack. "It's happened. I've had a call from the kidnapper. She's finally contacted me, asking for ransom. You've got to help me decide what to do."

She . . . Lydia!

Daniel's expression didn't change, but inside, where nobody could see, he was smiling. "Have you contacted the police? Who's the investigator on the case?"

"Detective Walsh from the Sheriff's Department," said Pierce. "And no, I haven't told anyone, except you. The call came this morning, through the bank's main number, someone insisting on talking to me. It took a while to get through all the barriers we set up for such things, but she stayed with it and eventually was put through to my office."

Daniel could imagine Lydia arguing with everyone from the lowliest assistant in bank transfers, to Ginny Poole outside Pierce's office. He would love to have heard the exchange between these two women, but right now, he needed to know what Lydia had said to Pierce.

He played his part. "It was a woman?"

"Can you believe it—yes, a damn woman."

Pierce was a sexist. To Daniel's sure knowledge, he was also a racist, an anti-Catholic, and bore a fear-based loathing for those in the grip of poverty. It had always worked to Daniel's advantage to know everything possible about his employers.

"What did she say? Did she ask for money?"

"She wanted two hundred thousand, by tonight."

He'd thought it would be more, but said, "That much?"

"It isn't the amount that's important. If it were me, instead of my granddaughter, I wouldn't give the woman a damned cent. But Paige is only a baby. For God's sake, I don't want to do anything to endanger her life."

"I think you should notify the Sheriff's Department." He knew Pierce wouldn't make that call, but it was important that the words were said, so that Daniel appeared to be on the right side of this. "They're trained in handling such situations. They're experts in—"

"Experts! Like the expert way they've bungled things so far? It's been two months, and the only reason two of the children were found was because a neighbor recognized Kordera's face from the news. The Police and Sheriff's Departments did nothing. I won't turn my granddaughter's life over to their hands—not when it's within my power to help her."

Daniel waited. He let the idea have time to become clear in Pierce's mind before he asked, "What do you want to do?"

Pierce didn't answer the question directly. Instead, he said, "Part of the finger of one child was cut off. Did you know that?"

"I hadn't heard. That's terrible. What kind of a monster would do such a thing to a baby?" It was a thought he wanted Pierce to dwell on.

They were silent. A moment later Pierce said, "I'm going to pay the ransom. God only knows what that woman might do to Paige."

"But, sir—"

"The money doesn't matter. She's my granddaughter, my flesh and blood. I'll pay it, and we'll get her back."

"I'm sorry to bring up the point, but this morning, on the drive over, I heard that they found the body of that man . . . what did you say his name was—Kordova?"

"Kordera," Pierce corrected him. "Jack Kordera. He was the one who called my daughter. Diane told me what he said to her. I'm glad the bastard's dead."

"But if this woman is the one who killed him, if she's capable of murder, then how do you know your granddaughter is still alive?"

"I heard Paige in the background. At least, I heard a baby."

Now was the moment Daniel had waited for. "How is the ransom to be delivered?"

"She gave me instructions, a place to drop off the money."

"You've decided to do this?"

"Yes. That child on the news, I saw her hand . . . what had been done to it. I can't let anything like that happen to my granddaughter."

"Then, let me help you, sir."

"What? This isn't your fight, Daniel. Believe me, you don't want to be involved."

"I am involved. And you're needed here, in case

this woman calls again. Anything could change. It's important that you be around to deal with her personally. Who else is there? The police? Your wife? Diane?"

Pierce reacted to each possibility as Daniel had known he would. There was no one else.

"Let me deliver the ransom money. I want to help."

Pierce's hesitation was palpable. "How could I ever repay you for doing this?"

"I'll think of something," said Daniel.

Pierce had the two hundred thousand withdrawn from his personal savings account. The money, stacks of twenties, filled a briefcase. Pierce handed over the briefcase to Daniel, with directions to the arranged drop-off location.

"Are you sure you want to go through with this?" Pierce asked. He had walked with Daniel to the parking garage, and the car. "It could be dangerous."

Daniel was enjoying playing the role of the hero. "Don't worry about me, sir. I'll be all right. I'm only dropping off the money."

"Don't take any risks," warned Pierce.

"No, I won't."

"Call me once you've made the drop-off."

Daniel nodded, and drove away.

He would call Pierce, but not after he'd left the money. It would be after he killed Lydia. When she was out of the way, he would deliver her new terms of negotiation . . . those he had planned for so long.

It was fate that Lydia had called Harper Pierce. She hadn't known Daniel worked for him. By calling, she had put her life in Daniel's hands. Now, he would willingly take it.

He took the freeway On ramp, moved into the fast lane, and set the cruise control. It was a long way to Barstow and a little town named Daggett.

Chapter Thirty-one

Daniel turned off I-40 and followed Hidden Springs Road. The drop-off for the ransom money was the Barstow-Daggett Airport. California poppies and blue-eyed grass bloomed along the green verge bordering the stretch of highway. It was the day after the vernal equinox, the first day of spring. This day marked another passage, the day Lydia would die.

Harper Pierce had agreed to meet the terms of the ransom. The briefcase containing two hundred thousand would be left in the shallow ravine outside the fence at the southeast corner of the airport property. Daniel followed Hidden Springs past the airport entrance, then west on the old dirt road toward Bristol Mountains and the Mojave River Wash.

The airport field was a huge concrete surface with row after row of long, open hangers. From the road Daniel could see an old DC-6 and a B-29 beside Pipers, homebuilts, and Cessnas. His attention was diverted by these only momentarily. He was looking for the southeast corner of the field, and the ravine.

He followed the dirt road past the main buildings, past the concrete tarmac and open field, to the end of the fenced tract. He stopped the car and got out. No one was around. The area was insolated, flat, and exposed. At the corner of the fence was a gully cut by the rush of water over the years, and four feet deep. He put the briefcase in this narrow depression.

The only sound was the sighing wind; the only witnesses, the ghostlike planes.

He got back in the car, made a U-turn, and drove to the gate of the airport parking lot, where he waited. Hidden Springs was the only road. If Lydia picked up the money, she would have to pass Daniel. And then he would follow her.

It was the beginning of a new season, the earth in flower, a time of rebirth. He was changing, too. After today, his life would never be the same.

For Lydia, the remaining moments of her life were counted in the steady heartbeat of the watcher, and the rhythmic pulse of Daniel's veins.

Lydia wished she had a gun. If Harper Pierce was waiting at the ransom point with a weapon, how could she protect herself? But Pierce wouldn't be there. She'd warned him she would kill Paige if he tried any tricks. She wouldn't, but he didn't know that. Still, she wished she had a gun.

Paige was like her kid, now. It was weird. Ever since they'd left the cabin in Wrightwood, Lydia had felt this closeness to the baby, as if they were in this together. In some way, they were both struggling for freedom. No, that wasn't true. Paige wasn't struggling for anything. She was happy enough with Lydia, like a mom and daughter. Lydia had no experience at such things. Her mother had been . . . it had been different.

Paige woke from her nap. Lydia changed the baby's diaper, then carried her around the cabin, showing her things out the window. It was pretty here, if you liked desert. Must be hell in the summer, but wildflowers were blooming now. The ground glistened with color. It was like a party, with bright balloons and ribbons in every shade of pink, yellow, red, and blue.

Lydia never had a birthday party.

Paige smiled at her.

What if she didn't give the kid away? What if she ran with her? They could be a family, the two of them. Who would know? It might be her only chance to have a family of her own.

And turn out like her mother? Scraping nickels and dimes together, bringing home men to pay the rent, and making the kid wish she'd never been born. Yeah, that would be a swell life. Paige deserved better.

"You've got a place to go home to," she told her. "You've got a mom and dad, sisters, and a fancy house with glass walls. You'll be okay."

Will I? thought Lydia.

It was time to pick up the ransom. She left the cabin and put the baby in the car seat beside her. If someone was watching the drop-off site, they wouldn't shoot if they saw Paige in the car. The baby was Lydia's insurance.

The plan she'd told Pierce was that she'd pick up the money, then phone him later to say where he could find the baby. That left her some leeway, a margin of safety. She'd leave Paige at the cabin in

Daggett, then, from someplace far away, she'd call Pierce and tell him where to get the kid. Paige would be all right. How much trouble could a fourteen-month-old get into, toddling around in a two-room cabin?

The answer didn't sit well, but Lydia ignored it and drove on.

She turned onto Hidden Springs Road and approached the Barstow-Daggett airport. The area surrounding the airport was flat ground, undisguised by tree or building. Flat, exposed land. Nothing to hide behind. No place for a gunman to wait. It was the perfect place for a ransom pickup.

Cautiously, she drove closer to the site. There was nothing there. No car. No gunman. No problem.

It was going to be easy, exactly as she'd planned. This was how it should happen. The money would be waiting for her, she'd get it, drive Paige back to the cabin, and she'd be on her way.

Make it be there, Lydia willed, as she veered across the road to where the airport property ended, and drove close to the fence and the narrow ditch. *Let it be there.*

It was. A black briefcase lay on its side along the bottom of the shallow ravine. She opened the car door, leaned out, and pulled the briefcase into the car. It wasn't heavy. She pushed the catches on either side of the padded leather handle, and released the lid. Inside, were ten stacks of one hundred twenty-dollar bills, five across and two deep. She counted one stack, twenty thousand in each. It was all there.

There wasn't time to do more than glance at it. The money looked genuine. Lydia shoved the briefcase under the driver's seat, made a turnaround, and headed back along Hidden Springs Road toward the Desert Flower Motel. She was thinking of April in Hawaii, or maybe England. She'd never been to England.

He watched her as she passed the airport. She was smiling, not thinking of Daniel, or Logan, or Gage. He had started the engine when he'd spotted her a few minutes earlier, on her way to pick up the ransom money. His car had been idling in neutral. Waiting. Now, Daniel shifted into drive.

He left the fenced parking lot, turned in the direction Lydia's car had taken, and followed at a distance. He was three blocks behind her, but he could see her turn signal flash when she made a right onto I-40 and drove out of his view.

Now, he floored it, hurrying to reach that corner. At the stop, he eased the car forward, and saw Lydia's old Dodge about a half-mile down the highway, making a left into the parking lot of the Desert Flower Motel.

Daniel waited at the corner. There was no hurry. Let her get settled, feel safe. He knew where to find her. Five minutes went by. Ten.

Slowly, with the patience of a man who knew his future, Daniel turned onto I-40, drove the half mile, and entered the parking lot of the motel.

He looked, but Lydia's car wasn't there.

The parking lot stretched the length of the motel complex, with marked spaces before each door of the building. There were less than fifty units. He circled the area a second time, and to his horror, noticed an unmarked exit on the northeast side of the lot.

All the time he'd wasted! If this led to the main highway. If she'd gotten away . . .

He drove to the exit, saw it was a dirt road, and began to hope. Maybe. The access road was a narrow, one-way passage through an isolated desert retreat. It was nearly half a mile before he saw the first cabin. And he knew it was going to be all right.

The first cabin was empty. He got out of the car, looked around, found nothing, got back in the car, and drove on. It wasn't tourist season. The place was deserted. He drove to the second cabin, and the third. She was here, he knew it. When he saw Lydia's car parked in front of the fourth cabin, Daniel felt a heat of excitement run through him. He was always this way before a kill. Like the nurse. Like Christine Campbell. Like the way he'd felt when he drove to the psychic's house. He was ready.

He parked far enough away from the cabin that Lydia wouldn't hear the sound of the car's engine, or the noise of the driver's door opening. She wouldn't hear a warning of any kind. Let her imagine she was safe, until it was deadly clear she wasn't. He would walk in, put a bullet between her pretty eyes, and—

The cabin door opened. Lydia stepped into view. Screamed, "No!" and ran.

Daniel lifted his arm and took aim, but she zigzagged across the rough ground of the high desert. She ran, screaming for help, far ahead of him and running for her life. He didn't fire. In this open terrain, even with the silencer, the sound would carry. He could risk only one shot, and it must bring down the kill.

"Help me!" Lydia cried, her voice ragged with terror. "Somebody help me!"

300

There was no one to hear her. Only Daniel.

He chased her, stumbling once, getting back on his feet and running. She ran faster than Daniel, weighed less, but her heart beat harder than his, from fear. She had more to lose. He would catch her.

"Logan, don't!" she shrieked. Running. Her head thrown back and her thin arms pumping the wind at her sides. Needing the earth to open up and swallow her. Needing the sky to lift her into its vacant eye. Needing—

He fired.

The back of Lydia's head burst open, spewing bits of white bone and red pulp. Her body ran two more steps . . . three . . . then dropped. It fell like a jointed doll whose strings had been cut.

Daniel approached cautiously. He wedged the toe of his shoe under the body and rolled it over. There wasn't much left of Lydia's face. The bullet's entry hole had shattered the back of her head, but its exit was much wider. Her face had blown apart, creating a bloody maw that looked like a hideous mouth, red-bordered with puffy scarlet lips.

He stared at her, and a plan evolved in his mind. Lydia's body must never be found. No one would suspect him of the kidnapping and murder, because he would make it look as if Daniel Cantrell were dead, as if Lydia had killed him.

Harper Pierce had sent his assistant to Daggett, and knew where to look for him if something happened. Sooner or later, someone would check the motel, and the cabins. It was important to leave the right evidence—his blood and traces of his body hair to be found in the trunk of Lydia's car. He'd leave his car

301

parked here, as if he'd found her, and then never driven away. Couldn't. Because she had killed him.

In reality, he had come here to kill Lydia, and had brought along a large plastic tarp for the body. What he hadn't known until now was that she would be his alibi. It was hard work, going back for the tarp, wrapping the body, and hauling it over his shoulder to the back seat of Lydia's car. The Dodge's door was unlocked. The corpse made a *whooshing* sound as it hit the seat. Then, he retraced his steps into the desert, brushed away both sets of footprints, and covered Lydia's blood with dirt.

Everything had gone much better than he'd imagined. It was time to call Pierce. After a moment to catch his breath, Daniel headed back to the cabin to get Paige. The door stood open, as Lydia had left it. The cabin was small, only two rooms, a bedroom and small bath. It didn't take Daniel long to see the problem.

Paige was gone.

Chapter Thirty-two

He looked everywhere. He called to her and listened for the sound of crying, but there was no answer, no trace of the baby. While he was chasing Lydia, killing her, and carrying the body to the car, Paige had disappeared.

If Paige had been with Lydia at all.

Now that he thought of it, he wasn't positive she'd ever been here. He hadn't seen her. Maybe Lydia didn't bring her here. Maybe she stashed the kid somewhere else, in case someone gave her trouble. *Someone like me,* thought Daniel.

How far could a fourteen-month-old baby wander? He ought to be able to see her, if she was here. Kids made noise. He should hear her cry. But he heard nothing, and he saw only desert.

Time was running out. Pierce wouldn't wait long before concern for his granddaughter's safety would drive him to contact the police. Daniel needed to call him soon. Now. He needed to do it now. If he could only find Paige . . .

Frustrated. Angry. Lydia had cost him everything. And then, the idea unfolded as effortlessly as night. None of it mattered. Pierce assumed Lydia had the child. He'd paid the ransom to get his granddaughter back. Daniel didn't have to prove it, and he didn't have to find Paige. Let her die wherever Lydia had hid her, if it came to that. What difference did it make to him?

To Daniel, the answer was *none*.

He brought a suitcase from his car and put it in Lydia's. He laid the briefcase full of money beside it. In the cabin, he found her purse and keys. He took them. Lydia's suitcase was on the floor, still packed, as if ready for her to grab at any minute and run.

She wouldn't run anymore. Never again.

Everything that was hers, Daniel took with him. He drove Lydia's car. His leather gloves would leave no fingerprints on the steering wheel. He took a back road toward Los Angeles, avoiding the main highway, driving through Lenwood, Hodge, and Helendale. Outside of Victorville, he dumped Lydia's body in a shallow canyon along a barren strip of land between George Air Force Base and Ord Grande. Her corpse couldn't be seen from the road. It lay hidden within the crumbling rock walls of a gouge in the canyon.

He kept the purse, helping himself to the money in her wallet—seventy-six dollars. When he reached the city of Victorville, he drove to the alley behind an apartment complex, found the apartment's trash dumpster, and threw the purse inside.

From Victorville, Daniel turned onto Highway 18 and headed for Pearblossom. There, he pulled up to a phone booth outside a gas station. Time to call Harper Pierce.

It was answered on the first ring with an edgy, "Yes?"

"It's Daniel," he said. "I'm in Daggett." There was no point in telling Pierce where he really was.

"You've got her? You have Paige?"

"No. Not yet."

"Did you leave the money where I told you? Maybe you did something wrong. I should have gone myself. I should never have trusted anyone else to do this. You made a mistake, and my grandchild's life may be—"

"I didn't make a mistake. I left the money in the right place. I've spoken to the woman."

"You spoke to her? How?"

"She left a note on the fence, in the place where the ransom was to be turned over. It said to go to a phone booth in Daggett and wait for her call. I did that."

"And?"

"And, she wants more."

"More! What is this?"

"It gets worse," said Daniel. "She's asking for a transfer of funds from the bank, a large transfer."

Daniel waited, giving Pierce time to let this news sink in.

"Tell me everything," said Pierce.

While cars whizzed past him on the highway, Daniel told Pierce the details of the kidnapper's demands for Paige's ransom. The money was to be transferred by international wire to an unnamed numbered account in Bolivia.

"I wouldn't have thought the woman I spoke to could think of something like this," said Pierce. Then he asked the question Daniel had been waiting to hear. "How much?"

"Two million."

"What! That's impossible. I haven't got that kind of money. Did you tell her? Did you explain that I—"

"Sir, she said, 'Tell him to borrow it from the bank, against his properties.' I don't know how she did it, but she knows the value of your home, and of your other holdings in real estate. She listed the net worth of your shares in the stock market, and quoted the exact figures in your savings accounts and IRAs. She says the wire transfer must take place today, or Paige dies."

"This can't be happening," said Pierce. The sound of anger was gone from his voice. What was left was a tremor of shock and disbelief.

"I don't want to press you, sir, but there isn't much time," Daniel reminded him. "She pointed out to me that Bolivia is four hours ahead of us, and that there is only one international wire per day into the country. That's two hours from now."

"How could she know so much?"

"I don't know, sir."

"Two hours! You expect me to raise two million dollars in two hours! It can't be done. Even if I knew I could trust her—and I have absolutely no reason to believe that I should—I couldn't possibly raise that amount in so little time."

Daniel didn't push. He waited. Give Pierce a chance to think about the consequences of saying no. Give him time to remember what happened to Chelsea Cole, and Jack Kordera. Keep the baited line dangling before him . . . until he bit.

306

"What do you think, Daniel? You spoke to her. Did she sound like the kind of person who'd—"

"I think she'd kill the child." He said it bluntly, leaving that hard thought for Pierce to mull in his mind.

"And if I raise the money?"

"After she knows the wire transfer has been made, and checks to make sure it's valid, she said she'd call me at this number and advise us where to find your granddaughter."

"You think I should do it?" Daniel had never heard Harper Pierce sound so powerless.

"I wouldn't want to speculate on something so important."

"Dammit, man. I need your counsel. In my place, what would you do?"

"I think it's Paige's only chance."

There was a break in the conversation, a lull while Pierce seemed to be considering his options. Daniel watched the cars go by on the highway. He began counting them. Five. Six. Seven.

"All right. When she calls again, tell her I'm going through with it. She'll have the money. It'll be in the account today. Tell her that."

"Sir."

"What is it?"

"The account number, let me give it to you."

It was that simple.

"Jack Kordera's dead," said Diane. "I heard it on the radio just now, when I was making coffee."

"Yes," said Rowena, sounding unsurprised.

"You knew," said Tripp. It was a statement, not a question.

"I've been wrong about things before, but yes," Rowena admitted, "I knew."

"Why didn't you say something?"

Her eyes were cool, defiant. "Would you have believed me?"

"I damn sure would've liked the chance."

"Good," she said. "Maybe we're getting somewhere."

"Yeah, we're getting somewhere," said Tripp. "Getting crazier and crazier."

Diane stood between them, looking from one to the other. "What does it mean? My little girl's still missing, and this man's dead. I thought he was the one who had her. What's happened?" She turned to Rowena. "You said you knew this. If you know anything else, I want you to tell me."

"She's waiting till she hears it on the news," said Tripp, feeling argumentive.

"There is something," Rowena had their attention.

"I want to know," said Diane, "even if she's dead. I want to know."

Suddenly, Tripp wasn't sure he wanted to hear this. If Rowena said that Paige was dead, he wasn't convinced Diane could handle it. All he needed right now was another suicidal mother, one like Carin Sayers. "Hey, look. I don't know where you get these things, but—"

Rowena stood. "You said you wanted the chance to believe me. Remember?" She moved around the room distractedly. "Do you have a map of California?"

"What?" Tripp didn't have a clue abut where she was heading with this.

"A map, a big one, please. My eyes aren't too good on little-bitty print."

"I have an Automobile Club map," said Diane.

"Nothing bigger?"

Diane shook her head. "No, I—"

"That's all right, honey. Go get it. Mr. Tripp can help me read it." She gave Tripp a glance that made him feel as see-through as glass.

When Diane went to find the map, he asked Rowena, "What's the deal?"

The look on her face startled him. It was so intense, as if he could see the movement of her thoughts under her skin. She was pale and perspiring.

"I've been seeing the baby, right along."

He listened without interrupting.

"A woman had her, drove her someplace in a blue car, away from the mountains. I saw stars, a dreamy night of them, then a long stretch of black, nothing but dark highway."

Diane returned, carrying the map. Tripp motioned to her to put it down and keep silent. She pulled a chair close to Rowena. The fear in Diane's eyes reflected the startling vision of the psychic. Rowena was pale and perspiring. Diane looked ready to crack.

Tripp felt the tension in the room. Oppressive. Powerful. Threatening.

"She took Paige into the desert, drove through that flat wilderness. Plants growing. Wildflowers. And stars shining above them, brighter now. And . . ."

"What?" Tripp prodded. "What do you see?"

Rowena turned and stared at him. "Airplanes, rows and rows of airplanes."

He stood, walked to the table, and spread open the map. "An airport?"

"Yes, I think . . ." She hesitated. Then said, "There were open buildings. They looked like upside-down L's. I saw long tracks of them, on a field of concrete."

For Tripp, Rowena's words triggered a memory. One year, on the impulse of a friend, he had spent a miserable weekend prospecting in a remote area called Devils Playground, between Barstow and East Mojave. On the way there, they'd passed a town called Daggett. That was where he'd seen the airport, with its wide expanse of concrete, and row after row of hangers running across the tarmac.

"I think you're talking about the Barstow-Daggett airport." He showed them where it was on the map.

Rowena let her finger trace the line from Wrightwood to Barstow, and then to Daggett. "Yes. It's right. That's where we'll find her. Come on, Mr. Tripp. I'll need you to drive. I'm not so good at navigating anything beyond country roads. We'll have to hurry."

"Hang on." Tripp was backing away from this, putting on the brakes. "You expect me to drive two and a half hours so you can look at this place?"

Rowena met his gaze. "A few minutes ago, I asked if you would have believed me if I'd told you about Jack Kordera's death. You said you would have liked the chance. Remember?"

"Yes, but—"

"I'm giving you that chance right now. I can see the baby. I know where to find her. You take me there, and we'll bring her home to her mama."

He didn't want to make the drive—good God, two

and a half hours—but couldn't think of any argument strong enough to match Rowena's challenge. And if she was right . . .

Diane looked depressed.

"Okay," he gave in, "we'll go."

Rowena had the grace not to look triumphant.

"Could I use your phone?" he asked Diane. "I've got to call my office, tell them where I'll be. Grodin will love this one."

"Tell him there's been a sighting," Rowena suggested.

He did. Grodin was thrilled to hear it. He just didn't know what kind.

When he came back into the room, Diane was standing by the front door, sweater on, purse in hand. "I'm coming with you."

"Not this time," said Rowena. "There might be a phone call. You need to be here to answer it."

"A call?"

Rowena nodded, took Diane's purse from her, and laid it on the table. "You stay here, honey. I'll find your girl for you. Trust me."

Determination died in Diane's eyes. Tripp saw it happen. Her shoulders slumped, and a slackness of muscle pulled at the attractive face. It was hard to witness, pitiful.

They left, supplied with a road map, Paige's musical lamb, and Rowena's visions.

He took the 2 to the 210, and headed for the Antelope Valley Freeway. It was going to be a long drive. For a while, he was silent, but then he asked Rowena the question that was bugging him. "Why didn't you let Diane come along? Did you see the disappointment in her face?"

311

"I know, but I couldn't let her come with us."

"Why not?"

"I saw her baby, stretched out on that desert, lying still as death."

Tripp almost veered into the next lane. "Jesus! Warn me when you're gonna say something like that. The kid's dead?"

"I don't know," said Rowena, "but I think we'd better hurry."

Everything of Tripp believed her. He pressed his foot heavier on the accelerator, and floored it.

Chapter Thirty-three

Daniel drove straight through for the next two hours, from Victorville to Los Angeles. Time enough for Pierce to have arranged for the international wire. He stopped at a phone booth outside a 7-Eleven in Inglewood, and placed a call to Tomas Villemarquez, his contact at Bank of Bolivia.

"Did the wire transfer come through?" he asked Villemarquez.

"Yes, my friend, one hour ago."

Daniel was impressed. Pierce had worked fast. "Any flags on the transfer? Any qualifiers or holds on the money?"

"No, it cleared immediately. I followed your instructions, withdrew all of it from the numbered account, deducting my share, then placed the remainder into the new holding account you established in the other bank."

Villemarquez gave Daniel the numbers and bank branch for the new account. The branch was two hundred miles from the main offices of Bank of Bolivia. Villemarquez knew the location, but only Daniel had access to the funds.

"You have done me a favor, Tomas. I don't forget such things."

"I have been paid well for my services."

"Yes," said Daniel, "but I will pay you again, when I arrive."

Daniel was not a man comfortable with being obligated to anyone. He would discharge his debt to Tomas when he reached Bolivia, through the barrel of a gun.

He made one more long distance call, this time to the bank branch which held his numbered account. He checked the amount. Tomas had been more than generous to himself than Daniel had instructed. He'd expected that. The two hundred thousand dollars he carried in the briefcase more than made up the difference. It gave him all the more reason to pay Tomas a visit, and justified that would have happened anyway.

Now, there was nothing to stop him. Only one last thing to do.

The 7-Eleven was in a rough area of town. Daniel felt safer here, less chance of a cop dropping in, or someone recognizing him. He bought a packet of razor blades, a box of Band-Aid bandages, and a tube of Neosporin Ointment. Then he drove to an empty lot.

With the car facing the street and the trunk lid up, so passersby couldn't see what he was doing, he held his arm over the inside of the trunk, and made the cut. His arm bled profusely. When there was enough, he spread the ointment over the cut, opened the box of bandages and taped the wound.

Next, he pulled hair from his arms, chest, and the back of his head. He scattered these over the inside surface of the trunk, as if his body had been there—injured or murdered by Lydia.

He wanted the police to find the car. When they did, it would look as though Lydia had killed him, disposed of his body, and taken a plane to Bolivia. After a while, no one would continue looking for him. He would become one more murder victim in a city that bred homicides like roaches behind the cracks of a wall.

He put down the trunk lid, got back into his car, and drove to LAX. The next flight to Bolivia was in exactly one hour. It would leave him just enough time to present his passport and visa, before leaving the country.

Bolivia. The sound of it sang in his mind like a caged bird. When he got there, the cage would be opened, and Daniel would be free.

Diane waited for the phone to ring. She sat beside it and stared at the receiver, as if willing the call to happen. Rowena had told her someone would call, but the phone didn't ring.

Charles would be home soon, with the children. He picked them up after school. Diane had stopped doing that. Since Rowena arrived, she'd spent as much time as possible with the psychic, letting everything else go. Even her children. They were safe. Other people looked after them. But Paige . . . Paige. Who looked after her?

She heard Charles' car in the driveway, and the noisy voices of her daughters. Emily and Noelle ran into the house.

"Mama, Mama, Emmers hit me."

"Did not," said Emily.

"Did so," Noelle insisted. "See."

There was a small red mark, no bigger than a nickel, on Noelle's wrist. Diane bent over her three-year-old's hand and kissed it. Noelle was a baby, too. She needed her mother.

A flood of sudden tears rushed from somewhere that had been held back and restrained too long in Diane. She pulled Noelle onto her lap and hugged and kissed the small, adorable face. Warm, salty tears washed over Diane's cheeks.

"Don't cry, Mama," said Noelle, her wide eyes full of concern. "It's all better."

"I'm sorry," cried Emily, clearly upset to see her mother's tears. She threw herself onto Diane's lap, too. Needing her mother's attention—as much as her missing sister did. Needing to be noticed, cared about, loved.

Diane held them both, her little girls, no longer her *other* children. It had taken her a long time to remember them, to recognize their needs, as well as Paige's. She was mother to them all. From this minute, she'd begin to act like it.

"What's happened?" asked Charles. It was obvious something had changed.

"I've come home," said Diane, taking his hand. "I've been living as if I'm far away from you, and I've been gone too long. You've taken care of everything, work, the girls, making a life for us, while I—"

He stopped her with a kiss. "If you're really back with us, part of our lives again, that's all I want. I don't need apologies. I just need you."

She felt as if she'd been lost, and finally found her way. This was her home, her family. This man, these children. Whatever else happened, this was where she belonged.

She wasn't forgetting Paige, could never do that, but from this moment, Diane made the conscious choice to let life go on.

"I love you," she said to her husband. It was the first time she'd said those words in two months.

"I love you, too."

It was a new beginning. If they were lucky, their love for each other, and for their children, would be strong enough to hold them together.

"Mama loves *me*," said Noelle with a greedy little scowl on her face.

"I do, munchkin," said Diane. "And Emily," she added, "and Daddy."

"Mama, are you okay, now?" asked Emily. The expression on her face said she wasn't talking about just the tears.

"Yes, baby. Everything's going to be okay. I promise."

And for the first time since all that had happened, she believed it was true.

"She's been here; I feel it."

Rowena got out of Tripp's car and walked along the Hidden Springs Road. The highway turned into a dirt track, after the entrance to the airport. She stood in the center of the road, held the toy lamb, and closed her eyes.

"You're going to get hit by a truck!" yelled Tripp. "Keep closing your eyes in the middle of the highway. See what happens."

"Hush!" she called back to him.

The child was out here, she knew it—not in this place, but close by. She could feel it, hear Paige's breathing, get inside the child's mind, and—

"Get out of the road!" Tripped yelled again, louder this time.

She opened her eyes and saw a gravel-loaded truck bearing down on her. A hand grabbed her arm and yanked. She was pulled to the side of the rad, just as the truck roared by.

Tripp was glaring at her. "There are easier ways to kill yourself."

"I didn't hear it."

He looked incredulous. "You didn't hear that engine? You'd better get your ears checked. Who saves you when I'm not around?"

She ignored the question. "I was thinking of something else."

"That kind of thinking is bad for your health."

"I was trying to think of where Paige might be. She's out here. Not far away. Could we drive around?"

"Drive around?" He looked at her as if she were crazy, and then said, "Sure, I've got nothing else to do. We've only been trapped in that car for the last two and a half hours. What's a little more? Where do you want to go?"

"Drive around town," she told him. "I want to have a look."

"A look?"

She nodded. "And thanks," she said, "for dragging me away from the truck."

He sighed, got back in the car, and drove them toward the main boulevard of Daggett. There was only one motel in town.

"Stop there," she said.

Tripp pulled into the parking lot of the Desert Flower. Rowena hurried from the car. He trailed her to the motel office. "I'll ask the questions when we get inside," he said. "All right?"

"That'll be fine."

The desk clerk was a young man whose badge said he was Matt Parker. "Hi there." He greeted them with a lopsided grin. "You folks needing a room?"

"No, but we need some information," said Tripp.

"Go ahead, shoot," said Parker. "Nothing else going on."

"We're trying to locate some people for an insurance benefit."

"You mean you've got money for them?"

"That's right. A woman and a baby girl. They've been seen by a couple of other people out this way, and we thought you might have rented them a room?"

"When are we talking about?"

"The last couple of days."

"No, I don't think so. Let me look at the ledger."

Rowena heard their conversation, but she heard something else, too. She was still holding Paige's toy lamb, and she heard the baby—not with her ears, but with the hearing of her mind. Paige was somewhere around here. She was close.

"There was a woman with a baby boy," Matt Parker offered.

"You're sure it was a boy?" Tripp asked.

"Oh, yeah. I heard the mother talk about him."

"Well, thanks." He moved toward the exit.

"Wait!" Rowena grabbed Tripp's arm. "She's here. I know it. She's somewhere in this place."

Rowena felt panic grow within her, hear the quiet breathing, and the beating of Paige's heart. She felt danger. The child was alone. But where?

"The woman with the baby," Tripp confronted the clerk, "which room was it?"

The boy's eyes looked wary. He backed a step away. "I probably shouldn't be telling you that."

"It's all right. We're not here to hurt anybody," said Tripp.

But the damage was done. Rowena didn't have to be psychic to get a quick sense of this boy's mind. She'd been too anxious, and she'd scared him.

"I don't know what's going on here," said Parker, "but I don't want to say nothin' else."

"She's not in the room. She's in the desert." Rowena felt sure of it. "Come on," she pulled Tripp away from the desk. "Hurry. We have to find her. She's alone out there."

They got in the car. "Where do I go?" asked Tripp.

"I don't know." She glanced around the parking lot, and at the street before the motel. There was nothing. Nothing. Paige was lost. It was a desolate wilderness and the child was alone in it.

And then, as if through her strong connection to Paige, through the toy, and through her heightened senses, Rowena turned her head and saw something she'd overlooked. The access road.

She ran, not waiting for Tripp.

"Where are you going?" he shouted.

"This way," she cried. "Help me. She's over here."

She ran, heart shuddering, seeing the image in her mind of that place where Paige lay. There was death there, and terrible danger.

"Paige!" Tripp shouted. "Paige, where are you?"

Rowena ran in silence, knowing the baby would not, or could not answer.

Tripp ran toward the cabins, toward the one with the car parked in front. Rowena turned the other way, toward the desert.

She ran across the hard ground, her breath labored, her chest heaving with the strain of drawing air. *Where are you?* she wanted to scream.

The desert was blinding, and a sea of silence. It was overwhelming. The baby could be anywhere. Mile after mile stretched before her, and there was no way of seeing a little lost girl.

In frustration, Rowena's hand squeezed the toy, touching the metal key. It produced a sound. A single note. She wound the music box, and let the tune play *Mary Had A Little Lamb*.

In that magical moment, Paige Kendall stood, woken by the familiar sound, and walked halting baby steps across the desert, arms reaching for the toy, Rowena, and home.

Chapter Thirty-four

Harper Pierce began putting the pieces together, soon after Paige was found and returned home. The money was gone, and so was Daniel. As soon as he knew his granddaughter was safe, Pierce phoned Detective Walsh, telling her that he'd been forced to pay a ransom. Then he paid a visit to PI John Tripp.

"You're the one who found the child," Pierce told Tripp.

"With the help of Rowena Crawford."

"I don't hope to ever understand such ideas as spiritual connections, but I am impressed with the work you've done. You succeeded in rescuing the baby, when the entire Sheriff's Department's efforts failed. That's why I've come to you now. I have my doubts about Daniel Cantrell, and questions that won't go away."

"Like?"

"Daniel knew how to arrange international wiring transfers."

"Was that the means of delivering the ransom?"

"Yes. Someone without banking experience wouldn't have known there was only one time per day for all international wires to South America. How did the suspect come by that knowledge unless . . ."

"Unless she was working with Daniel?" said Tripp.

"Exactly."

"I don't know if Detective Walsh has made you aware of this," Tripp said, "but forensics found traces of Cantrell's blood and body hair in the trunk of the suspect's car."

"They think the woman killed him?"

"It looks that way. Her car was found at the airport. Daniel's car was still at the cabin."

"But they haven't found his body, have they?" said Pierce.

Tripp could see where Pierce was heading with this. "You think Cantrell was part of it?"

"I think he planned the whole thing. He was my personal assistant, but I was a damned fool to have trusted him. I confided in the man, gave him certain information he must have found useful. I told him about the psychic. He offered to fly to West Virginia, to warn her to stay out of Diane's life. God knows what would have happened if he'd found the woman."

Tripp's hands went cold at the thought. After what they'd gone through together, finding the child and bringing her back, Rowena had become a friend to Tripp, a good one. She had gone home to West Virginia after Paige was found.

"Everything you've told me is suspicious, I'll grant you," he told Pierce, "but it's not enough evidence to accuse the man of kidnapping and murder. If he did all this, why did he wait so long to arrange the ransom?"

"He was being careful, that's his way. And part of the time, he wasn't able to contact me."

"Why not?"

"I told you he went to West Virginia."

"Yes, but he never saw Rowena."

"He was on the way to her house when his car hit a hay wagon. He was nearly killed in the accident, and spent the next three weeks in the hospital. Two of those weeks were in a coma."

"You believe his story?" Tripp asked.

"He looked like hell when I saw him, bruises under his eyes, his face gaunt, and walking like a man who'd been badly hurt."

Tripp kept his reaction to himself, but if this was true, Cantrell's accident accounted for an unexplained block of time. Tripp had never understood why the kidnapper had waited so long to make a ransom demand.

"It's possible," he admitted, "but not proof."

"I may never have your kind of proof," said Pierce, "but I know what my gut tells me. He got away with it all. He's smart, a near genius, that's why I picked him as my assistant. He never had any friends among our other employees, the kind of man for whom work became an obsession. I thought I understood him; I'm a little that way myself. He's alive all right, and living in Bolivia on my two million."

Pierce left, and Tripp let the confusion about Daniel Cantrell's whereabouts disappear with him. Detective Walsh had searched Cantrell's apartment and found nothing to indicate the man had planned on leaving the country. His clothes were still in the closet and chest of drawers. His suitcase was still on the shelf, unpacked. Even his toothbrush was in a glass on the bathroom sink.

Pierce was desperate, two million was a lot of money. In his place, Tripp might be turning victims into criminals, too.

It was later that day—Tripp was stretched out on his sofa in slovenly comfort, his feet propped on its well-padded arm—that he remembered the package with Chelsea's fingertip. It had been mailed from somewhere in downtown Los Angeles. Los Angeles . . . where Daniel Cantrell worked.

"You're home. I've been trying to reach you."

Hearing her voice again brought an instant flood of memories to Tripp. "Alix, how are you?"

"Better now. This house doesn't feel unhappy anymore. It's made such a difference, having my daughter back. I have news about Chelsea, something I wanted you to know."

"What?"

"When she was examined at the emergency room, the doctor said I should take her to a specialist, about her finger. I did, and you know what he told me?"

Tripp wasn't sure he wanted to hear this. He remembered staring at the severed tip of that finger lying in the box.

"What did he say?"

"He said it will grow back."

"What will?"

"The tip of her finger. If a baby under a year old loses the first joint of a finger, the body replaces it. The fingertip grows back."

"Are you sure?" He couldn't believe it.

"That's what he said. He's an expert in pediatric orthopedics, the specialist everyone recommended."

"I've never heard of such a thing."

"Neither had I, but it's happening. It only works with infants. He showed me where the tip of her finger had been severed, and how much has already grown back."

"That's great news. I'm happy for you, Alix. Happy for Chelsea, too."

There was a long pause in the conversation. It was the place where Tripp should have asked if he could come see her, but he didn't. Whatever had been between them had more to do with getting through the trauma of the kidnapping than it did with love.

"Take care of yourself," she said.

"You, too."

It was over, ending as abruptly as it had begun. In one moment, Alix was still a possibility for him, and in the next, she was gone. He regretted the decision, missing her already, but some things weren't meant to be. Alix was Rick's wife, divorced or not. Tripp couldn't forget that. Not because he was afraid of the ex-husband, but because he had seen how much Rick still loved her.

Tripp didn't love her that much, and never could. It was time to say goodbye.

In the interminable quiet of her house, Carin Sayers lifted the razor to her wrist. She had waited. In the early weeks, Zack had promised her that Sydney would be found. At first, she'd believed him.

But Sydney didn't come home.

It had been so hard, waking each day and realizing

326

that she hadn't dreamed this nightmare, that Sydney wasn't asleep in the next room, and that another day must be lived without her. So many mornings, but no new beginnings.

She pressed the thin edge of the blade to her skin. A single cut, and all the pain would be over. No more nightmares, no more waking to terrible truths, and no more falling asleep from the sheer exhaustion of being emotionally empty.

Zack's promises didn't comfort her anymore.

Carin had been told when the other three babies were found. Detective Walsh had come by this time, not wanting her to hear it on the news. First Chelsea and Jennifer, and now Paige. Their mothers could hold them, watch them through the night, be sure they were safe.

"Don't give up," Jessa Walsh had promised. "We'll find Sydney."

But she hadn't. No one had. The horror of each day was that nothing had changed. Only Carin's fear was bigger, like a cancer. It grew within her, a torment that couldn't be healed. Who had her baby? Had someone hurt her? Killed her? She fought sleep, but when exhaustion finally took her and she dreamed, she could hear Sydney screaming.

All the promises in the world couldn't help Carin anymore. She'd given up. One kidnapper was dead; the other had escaped. Sydney was gone, and so was Carin's hope. There wouldn't be a bright tomorrow. After tonight, there wouldn't have to be any tomorrows at all.

She made the cut. Pushed hard. Forced the razor into her flesh, and drew it from above the wrist bones to halfway up her forearm. A seam of blood opened.

Pain spilled from her. Fear. Worry. Anger. Like the red life draining from her body, she felt their loss.

"Carin!"

She heard Zack's shout. Saw his terrified face. It was the last she heard or saw, before all the sounds faded, and the world slipped away.

Chapter Thirty-five

"They don't know if she'll live. I was there when it happened. Saw blood everywhere. I tied a tourniquet below the elbow, carried her to the car, and rushed her to the hospital, but what if she . . ."

Jessa heard the agony in the husband's voice. Zack Sayers had warned her. *If our daughter isn't found soon, I'm going to lose my whole family.* Now, that prediction might be coming true.

The emergency room of Verdugo Hills Hospital was crowded. One mother held a baby whose labored breathing sounded like pneumonia. A young woman with no obvious injury sat quietly in the corner of the room, as if she were waiting for a patient. It wasn't until she stood that Jessa saw her support her wrist and elbow, because her arm was broken.

All around them was pain and suffering. She knew that didn't make this any easier for Zack. He'd been living like a man walking on shards of glass, afraid to make the wrong step. Finally, the cut had happened—only it was to Carin.

"I don't know what I'll do if she . . ."

"Don't," Jessa told him. "Come on, take a deep breath. Let me get you some coffee."

"No, stay here. Please," he added, and there was fear in his eyes. "I keep watching that door, expecting the doctor to come through and tell me—"

"Do you know if Carin had any further contact from the kidnapper?" The question was meant to distract him. Anything to make him stop thinking about that emergency room door, and his wife in one of the cubicles beyond it.

"I don't think so. At least, nothing she's told me about. Carin's been so quiet, ever since they found the third baby. It's like she's been dying every minute since then. I think watching the TV coverage of Paige going home made it worse for her. She wouldn't talk to me, after that."

When Zack Sayers had dialed 911, the Sheriff's Department had been notified of a possible suicide attempt. Carin's name had twigged a connection in the computer files, and the information had been passed along to Jessa's office. It was her responsibility to be present, in case there was a deathbed confession. She didn't expect anything as dramatic as that.

What Jessa expected was that Carin Sayers would die.

"Do you think Sydney's dead?" He asked it without looking at her.

"I don't know."

"I asked what you think."

She decided to tell him the truth. "I thought all the children were dead, but I've been wrong three times."

"Why don't they tell us something? Why is it taking so long?"

She wasn't sure if he was talking about the kidnappers or the doctors.

"If Carin dies, I'm going to—"

"I don't want to hear that." Jessa knew he was going to make a reckless threat. She didn't want to have to put it in the file. The man had enough trouble without a record of a criminal threat being logged in department files. "I know you're angry. You have every right to be. Don't take it beyond that."

She saw the look he gave her and felt his contempt. What had she done for him or his wife? Nothing. What had all the questions and prying into their personal lives accomplished? His wife had tried to kill herself, and their baby was still missing.

"You need to hold it together," she told him, "so when your wife comes home, you can rebuild your lives."

He broke down and started to cry. Loud, gut-wrenching sobs. She noticed the eyes of everyone in the waiting room, even the baby, staring at him.

"Come on," she said, and led him outside to the parking lot and the night air. It was cold. The moment felt timeless, as if the world had stopped and held its breath while they waited.

When he was calm again, she said, "Tell me about when you met your wife."

"I—I couldn't. Not now."

"Please. I want to know what she was like, before this happened? Go on, tell me."

It was as if a door opened and Jessa stepped through it into their lives. She listened as Zack introduced her to the woman he'd fallen in love with, to the woman he'd married. She saw Carin through his words, his memories. Not the distraught mother Jessa

331

had met, but the strong and beautiful woman who had captured Zack's mind and heart.

As he spoke, the choking sobs lessened and the tears stopped. "We met on her brother Andy's sailboat. I was a friend he'd invited for the weekend. She was his kid sister, her hair in a ponytail, and dressed in blue jean shorts with rolled up cuffs, and a thin white blouse tied high on her waist. She was the prettiest girl I'd ever seen."

Jessa listened. Until this moment, she'd thought of Carin Sayers as a victim. She'd been able to hold her at a distance, classified in her mind, filed under suspect, victim. Now, through Zack's words, she saw her as a person, a woman someone loved, part of a family. And she saw the hurt that losing this woman would inflict. To Jessa, Carin Sayers became a real human being, one she could never hold at a distance again.

Dawn was a pink promise in the sky, when the emergency room's exit doors opened, and a young doctor stepped out into the parking lot.

"Are you Mr. Sayers?"

Everything was in slow motion, a moment stretched in time. She saw Zack swallow before answering. "Yes. Is she—"

"Ninety-nine times out of a hundred, suicides who cut themselves like that are fatal. You must understand, there was so much damage to the vein."

Jessa hated him for telling Zack like this. He should have offered sympathy, a word of comfort. The man was hurting, for God's sake.

"I'm sorry," said the doctor.

Here it comes. Should have started that way. Should have—

"We tried to save the damaged muscle, but I'm not sure she'll have full mobility in that arm. It's something we can't know for a while. The vein repair went pretty well. I think—"

Zack gripped the doctor by the shoulders. "You mean . . . she's alive?"

"Yes, we saved her. Didn't I say that?"

Zack began to cry again. He turned away, hugged his arms to his chest, and cried.

The doctor looked genuinely confused. "You don't understand, we saved your wife. She's going to be all right."

It was the doctor who didn't understand, but that didn't matter. It was morning. A new beginning. A new chance. Jessa felt the warmth of this day spread over her like the radiating heat of love.

Another chance at getting it right, she thought. One more day. A life spared. God help us, but the bastards hadn't won. Not this time. One for the good guys.

Jesus, it was a beautiful day.

Tripp was slow at waking. It was his nature. He needed time to stare bleary-eyed at the world before he could be expected to really see it. And he needed coffee. The memory of sleep was still a heaviness in his mind, numbing all his senses, when he turned on the TV and held the coffee mug an inch from his lips, inhaling the heat and aroma.

Good Morning America was showing its viewers how to create holiday centerpieces for their Easter or Passover tables. Something about dribbling hot wax on hollowed eggshells. This was about as complicated as Tripp wanted to get first thing in the morning.

"We interrupt this program for the following news bulletin."

The picture changed to a woman seated behind a dozen or more microphones at a table. Tripp looked closer and saw that the woman was Detective Walsh. She read from a prepared sheet of notes.

"I have asked local news stations for time this morning in order to issue a statement about what has been happening in the Campbell day care kidnapping case. I am pleased to report three of the children have been returned to their families. One suspect has been found dead. We are still searching for a woman suspect believed to be connected with the case, whom we think may have fled to South America.

"Last night, in the anguish of depression, Carin Sayers, mother of kidnap victim Sydney Sayers, attempted suicide. Sydney is the last of the four kidnapped children, the only one who remains missing. Last night, I waited outside the emergency room with Zack Sayers, Carin's husband. These are real people, not nameless, faceless victims you may hear about on the news and forget. I don't want you to forget them. I want you to look at this photo, and remember this child's face."

She held a picture of Sydney Sayers to the television monitor. "I'm asking for your help. Anyone who has seen this child, please notify your local authorities. Sydney's looks may have changed in the two months since this picture was taken. Look carefully at her face. I speak for her, because she cannot. I speak for her mother and father. Help us. Someone out there has seen this baby."

Tripp felt his guts clench, thinking of Carin Sayers, and how she'd looked the last time he'd seen her.

"I stayed with Zack Sayers until early this morning, when doctors were finally able to tell him they expected his wife to recover. Help us find her child, I ask you, before this tragedy becomes one that doctors cannot heal."

"That was Detective Jessa Walsh of the Foothill Division Sheriff's Department, speaking this morning from the conference room of Verdugo Hills Hospital," said the news correspondent.

Tripp switched off the set. He couldn't sit still. Too much had happened to these four families. Too much for Carin Sayers. Guilt that he knew was irrational told him he was somehow responsible for her desperate act. If he'd found her child . . .

He tried not to think about it. For two hours, he tried. Then, when he thought enough time had gone by for her to be back at her desk, he left the house and drove to La Cañada, to see Detective Walsh.

"I know what Harper Pierce thinks," said Walsh. "He doesn't leave people in doubt about his opinions." Walsh looked tired, probably physically and mentally exhausted by the night's ordeal at the hospital.

"If you put it together," Tripp told her, "there's sense to what he says. Daniel Cantrell did know about international wire transfers. He had access to all the information needed to set up the ransom."

"I know that. I'm not ignoring him as a possible suspect, but there's nothing substantial to indicate his criminal involvement. You can't bring charges on a man because of his knowledge of banking procedures."

"But the time factor matches his," argued Tripp. "Cantrell was missing for three weeks, hospitalized in West Virginia. The ransom demand wasn't made until he came back. It fits with his absence."

"Cantrell's blood and samples of his hair were found in the trunk of Lydia Spencer's car," Walsh reminded him.

"Which makes it look as though she killed him," Tripp admitted, "but I don't buy it."

"Why not?"

"Because from what I've been able to gather from those who knew her, Lydia Spencer didn't have the education or the needed expertise and access to banking information to have pulled it off. When Cantrell phoned Pierce from the ransom site, he quoted Pierce's financial statement, dollar by dollar. He'd been inside locked files. How would Lydia Spencer have done that?"

"I don't know, and you don't either." She stood and walked restlessly around the office.

"Did you know he paid for his airline ticket, rental car, and hospitalization in West Virginia with a fraudulent credit card?"

"We verified that."

"Look," he began—

"No, you look." She turned around to face him. "I understand what you're trying to say to me. Dammit, I agree with you. If I were God, I'd pick Daniel Cantrell to be our suspect. I'd charge him with kidnapping and murder, and I'd bring him in—if I could find him. But I'm not God; I'm a homicide detective. I have to go by the rules."

"Rules! There's a baby still out there."

"Don't you tell me that!" said Walsh. "Don't you dare!" Her face was livid. "I know all about that baby, and I want her back as badly as you do, but I can't invent my own laws to bring Cantrell to charges. They wouldn't hold up in court. Do you understand that?"

"Too goddamn well."

"The man is probably in Bolivia," said Walsh, "but I can't extradite him from there. I don't have the jurisdiction, not on what we can prove against him. We have no hard evidence. It would never come to trial. There's nothing I can do."

But there's something I can do, thought Tripp. His fingers touched the slip of paper in his pocket. The phone number of a drug dealer . . . and murderer.

Time to pay the Devil his due.

Chapter Thirty-six

Tripp thought about it long and hard before he placed the call. If Cantrell was dead, as the evidence suggested, it wouldn't matter. If he was in Bolivia, he was guilty.

He dialed.

A man answered, not Rick.

"Rick Cole," he said. "This is John Tripp." Tripp's high school Spanish was long since forgotten. He didn't make an effort at reviving it. Either they'd know who Cole was, or they wouldn't.

He heard the receiver laid down, and waited. A couple of minutes later, he heard it picked up again.

"What do you want, Tripp?"

It was Rick. He could never forget that voice.

"It's what you want," Tripp told him.

"I don't want anything. My kid's back. I've got nothing to say to you."

"I have something for you. A name—Daniel Cantrell. If he's in Bolivia, or anywhere in South America, he's the one who kidnapped your daughter and mutilated her hand. Give me a fax number and I'll send you a photo of him."

There was a delay of seconds before Rick spoke again. "Why aren't you going to the police with this?"

"I did."

"And they're doing nothing?"

"No evidence that would stand up in court. It's out of their jurisdiction."

"What do you expect me to do about it?"

"I don't know."

But he did know. He knew what he would do if he were Chelsea Cole's father, and if he had the power of a drug lord in a South American country. And he knew what would happen to Daniel Cantrell if Rick found him.

"I'll look around," said Cole.

Tripp knew he would.

Cole gave him the fax number, then asked, "You still sleeping with my wife?"

He would like to have answered, *Just a minute, I'll ask her. She's lying right here beside me.* But he didn't want to spend the rest of his days looking over his shoulder for Cole or one of his thugs to be following him down some dark alley. And there wasn't any pleasure in driving the guy crazy. It was clear to Tripp that Cole loved Alix—like the fact that he still called her his wife, even though they were divorced.

"You don't need to worry about it."

"Did I say I was worried?"

"I'm out of her life."

"That's good. You're a wise man."

The conversation was starting to sour. "There's one more thing," Tripp said. "If you find him, I want to know."

"Who said I'd be looking?"

"Just in case."

The click on the line said Rick had hung up. No goodbye. Tripp laid down the receiver.

"That was for Carin Sayers," he said to his conscience, "and for Christine Campbell."

He wasn't feeling so good. The day had barely begun and he had already sentenced a man to death.

"Detective Walsh," Jessa answered the phone in her office.

"Hello, I—I'm not sure how to begin this," said the caller, a woman, sounding nervous. "I saw the news bulletin this morning . . . about the missing baby."

Jessa sat up straight and put the call on speakerphone so Dillon could hear it, too. "You have some information for us about the child?"

"No. I mean—I shouldn't have called. It can't be true."

Jessa could hear the strain of emotion in the woman's voice.

"Take your time. What's your name?"

"Linda Norton."

"All right, Mrs. Norton—is it Mrs. Norton?" Jessa asked.

"Yes."

Jessa glanced at Dillon. She held up two crossed fingers and said, "Take a deep breath, Mrs. Norton, and tell me why you called."

"I have to know the truth. You understand?"

"Go on."

"We haven't had her very long, but she's our baby, our little girl. Bob, my husband, he loves her so much. He doesn't know. Oh God, how am I going to tell him?"

"Are you telling me you have the Sayers' child? You've got Sydney?"

"He told us it was a private adoption, that everything was legal." The woman was crying, her voice so broken, Jessa couldn't understand the next words.

"What? What did you say?"

"I said"—there was a pause for a shuddering breath—"we call her Amy."

Jessa could feel the rush of adrenaline through her. "Give me your address, Mrs. Norton. I'll be right there."

Dillon wrote down the address as Jessa hung up the receiver, "I'm not going to believe any part of this until we see her," Jessa told him.

"Good."

She grabbed her suit jacket and purse. "An announcement like this morning's brings out all the crazies."

"I know," said Dillon.

"Just don't get your hopes up, that's all."

"I won't. But, Jessa—"

"What?"

"How about you?"

"C'mon," she hurried him. "Let's get there before she changes her mind. And I'm driving; you're too slow."

The Norton home in Palos Verdes was high on a seaside cliff overlooking the Pacific Ocean. It was in a gated community with an overweight armed guard standing before a pretentious-looking gatehouse.

"Crane your neck at these beauties," said Dillon. "Do you realize how much these places must cost? Big bucks. Take a look at the neat rows of them, will you? They're arranged like somebody's garden along every habitable space on the cliff."

"And some not so habitable," Jessa observed.

Dillon couldn't seem to get over it. "Places like these, commanding such fabulous views and the snob appeal of gated living, you've got to be rich to live here, or a longtime resident who got lucky."

Jess was willing to go along with Dillon's guessing game. It distracted her from the worrying thoughts that were racing ahead in her mind. "Given the sound of Linda Norton's voice on the phone, I assume she's a young woman, and that the Nortons have money, a lot of it."

"Enough to pay the cost of a private adoption," added Dillon. "I'll bet it wasn't cheap."

"Or legal."

Jessa pulled into the driveway at the address Linda Norton had given them. The place was a two-story Mediterranean-style villa, newly built, and polished as a pearl in the sunlight.

"Doctor, or lawyer?" asked Dillon, getting out of the car. "No, maybe old money."

Jessa didn't answer. She was through playing the game. This wasn't fun or funny. Her mouth was dry with nervousness. She wanted the child to be Sydney Sayers, wanted it more than anything, but as she stood at the Norton's doorstep, she tried to prepare herself that it might not be. She'd been damn lucky finding three kids. Four out of four—was it asking too much?

Hell, no.

She rang the bell.

A pleasant-looking Mexican woman answered the door.

"I'm Detective Walsh, and this is my assistant, Detective Rhys."

The woman nodded. "I am Lupe. Mrs. Norton waits for you on the patio. Please, you come with me. I take you to her."

Lupe led them through the wide, cool areas of living room, dining room, kitchen, and to the back of the house where a sliding glass door overlooked a flower-decked patio.

"Mrs. Norton?" Jessa addressed the dark-haired woman holding the baby.

"Forgive me if I don't get up," said Linda Norton. "She's sleeping. Babies are so warm, aren't they?" She ran her finger over a wisp of the child's straight blond hair. "I can feel her heartbeat pass right through me."

She looked up at Jessa then. "I've spoken to my husband." She sounded composed and resolved, not the tearful woman Jessa had spoken to earlier. "Bob can't be here, he's out of state on business. We've discussed what to do. We've had her less than a week, you know?"

"I'm sorry," said Jessa.

She hadn't been asked to sit down, and didn't.

"I knew," said Mrs. Norton, "the minute I saw the picture on that news bulletin this morning. Do you have that picture with you, Detective?"

Jessa pulled the photo from the folder and handed it to her.

Mrs. Norton studied the picture, comparing it to

the child in her arms. "She's changed a little, but you can see the resemblance, can't you?"

"Yes, I can." Jessa didn't rush anything, but her gaze had been fixed on the baby in Linda Norton's arms since the moment she saw her. There was no doubt. This was Sydney.

Mrs. Norton handed back the photo. "You'll have to take her today, I suppose?"

"I'm afraid so."

There was a slight nod of her head, an acceptance, and then she stood. "I want that doctor prosecuted. His name is Walker Reinhard, of Bel Air."

Dillon wrote down the information.

There was an awful moment when Jessa wasn't sure Linda Norton would hand over the baby. If the woman didn't give up the child willingly, it could mean a long, drawn-out case in court. Carin Sayers wouldn't survive that.

"If it's any comfort," she said, "I can tell you that the baby is going back to someone who loves her as much as you do."

"Here, said Linda Norton, and thrust the child at Jessa.

She had her! The baby was in her arms.

"I know the Sayers will want to thank you personally for what you've done."

"No. I don't want to see them. Not ever. I don't want them to call, or write, or visit. I never want to hear about them or this baby again."

Jessa understood raw pain, and heard it in Linda Norton's voice.

"If you would please go now."

"Thank you," Jessa said, turned, and hurried out of the house.

"My God," said Dillon. "We got her."

"You drive," Jessa told him when they got to the car, "and take it nice and slow."

Sydney Sayers opened her gray-green eyes and stared at Jessa.

The Mexican woman, Lupe, came running out of the garage, carrying a child's car seat. "Mrs. Norton says please, you take this." She reached a stubby brown hand to the baby, touched its face, and said, *"Vaya con Dios, infanta."*

They drove away, Sydney snug in her car seat, Dillon taking the curves like somebody's grandmother, and Jessa trying to make herself believe it had really come true. The babies were back—good God, all four of them.

Jessa stepped out of the hospital elevator and saw Zack Sayers sitting in the corridor outside his wife's room. His elbows pressed to his knees, his head was cradled in both hands, like a man who'd been praying, or weeping. She knew he'd done both.

He didn't seem to hear as she approached. "Zack," she said, "I brought someone to see you."

He looked up, and she saw the change come over his face. He stared, then squinted his eyes and stared harder, as if trying to be sure. "Is it really her?"

Jessa nodded. She didn't trust herself to speak.

He got up and walked toward them. "You got her back?"

She held the baby out to him, and when he was close enough, put Sydney into her father's arms.

He held Sydney gently, looking into her eyes as if

345

trying to recognize the child he remembered. "It's me, angel. It's Daddy. I'm going to take you home."

And then, as Jessa watched, he carried his daughter toward his wife's room. Dillon started to follow, but she grabbed his hand. "No," she said, "leave them alone."

Jessa waited in the hall, and standing there, she heard Zack Sayers open the door of the hospital room and say, "Carin, open your eyes honey. It's our baby, she's come home."

Chapter Thirty-seven

The four babies were home again and safe, but it was hard for Tripp to stop thinking about the case. There were memories about it which still haunted him, thoughts which kept him sleepless through the long nights. The way he figured it, every case had an afterlife, and this one was hanging on like a ghost.

He'd been meaning to go back to work. Grodin had been calling him, putting on the pressure, but he hadn't gone in yet. Maybe he wasn't ready, or maybe he'd pushed it too far with this one. Gone over the line.

The phone rang. He let the machine answer.

"Are you there? I hate talking on these things," said an unmistakable voice.

He picked up the receiver. "Rowena. Don't tell me you're back in town."

"You wouldn't get me back in that busy place. I'm here at home, where I belong."

"It's great to hear from you," he said, and meant it.

"Thought I'd call and see what's happened since I left."

He told her about Sydney.

"That's good news. I figured it'd turn out all right."

"Oh, you did? You might have let me know."

"You had other things on your mind."

"Are you trying your mind reading on me now, Rowena?"

"I thought I'd call and talk with you about it."

"About what?"

"About what you did, and about letting go of the guilt."

"Jesus," he said. "You're good."

She laughed. "You're learning. Look here, Tripp, I don't know exactly what you did, and I don't want to know. One thing I'm sure of is what kind of man you are. You're decent, and a caring human being. Whatever you've done, it's time you forgave yourself for it."

"Right."

"I mean it," she came back at him. "Let it go, or it'll eat you alive. Whatever you've done, it's over. Forgive yourself and go on."

"Is that what you do?" he asked.

"Sometimes. I'm not always right, but I generally mean well, and so do you."

He wanted to confess it to her, offer an Act of Contrition and say, *Bless me, for I have sinned,* like he had when he was eleven. But Rowena wasn't a priest and Tripp wasn't a schoolboy. He was a man, and no forgiveness by Rowena, a priest, or anyone, would erase how he felt. The sin would stick. He'd carry it the rest of his life.

"Would you do it any different?" she asked. "If you could change whatever happened—would you?"

He didn't have to think about it. "No."

"I didn't think so," she said. "You'll be all right now, Tripp. I can see that. Fact is, I can see a lot of good things ahead for you."

He felt better after she called. Maybe it was knowing he'd do the same thing over again, if given the chance. Or maybe, it was seeing himself the way Rowena saw him. She was right. It was time to let go of the guilt. That afternoon, he shaved, dressed and reported back for work at the office.

"So, he's going to jail?" Tripp asked.

He'd called Detective Walsh as a follow-up to the Campbell day care case. Grodin liked his files complete.

"Reinhard wouldn't cooperate," she told him. "He refused to tell us who sold him the baby. He'll spend some time in prison, but he's got money and a good lawyer. With good behavior, he'll be out before you know it."

"Why can't they press the kidnapping and murder charges on him and make them stick?"

"We've got no proof of that. My guess is, Reinhard's afraid to give us the name. More scared of that person than he is of prison."

It was frustrating to Tripp. "The system doesn't always work, does it?"

"Not always. Sometimes the bad guys get away with it."

And sometimes they don't, he thought.

"I don't care about Reinhard," Walsh told him. "Oh, I'd like to nail his ass to the wall," she said, "but hey, we got back what we wanted most. Those babies are alive and home. That's more than I thought possible."

He had to agree. With a high-priced lawyer, Dr. Reinhard would probably never serve a day behind bars, or if he did, it would be in some country club prison set up for the rich. The ransom money was gone. That was a black mark against PIC, and Harper Place was two million dollars poorer. All of these were things Tripp should care about, but didn't.

"You know, when it comes down to it," she said, "I'm not going to sit in my rocking chair someday and remember sending a guy away to prison, but I will remember finding those babies, and bringing them home. Till the day I die, I'll remember."

Tripp nodded. He knew he would, too.

A week later, Tripp was getting ready for work when the UPS truck pulled up in front of his house. It was a small package, overwrapped in brown paper and tied with string. It bore no return address, but was postmarked Bolivia. He pulled the string over the corners of the box, undid the paper wrapping, and lifted the lid.

Inside, lying at the dark center of the box, was a man's severed finger.